Rising From Darkness

Small Town Secrets Book 3
A.K. Hughey

Ravens Call Publishing

Contents

Chapter 1
CHAPTER ONE

Tuesday, December 5th

L ucia watched in silence as white, fluffy snowflakes flew in a blur over the hood, each brightened temporarily by the headlights of her truck. Combined with her exhaustion, the whirling snow added to the sensation of tunnel vision. The way the streaks of snow flew straight at the windshield, brightened against the darkness, reminded her of Star Trek's "warp speed."

Dawn hadn't yet broken the horizon to give her eyes a break, and, given the blizzard conditions, its rays wouldn't lighten the thick cloud cover for another three hours.

In dry conditions, the drive back to Pine River would have been just over an hour, but, considering the weather, they'd been on the road almost two hours and still hadn't made it home.

The taillights of Sam's small pickup glowed ahead of her. Without him leading the way, she wouldn't have risked the drive. He hadn't said a word to her directly before they'd left the crash, and Lucia couldn't begin to fathom the right words to say. To apologize.

Or to thank him.

Shelby shifted in the passenger seat, then lifted her head and yawned. "Where are we?"

"Close, I hope," Lucia replied simply, keeping her eyes glued to what little she could see of Sam's truck and the road in front of her. It was snow-packed and unplowed, its edges uncertain, and the world around them was obscured by the blizzard and the enveloping darkness beyond their headlights.

"Wake me when you know we're close." Shelby leaned against her door and shut her eyes again.

"How can you possibly sleep?" Lucia asked in bewilderment as Sam slowed to a stop at a crossroads. There wasn't another car in sight. Lights from any source other than their vehicles were nonexistent in the blackness of the early morning hour.

"Why not?"

"That man is dead!" Lucia half-shouted, unable to contain her frustration. "You almost died, Shelby."

"But I didn't," she said nonchalantly, shrugging.

"We need to talk about this. You can't–"

"Can't what?" Shelby interrupted. "We set out to save that girl, and we did. Hell, we saved her and another we didn't even know about. Damn the consequences. As far as I'm concerned, that's worth risking my life for."

"I'm sorry, I just–"

"Don't apologize, and don't you worry about me. I'm good with the blood, fire, and ash. You need to worry about Sam. He's the one you need to have a conversation with. Leave me the hell out of it."

"Sure," Lucia mumbled as Shelby leaned back again and closed her eyes.

As much as Lucia hated to admit it, Shelby was right.

Lucia pulled her phone from the center console and opened the maps program. She watched in frustration as it stalled on the loading screen.

No signal in the country meant no GPS.

Without GPS, they were guessing.

Thankfully, it wasn't hard to guess the right way in rural Michigan. Most of the roads were laid out in a grid, running east and west, and north and south. Few rural roads ran diagonally across the landscape or curved significantly.

True to the pattern, Sam carefully turned his truck left onto the unplowed country road. Lucia followed suit, wishing all the while she could talk to him.

If they took enough rights for east and lefts for north, they were bound to hit M-46 eventually, and then they would know the way home for certain.

Lucia chewed her lip as she considered what she would say to Sam. He was the love of her life, the man she never thought she deserved, and her fiancé. But she'd been keeping secrets too long now.

Deadly secrets.

And last night, Sam had stumbled upon those secrets and their vast, unavoidable implications.

Worse, he had gotten involved in the mix just as another officer arrived on the scene.

Sam's truck braked at another stop sign as a plow truck roared past along the crossroad, spraying snow aside and dropping salt behind. The frigid wind whipped at the debris, carrying the snow and salt far enough to pepper Lucia's windshield as she stopped behind Sam.

"We're close," she informed Shelby.

Shelby groaned and sat up in the passenger seat before stretching and cracking her neck. "Are you sure?"

"This is M-46." Lucia turned the truck east onto the road. "We're probably just a few minutes away now."

"Damn. I wanted a little more sleep." Shelby stretched her arms out toward the dash and cracked her knuckles.

"Stop that," Lucia begged, shuddering.

"No," Shelby replied evenly. "Have you thought about what you're going to say to Sam?"

"No. All I can do right now is..." She let her words trail off.

Shelby chuckled, but it was a bitter sound. "Pray."

Lucia didn't bother saying anything else. She recalled every time Shelby had warned her over the past two months. Her secrets were too big to keep and just big enough to swallow them all.

In two more miles, she began to recognize the landscape despite the darkness and the wind-whipped snowfall that hadn't slowed since noon the previous day.

As they reached the long driveway to Sam's house, his truck slowed to a stop just beyond the short wall of plowed snow that blocked the turn. His tires turned, and he punched through the snow. Lucia carefully pressed the gas, climbed the mound of snow, and followed him up the driveway. She was halfway up the drive when her phone rang.

Glancing down into the console and saw Sam's picture staring up at her from her lock screen. When she lifted her gaze again, she found Sam had stopped just ahead.

After hitting the brakes and stopping, her fingers flew over the screen as she picked it up and answered. "What's wrong?"

"The power's out," Sam said, his voice low.

"That's fine, right? We have a generator."

"Yes," he replied, annoyance tinging his voice. "I do have a generator, but that's not the problem."

"Okay." Lucia couldn't help but sigh, an open indication of her growing frustration. She was exhausted. They'd been through hell.

Slippery roads. A crashed car. Fire. Victims. A woman she never thought she'd see alive again.

Blood and bodies.

She didn't have patience for his quirks right now, even if she did owe him more than a little in the way of an explanation.

"Look around," he pressed.

Shelby perked up in her seat as Lucia followed Sam's instructions, and she mirrored the action.

"Lights are out at the house," Shelby muttered. She twisted in the passenger seat as she surveyed 360 degrees around the truck. Stopping suddenly, she turned back to Lucia, then threw a thumb back and to their right.

Lucia focused her tired eyes in the direction of the closest neighbor. Although the neighbor's house couldn't be seen through the trees, the glow of their floodlights lit the falling snow well above the trees.

"Did you figure it out yet?" Sam's voice came through clear and steady.

"I think—"

"Or was it Shelby?" he interrupted.

Lucia flinched, his words striking her in a way she hadn't expected. She glanced at her friend before turning her gaze back to Sam's house again.

"If the blizzard had caused a power outage, the rest of the houses around us wouldn't have their outdoor lights on," Sam explained. "Every house we passed on 46 had some light visible from the road. I'd bet money there are a few who don't have generators."

As his words sunk in, Lucia's blood chilled in her veins. She turned down the hot air that poured from the truck's vents. It seemed too hot as her senses sharpened, and alarms blared in her head.

"Put it in reverse and get the hell back here," Sam commanded, his voice snapping through the fog of her racing thoughts.

With the phone in her left hand, Lucia dropped the shifter into reverse, turning in her seat as she backed out of the driveway.

Another thought stopped her as quickly as she had begun.

"Penny," she whispered, sucking in a breath.

Lucia turned forward again and flung the shifter into drive before gunning it.

"What the hell?!" Shelby cried out, hands flying out to grab the door handle as she slid back in her seat.

The truck fish-tailed for a moment when she rounded Sam's truck, its tires hungry for purchase in the deep snow, but Lucia corrected it with ease and picked up speed to close the remaining distance to the house in less than sixty seconds.

"Penny!" Lucia cried as she threw the truck into park. She reached under her seat and grabbed her loaded Beretta 9mm. After shoving open the door and flinging herself out into the snow, she racked the slide and switched off the safety.

With a few leaping steps, she picked up momentum and ran up the porch steps to the front door. She skidded to a halt at the top, heart thudding in her chest, and reached out her left hand to the door handle. It turned freely, squeaking against the cold.

Lucia was only vaguely aware of how foolish it was to run into this situation without Sam and Shelby, without a plan and knowing it was probably a trap.

A frightened bark sounded from inside, giving her the final push she needed to ignore her better judgment. She pushed open the door and stepped over the threshold, her Beretta at the ready, finger resting on the trigger.

A high-pitched whine greeted her from the darkness. Her truck's beams shone through the windows, slicing past the vertical blinds in the living room and giving her enough ambient light to avoid running into any furniture.

Lucia's breath fogged in the air, and she fought the shiver that threatened to break her readiness. It was far colder in the house than it should have been, and she wondered how long the power had been out.

Pausing in the living room, she took a moment to listen while her eyes adjusted. Only stillness greeted her as the room and furniture solidified in her vision.

Another whine from Penny, and Lucia could no longer wait. Her snow-covered boots made no sound as she stepped lightly across the carpet. There wasn't any noise apart from Penny's whining and her nails slipping on the tiles of the kitchen floor.

As she reached the kitchen, Lucia raised her Baretta and moved slowly, "slicing" the inside corner with her field of fire. Even if she hadn't already been using the technique on her and Shelby's "missions," she could never forget any of the tactical marksmanship training her parents had drilled into her throughout childhood. It was second nature now, muscle memory, and she was grateful for how she was raised now that earthly evil had marched into her life.

She cleared the kitchen quickly and crouched as she approached Penny on the other side of the kitchen island. Her faded red dog leash was attached to her collar, the other end pinched inside a cupboard hinge. The big Rott whined and groaned, wagging her tail furiously and straining against the leash as Lucia approached. Jumping up, she lunged and tried to lick Lucia's face.

"Down," Lucia scolded quietly. Penny whined but obeyed, dropping to the floor.

Her tail still flew furiously back and forth as Lucia opened the cupboard and freed the leash. Once it was free, Penny let out a soft bark as she jumped forward and pushed Lucia off balance. The sound was filled with fear. As scary as she might rightfully look to strangers, Penny was a scaredy-cat and a couch potato. Even with training, she had never been fit to be a guard dog.

"Easy, girl," Lucia spoke softly, trying to comfort Penny while keeping her eyes on the darkened corners of the open space between the kitchen and the hall that led to the bedrooms and the basement.

When she was sure nothing was moving in the shadows, she glanced back toward the front room and noticed her headlights were not the only lights shining through the blinds. The faded colors of flashing red and blue lights broke around the edges, and she wondered if Sam had already called for backup.

She turned back to Penny and stroked her fur, hoping to calm the stressed-out dog. Lucia stopped abruptly when her hand touched something sticky and wet. Her breath caught in her throat, and her stomach turned.

Chapter 2
CHAPTER TWO

S helby flipped on the kitchen light, temporarily blinding Lucia. As her eyes adjusted, she could only pray the wet, sticky substance on Penny wasn't blood.

"What the hell?" Sam's voice called out, his footsteps pounding through the front of the house.

Lucia ignored him, instead focused on Penny. Her eyes finally adjusted, and the red blotch on her hands became brighter.

Spray paint. Not blood.

Something about it felt too familiar about the scene, but she dismissed it. Turning Penny's body to the side, she inhaled sharply as she surveyed the dog.

A giant red X was sloppily spray-painted across the rottweiler's black fur from her shoulder to her hip. Shock and silence stilled Lucia, and she hardly heard Sam and Shelby next to her.

"Two sets of boot tracks through the snow leading in and two leading out," Shelby said.

"Dammit!" Sam strode toward the backdoor, Shelby following in his wake.

Lucia remained on the floor, hugging Penny close and stroking her fur. The canine's fierce appearance and Rottweiler breed reputation did not match her scaredy-cat personality. It was easy to imagine Penny whimpering and cowering as the intruders spray-painted her.

"You poor thing," Lucia muttered, pressing her face against the dog's neck. Penny let out a pitiful, high-pitched whine in response. The exhaustion of everything that had happened over the past twenty-four hours finally caught up with her as she sat on the floor, embracing her frightened dog.

Her eyes stung with tears as she remembered the man who'd died only hours ago. It was like a loop she couldn't shut off: the man aiming his gun at Shelby, the blood blossoming on his chest after a bullet tore through flesh and bone, the car engulfed in flames, Natalie's sallow face and frightened eyes staring back at her. It was too much for her mind to bear, especially without sleep.

Footsteps warned of Sam and Shelby's return, and she listened, uninvested, as they argued.

"They're gone," Shelby said.

"How could you possibly be sure?" Sam challenged.

"I followed the tracks through the woods to where a vehicle had been parked on a two-track."

"You can't be serious. You did all that in five minutes?"

"I sure as hell did. They're gone, Sam."

"I need a drink." He ran his hands over his short hair, stretching, then began unbuttoning his uniform shirt. "Lucia, we need to talk."

She turned to gaze up at him, knowing a few stray tears had escaped and trailed down her cold cheeks.

Whatever Sam was going to say, he stopped, his eyes softening ever so slightly. Lucia knew he loved her, and he hated to see her upset. She had rarely let him see her cry. Now, she was on the verge of a breakdown.

He bent down and grabbed her hand, pulling her to her feet before leading her to the living room. After settling her on the couch with a blanket, he worked with Shelby to secure the rest of the house and close all the doors and windows.

Lucia wanted to help, but her limbs wouldn't obey her. Her entire body ached, and her tight stomach threatened to upturn whatever remnants of yesterday's lunch remained. Penny jumped on the couch and lay her head on Lucia's lap. She needed to move, talk to Natalie, and clean up everything–her truck, her pistol...her body.

She didn't know why the detective had let them go, but she didn't trust it. By all rights, they'd been caught doing very illegal things, regardless of their intent to save a woman's life.

Most law enforcement hated vigilantes and, from their perspective, rightfully so. But when the system failed, someone needed to step in and right the scales of justice. In this case, they'd tried to do everything right, to call the tip line so the cops could save Kaylie. But the legal system made it impossible for the police to act. Without enough evidence for a search warrant or permission from the property owner, they couldn't save Kaylie.

The same thing had happened up in Manistee. Miranda had suffered several weeks more abuse than needed due to the exact property issue. As it turned out, tips didn't mean jack. They were quickly becoming a check in the box for Lucia to feel like she'd tried to do the right thing and respect the law and the justice system. As much as she appreciated the U.S. Constitution and Bill of Rights, they protected monsters equally, and innocents suffered for it.

"Lucia," Sam's voice broke through her thoughts, bringing her attention back to the present. She looked up and locked eyes with him. His green eyes were softer than she expected, given how pissed she knew he had been.

"I'm sorry," she whispered, her voice quieter than she'd intended.

Sam hesitated, then sat beside her and pulled her into his arms.

Lucia wrapped her arms around his neck and squeezed tight, as if being closer to him would ease the burden on her heart and mind, as if he could chase her demons away. They stayed like that for what felt like forever.

A creaking sound broke through the quiet power of the moment, and Lucia looked over Sam's shoulder to find Shelby rocking in the recliner with her feet tucked under her thighs and her knees falling together to one side. She was using her Bowie knife to clean her nails. She looked as calm and collected as if nothing had happened only hours ago. What the hell was happening in that woman's mind?

She looked up then and caught Lucia staring at her. "Are we going to get this talk out of the way, or can I get some sleep first?"

Sam sighed and released Lucia from his embrace, giving her more space than she wanted at that moment. "Let's talk first. Is that okay, Luce?"

Lucia said nothing, letting her gaze fall to Penny, who had moved to the other side of the couch when Sam sat down.

"What the hell is going on with you two?"

She could feel Sam's eyes burning into her, but she wasn't ready to meet them yet, especially now that the conversation had begun.

Shelby said nothing, and Lucia imagined she was staring, too.

"Lucia," Sam pressed. "I need you to talk to me because the proverbial shit is about to hit the fan."

Lucia shrugged, steeling herself before finally looking up. "Where do I start?"

"Sam," Shelby interjected, her tone casual. "We had information about where a kidnapped girl was located. We called in the tips, but nothing happened. Our contact said she didn't have long, so we did whatever we could to save her."

His eyes went wide, and the color drained from his face. "You can't be serious right now. There's no way…" He rubbed his temples and closed his eyes for a moment. "You cannot be saying what I think you're saying."

"Take it how you want to," Shelby interjected defiantly, then returned her attention to her knife. She practiced spinning it, her nimble fingers handling the deadly sharp blade with ease.

"I'm sorry I didn't tell you," Lucia interjected before Sam could snap. If Sam and Shelby fought, it would be disastrous.

"Of course you didn't tell me because you know what I'd say. At least you thought you knew what I'd say. Things don't turn out the way we want; I understand that. The legal system can fail everyone, the innocent and monsters alike. That doesn't mean we can't take matters into our own hands, or we wouldn't have law and order. Which, I believe, is the basis of a peaceful and prosperous society. But things have gotten out of hand."

Lucia froze, locking eyes with him.

"I didn't get a chance to tell you. The judge dismissed all charges against McNamara. He's walking free."

She felt her jaw drop as she jumped to her feet and ran her fingers through her hair, raking the loose strands away from her face. "No. No, dammit. He shot you!"

Sam said nothing, only stared back at her, his eyes hard again, and threw up his hands. "I guess that doesn't matter. He's free, Luce."

Lucia's mind raced, and her body quaked. She wanted to hit a wall or destroy something, but looking around, she knew she couldn't disrespect Sam like that. She couldn't bear to bring harm to any part of the life they'd begun to build together. Striding across the living room, she yanked open the front door and sprinted out into the deep, unblemished snow in front of the house.

She ran into the darkness, her wavy, long black hair whipping behind her as the wind and flying snow blinded her. As hard as she pumped her legs, she didn't make it far through the knee-deep snow. Her muscles failed, lungs burning as she collapsed into the frozen, white sea.

The howling wind and the rushing blood in her ears drowned her ven-
omous thoughts, her chest heaving to take in breath. Frozen chunks of
snow burned cold against her bare face, but she was numb to the pain and
the danger.

It couldn't be true.

"He can't be free," Lucia muttered, her frozen lips causing her to slur.
"He has to pay."

It was clear now. The paint on Penny was a warning, just like the spray
paint on her ex's car had been a warning before. Phil McNamara had
swatted aside justice, and now he was ready to punish her.

Chapter 3

CHAPTER THREE

Tyler dialed Derek's number for the fifth time that hour and pressed the speaker button. Four long seconds of tense silence passed before the voicemail message began.

"Please leave a message for 313—"

He ended the call. Although he wasn't supposed to make direct calls, he'd already sent more than a dozen texts and left three voicemails since midnight.

But something was wrong. He could feel it.

Derek should have called hours ago, especially considering the cops had just busted into their house with a warrant. Even with blizzard conditions, if Derek had decided to stay overnight, he should at least have answered Tyler's calls. His delivery was too important, his cargo too precious. Any delay could mean losing the job or, far worse, horrendous torture and a slow death.

Dropping Jeff's phone on the center console, he glanced at his watch again. It was already 3:07 a.m.

Tyler only now realized the error in his judgment. He shouldn't have left this job to Derek alone. He should have taken the mission himself or at least ridden along.

He glanced around the rural carpool parking lot, surrounded by trees and hidden from the road. A single lamp post cast a weak glow in the snow-laden gale.

"Any luck?" Jeff asked through a yawn as he rose from a brief nap. The pair had spent most of the previous day and the late evening cleaning the house. They hadn't dared sleep as they waited for word from Derek, but eventually, the exhaustion had overwhelmed Jeff. Tyler had encouraged him to get some rest while he kept watch and tried to reach Derek.

He shook his head. "Not yet."

"It's not looking good." Jeff crossed his arms and leaned back in his seat, his eyes closing. Tyler studied the younger man. "We should just go."

"Go where?"

"Well, we could either go find him or–"

"Absolutely not."

"Or," Jeff continued sleepily, "we can head to the cabin and settle in until everything cools down."

"I guess the cabin's not a bad idea," Tyler admitted. He'd jumped at every shadow all night. Each bluster of the freezing wind against the truck was an omen. He tapped his fingers anxiously on the steering wheel. "Stop it. He probably doesn't have signal out there."

"He is pretty deep in the country." Jeff tried to stretch his legs. "But it's been too long for him to be okay."

"And this blizzard tore up the mid-state last night. There are probably power outages, network issues, and other shit. Too many things to count. And Derek knows he's not the best driver, so he won't take any more risk than he's got to. Especially not in the Prius."

"Sure, whatever. Let's just go lay low up north for a while."

Tyler chewed his lip as he mulled over the idea. His veins were buzzing with tension. He was too anxious to sleep or to be stuck in the truck for much longer.

A trip up to the cabin sounded better by the second. Only a handful of their closest associates knew about the hunting cabin up at Ryan Lake, and it wasn't connected to his name. He'd paid a lot of money to keep it under someone else's name on the public record while owning it entirely. He sent a single cryptic text message so Derek would know to join them up there when he could get on the road again.

"All right." Tyler dropped his phone on the dash and rolled his neck to release his tension. Time was getting short, and he wanted to get out of town before all hell broke loose. If Derek screwed up the job or failed, all their lives would be on the line. "You're right. Let's do it."

The snow seemed to fall faster as he pulled out of the parking lot and headed for I-75. It hadn't stopped snowing since the storm began, early the morning before. Giant, fluffy snowflakes beat down on his windshield, and he could barely see the white-blanketed world beyond the hood of the Tacoma.

How much snow had they gotten so far?

At least twelve inches, he thought, gauging by accumulation on the shoulders of the road.

In a few hours, his neighbors back in Southfield would be out to shovel their sidewalks and snow-blow their driveways. Those same average, mostly honest folks might notice when Tyler's driveway remained snow-covered. As was fitting in any suburban Midwest neighborhood, he expected one of his neighbors would push their snowblower over and clear the driveway for them. It would probably be Tammy across the street or Henry's teenage son, Jacob.

Of course, he supposed that only would have happened if the cops hadn't shown up in force and busted in the door.

Luckily, Tyler had a heads-up this time. It was a favor returned by someone at the Southfield Police Department. Now that their slate had been cleared, it wouldn't be repeated.

He only hoped his missing phone was in the duffel bag he'd hastily thrown in the backseat.

Best case scenario, they'd take a short vacation up north, spending their time drinking and snowmobiling. Worst case?

There'd be a bullet to the back of the head and a watery grave waiting for him, Jeff, and Derek.

"Sanitize your phone."

"Damn it. I forgot about that shit," Jeff grumbled, grabbing it from the dash. He turned off the location services, GPS, cellular service, Bluetooth, and WiFi before powering it off and tossing it in the glove box.

"Ugh. That means we have to listen to the radio. I hate the radio," Jeff complained.

"We'll just keep the noise to a minimum, okay?"

He was desperate to put as much distance as possible between them and Southfield as quickly as possible.

He pulled off the freeway at the next exit with a lit gas station he could see from the road. They headed inside to get snacks and drinks for the trip while Jeff filled the tank and the gas cans from the bed. A single employee sat on a stool behind the counter and glanced up when the door opened. Tyler spotted a thriller book in the man's hands—The Mechanic by Tom Fowler.

"I didn't think I'd see anybody this morning," he said, dog-earing a page before closing the book and setting it aside.

Tyler forced a tight smile and nodded. "Yeah, it's pretty bad out there." He slipped down the first aisle and headed to the ATM, withdrawing $400. Once the cash was in his wallet, he grabbed an armful of snacks and balanced them carefully atop two cases of bottled water.

"Taking a trip?" the cashier asked as Tyler set everything on the counter.

Tyler hesitated. The less he said, the better. He kept his mouth closed and only nodded.

The man shook his head as he rang up the items and bagged them. "Sorry. It's been slow."

"I can only imagine," Tyler replied as he paid for the items. "Can you give me a few extra bags?"

"Sure." The cashier pulled a few off the rack, folded them, and placed them with the snacks.

"Thanks," Tyler said, balancing the snacks on the water cases and hefting them off the counter. He pressed his back to the door and pushed it open, turning to find Jeff waiting for him.

"Don't fall." Jeff gestured to the packed snow covering the asphalt. He grabbed the bags off the top of the water cases and strode ahead to open the rear passenger door of the Tacoma.

By the time Tyler finished loading the water in the back, Jeff had already started the truck and buckled his seatbelt.

"I got cash and snacks, and if we can make it without any more stops, we might have a shot at avoiding more cameras."

"What about groceries?" Jeff asked as he double-checked the four-wheel was on high. He shifted into drive and headed back toward the freeway.

"The little store near the cabin. They're too poor for cameras, and they'll love us for using cash there."

"I'll feel a lot better once we're settled in." Jeff took the ramp onto I-75 North. "We don't need to make any other stops?"

Tyler shook his head. "We shouldn't."

Again, he ran through his mental checklist of all the things they might need or would have to do. He considered messaging the boss's men but quickly decided against it. He reassured himself it was better to wait until there was anything to report rather than worry the boss with low-level troubles.

After all, he wasn't sure that anything had gone wrong. Maybe Derek's phone simply stopped working, or he hadn't made it to an area where he could get signal yet.

"Dude, stop." Jeff broke the silence.

"What?"

"Your leg, man. You're so damn fidgety."

Tyler hadn't realized he'd been bouncing his leg. He stared down at the appendage, aggravated it was yet another thing in his life that seemed to defy him. Another piece of himself that he struggled to control. Especially when he was nervous.

The freeway was slick, and their progress was slow. What should have been a simple two-hour trip north would likely take two or three hours longer.

After nearly two hours, they finally hit the outskirts north of Flint. Out here, there weren't as many artificial sources to create the ambient light they had in the city. It was pitch dark, and the driving snow flew at the windshield with nothing but a black abyss looming just beyond the short reach of the headlights.

Jeff didn't use his brights; high beams made the light reflect worse off the snowflakes and made it much harder to see in a blizzard like this. Thankfully, they hadn't seen much traffic, and Jeff was a decent driver. He knew four-wheel drive didn't give him a license to drive at high speeds. He still had to be careful.

Especially now, when all the hands of hell could soon be nipping at their heels.

None of the cars they had seen so far had continued with them along the freeway. Tyler was counting backward from one hundred for the fifth time to focus his mind and calm himself when he spotted the hazards flashing ahead of them.

He snapped awake. In seconds, his fidgety limbs stilled, and the murky waters of his mind cleared.

"Slow down," he commanded.

"You said we can't stop—"

"Let's just see if they need help."

Jeff grumbled under his breath but slowed the truck. Turning on his hazards, he pulled up beside the vehicle. It was a four-door sedan, and its nose was seated snugly in a snowdrift on the right shoulder of the road.

Tyler rolled down his window, and a frigid breeze broke through the warm air of the truck. A pretty, pale face appeared from the driver's seat.

Unbuckling his seatbelt, Tyler sat up and leaned out as the woman rolled her window down.

"Are you all right, ma'am?" he asked, offering a smile despite the frigid air biting at his exposed skin. She looked scared, her pretty round eyes wide and glassy.

She was also shivering.

"I'm okay," she said, trying to hide the tremble in her voice.

"Is someone coming to help you?"

She hesitated.

"We'd help," Tyler added quickly. "But we don't have a tow strap. Unless you have one?"

"I don't." She shook her head. "I called my insurance. They said they'd find a service and call me back, but that was over an hour and a half ago, and I still haven't heard back."

"That sucks," Tyler said. He tapped his hand on the freezing exterior of the truck, then glanced at his friend.

Jeff slowly shook his head, his eyes wide and stern. He spoke in a low voice. "Absolutely not. Not right now. Stick to the plan."

"Come on, man," Tyler replied excitedly. "Damsel in distress."

"Damn it," Jeff growled, wrenching his fingers on the steering wheel. "Shit, shit, shit!"

Tyler turned back to the woman. "Where ya headin'?"

"One more exit up." Her voice was more relaxed now. "I was meeting my fiancé early for a family trip to the ski resort. He's waiting for me at our hotel. I work nights bartending. I didn't want this blizzard to ruin my vacation, so I headed straight up here after closing to surprise him."

"Why didn't he come and pick you up?"

"He's not answering his phone. It's pretty early, so he's probably not up yet."

Her eyes fell then. She was exhausted, unsure of her fiancé, and stuck out here freezing before dawn in the middle of a blizzard.

"I know it's a new day and age," he started gently, "but if you felt comfortable with it, we could give you a ride to your hotel. You're staying at the resort, right? Not somewhere else nearby."

She nodded, the war going on in her mind obvious from the furrow in her brow.

"I'm Tyler, by the way, and that's Jeff." He threw a thumb over his shoulder.

"Ellie," she introduced herself.

"Like I said, if you feel comfortable with it, you could grab your stuff, and we could drop you off at the hotel. If not, that's okay too. I don't mean to sound offensive, but you look like you're freezing your ass off."

She nodded and laughed lightly, a single tear sliding down her cheek. Her laugh was a bitter, mirthless sound bordering on a sob. "This damned car won't start."

"Probably better that it doesn't," he observed. "If too much snow drifts around your car and blocks your tailpipe, you'll get exhaust poisoning in there. People die like that."

She released a breath, shivered, then rolled up her window. Grabbing her things, she pulled her keys from the ignition, then took the car key from the ring and left it on the seat. Auburn hair peeked out from beneath the fur-lined hood of her blue parka.

"Are you sure it won't be a problem? If you get me to the exit, I could probably walk from there. I think it's only a mile or so."

"What kind of asshole would make a woman—or anyone else—walk alone in a blizzard?"

She smiled then, faintly, but it was unmistakable. Her walls were coming down.

"Let me help," Tyler offered, opening the door. He jumped out and took a small duffel from her as she pulled it from the back of her car. Setting it in the back next to their bags, he gestured to the front seat.

"Oh no, I couldn't–"

"But you can. You need the heater a hell of a lot more than I do. I can't deliver you to your fiancé with hypothermia."

"When you put it that way..." She let her words trail off as she climbed into the front seat. She held up her key fob and locked her car. "Thank you so much, guys."

Tyler climbed into the backseat. He closed the door before moving to the middle seat.

"No problem," Jeff shifted into gear and turned off his hazards. "Have you been skiing up here yet?"

"Yeah, a few times. You?"

"Almost every January. It's a family tradition."

Tyler listened as they chatted, making small talk. Once he spotted the one-mile sign for the upcoming exit, he bent down and reached under the passenger seat. He wrapped his fingers around the cold metal and sat up again.

"You sure this fiancé of yours isn't doing you dirty?" Tyler interrupted whatever small talk was going on.

"Excuse me?" Ellie asked, startled. "No, I don't think–"

"He didn't expect you, and you can't get a hold of him when you need him."

"He's probably sleep–"

"Sleeping through your crisis. How many times has he done this?"

"It's not like that," Ellie replied quietly. She stared at the road ahead, but Tyler watched as she fiddled in her purse. "Here's the exit."

Jeff didn't slow down. And when they reached the ramp, he didn't take it.

"You're missing the exit." Her voice was strained and trembled slightly.

"Roll down your window," Tyler commanded, lifting his pistol and pressing it to the back of her head. "You feel that?"

She whimpered and nodded, her shaking fingers feeling for the door handle.

Freezing air and icy snowflakes blasted into the vehicle. Keeping the muzzle against her head, Tyler leaned forward and reached into the purse on her lap. He pulled her phone from its hiding place and tossed it through the open window.

Chapter 4

CHAPTER FOUR

D aylight rose slow and lazy, barely lighting the blizzard-ridden skies. Mitch's eyes were blind to the rising natural light, having watched the remnants of the car finish burning out. The low visibility and treacherous roads meant it took longer for emergency responders to arrive after Mitch called them. It gave him more time to take statements from Kaylie and Natalie, ensuring they understood the importance of keeping their stories straight in the coming days and weeks.

The trio sat in his warm, running car. It was too cold to stand outside and wait for other first responders to arrive. Although he'd thought the blizzard had already reached its zenith throughout the night, it only worsened as the hours passed. This was no small storm that battered the mitten today. It might even be a record-breaker.

"Do you have any water?" Natalie asked from the backseat.

Mitch unlocked the car before popping the trunk and throwing his door open. He grabbed as many water bottles as he could carry in one arm, then slammed the trunk shut. Dipping his head down, he shielded his face with his free arm and jogged back to the driver's seat.

"Here," he said after closing the door. He passed back two bottles to Natalie, watching silently through the rearview mirror as she passed the first one to Kaylie, then opened the second one for herself.

Kaylie could hardly be bothered to accept the bottle. She did not look up at Natalie or at Mitch. Her red, teary eyes remained focused on some invisible point in the flying snow outside the car.

"Why did you let them go?" Natalie asked after gulping down half of her water.

It was the question he'd hoped to avoid, one he wanted to skirt when it was brought up by Collins or anyone else during the remainder of the investigation.

"Those Good Samaritans helped you after the crash," he said, looking away from the rearview mirror, "and I had to make sure they got out of the storm safely. There wasn't any reason to keep them out in these dangerous conditions once I arrived."

He met her gaze through the mirror.

"I know them," Natalie said softly, unblinking.

"What luck," Mitch said, fighting to keep his irritation from surfacing.

"Well, one of them anyway. Lucia. She used to date my big brother."

Mitch unlocked his phone and opened his email, ignoring the small talk.

"She's a good woman. I can't believe she was here." Her voice trembled at the end of her sentence, and her eyes glistened.

"Get out all these extra details now if you must," Mitch advised. "If you bring up irrelevant details when you speak on the record with anyone else, you will put that woman and her friends on the radar."

"What? Why? They didn't kidnap me."

"No. But how did they find you out in the middle of nowhere? There are about two houses in ten square miles. The more you talk, the more questions you'll create. And that could hurt the people who helped you."

He only had a few months left until retirement, and something like this just had to happen. It was far too complicated, even if he did save Kaylie like he swore to. Well, technically, someone else had saved her, and he just came to clean up their mess afterward.

He knew exactly what they were: vigilantes.

But even if they were vigilantes, they'd done what he couldn't and had saved Kaylie and Natalie. They'd also killed a suspect, and now he would take the blame for that.

"Who shot the man who hurt you?" He observed Natalie through the mirror.

Her lips pursed, and she hesitated before answering him. "You did."

"Why?"

"Because he had a gun. He was going to kill me, but then he pointed it at you."

"Where were you?"

"Outside of the car, lying in the snow. One of the women who stopped was pulling Kaylie from the backseat."

"Can you remember anything else?"

"I—"

"The answer is no. There's nothing else to tell. Not a single additional detail to relay. Do you understand? Do you truly grasp what's at stake?"

"I don't—"

"Where was he bringing you from?"

"A house in the city."

"Where?"

"I don't know exactly."

"Was there anyone else in the house?"

"Yes," she whispered, seeming to lose her breath. Her face turned hard, her body tensing. "Two other men. Tyler and Jeff."

"Okay, and what do you think happens if the investigation focuses on the good samaritans instead of Tyler and Jeff."

"The wrong people go to jail?"

"The focus on the people who hurt you could be diverted, and then they can run. They'll get away, and then they'll hurt someone else. And they won't have to face justice for what they've done to you and Kaylie. Instead, the good guys will be the ones who get punished."

Good guys and bad guys? Was he getting senile already?

"I understand. But who will protect them from the Fear Doirich?"

"The what?"

"That's what he calls himself. The Dark Man."

"Oh? That's Irish. Who is he?"

"He's the one who paid them to keep me. To hurt me."

A low-level pimp or a crime lord? He wondered before the memory struck him. He'd heard that name before in one of the reports from the state's intelligence fusion center.

"He'll want revenge. No one interferes with his business. No one takes his things."

Mitch studied her carefully in the reflection, worried momentarily that she was suffering from Stockholm syndrome or some gross fascination with the man who'd claimed her. But he didn't see that in her eyes. Her shoulders slumped forward, and she crossed her arms over her chest. Tears trickled down her red, soot-streaked cheeks.

"I'll see what I can do to help them." He couldn't promise anything to Natalie without raising suspicion, but he swore to himself that he wouldn't let any harm come to Shelby, Lucia, and Sam.

Before they could converse further, a line of responders' vehicles appeared through the driving snow on the road behind him, lights flashing and sirens blaring.

"Remember what I said, okay?"

Natalie nodded.

"I will," Kaylie said. The unexpected words came from the woman who'd been deathly silent until now, startling both of them. "But you have to protect my sister."

It was too late to ask what she meant, and if she mentioned it during the interviews, Mitch would have to be very careful about how he followed that thread.

"You're going to be okay, Kaylie. I promise I'll protect your sister, too." He'd said the words to calm her. He hoped his promise wouldn't be broken.

Chapter 5

CHAPTER FIVE

Dawn did not glimmer through the curtains as it usually would. Sunshine did not greet Phil as he woke with his alarm.

Today was special; it was his first full day of reclaimed freedom.

A combination of bribes and threats against the judge's family secured Phil's freedom. Regardless of how he'd gained it, he was thrilled to get back to work.

He'd never reclaim the use of his legs. Despite the encouragement of the gorgeous, young physical therapist in charge of his program, he knew that thinking positively wouldn't work miracles for him.

He was a realist, and anything he got came from his father or his own hard work.

And Phil loved his work.

With the judge bribed to secure his loyalty and others in the system on the payroll, Phil felt safe returning to his business.

After getting ready for the morning—which was no easy feat these days—Phil focused on his first order of business: connecting with his lieutenants. He needed to know if they'd made any progress acquiring the "pets" he'd requested. After settling in at his desk, he opened his phone. To Bran, the senior of the pair, he sent his coded message.

How is the adoption process moving along?

After a few minutes spent organizing his thoughts on paper, his phone dinged with a text.

Difficult. The paperwork is in order, but there are delays.

Phil chewed the inside of his cheek before replying. *Still? Help me understand.*

Bran's response came faster than expected. *After last night's events at the shelter, things have become more complicated.*

"What the hell?" Phil muttered, scanning the words. *Are you going to fix it or what?*

I'll do my best. The blizzard shut everything down.

Phil plucked a remote from the top drawer of his dark mahogany desk and pressed a button. The blinds on the wall of windows on the opposite side of the room curled upward. He rolled across the room to the wall of windows facing the garden and stared out over the blinding landscape.

It was unrecognizable. Flowerbeds and statuary took on bloated forms, masking their true shapes.

Damn it.

He returned to his desk and typed furiously with his thumbs. *Whatever you need, no matter the cost, make it happen. Move fast, or we'll lose the opportunity.*

Consider it done, Bran texted.

Phil snorted. *I'll consider it done once they're home with me.*

Phil locked his phone screen and cracked his knuckles before returning to his paper notes. Even though he wrote in shorthand, he'd still burn everything in the fireplace afterward. He couldn't take any chances, even if the DOJ seemed temporarily off his back. A few rabid dogs could still be hounding his tracks, scrounging for scraps of evidence.

Before reorganizing his business, he needed to collect those loose ends and burn the fringes. He couldn't move forward until he felt he was in control again.

The door to his study clicked, and he glanced up to find his father striding in. The older man walked a few steps into the room, stood erect, and cast his stony gaze downward at Phil.

"It's time to call your brother," Richard ordered before turning and leaving the room.

Phil nodded, even though his father couldn't see. The dominoes were stacked. It was time to knock them down.

Chapter 6
CHAPTER SIX

B rennan always took his morning coffee in the breakfast room with one tablespoon of cream and one teaspoon of sugar while reading the morning paper.

Soft hands surprised him, but he didn't flinch as long, silky fingers traced their way through his hair and down his neck. A gentle feminine voice whispered, "Good morning, my love."

He twisted in his chair to kiss her full lips deeply. Even after six years of marriage, it still felt like they were in the honeymoon phase. She was the perfect woman—a killer body, educated mind, and far more loyal than he could have dreamed. There was no one and nothing on the planet he loved more than his wife–save for their four-year-old daughter.

Cynthia stepped away for a moment before returning with her own cup of coffee. She was dressed in a short silk slip, and he didn't try to stop himself from staring at her lightly tanned thighs until she was seated. She grinned wildly, still glowing after a night of passionate love-making. He worshipped her in the bedroom, and she worshipped him too. When he looked at her, when he loved her, he knew he struck gold when he'd won her heart.

"Anything interesting in the paper this morning?" she asked before sipping her coffee. She leaned forward and stared at him with her sexy crystal blue eyes. Brennan wanted to carry her back to bed, but he refrained.

"Not much," he said, folding the paper and placing it in the center of the table. "A few charity events are coming up if you'd like us to attend."

Her eyes lit up at the suggestion, and her smile widened. "You know I'm a sucker for parties."

"I do." He smiled and reached his hand across the table, and she accepted it, gently stroking his fingers. Her touch was still electric to him, and he wanted to pick her up and take her back to bed.

"Mommy?" a sleepy little voice called out, firmly canceling the plans he was forming for his wife.

"Hey, honey," he greeted her with his arms outstretched. Her tiny bare feet pattered across the marble floor until she could jump into his arms. He pulled her into a tight hug and kissed her hair before setting her on the floor again so she could run and hug her mother.

"How did you sleep, Lizzie?" Cynthia asked as she seated their daughter on her lap.

"Good." Lizzie yawned and rubbed her eyes.

Brennan chuckled at her stubbornness. She could have slept in a while longer, but she wanted to be near her parents. The little one was determined to have what she wanted, and in that regard, she was like both of her parents.

His cell phone buzzed from the kitchen, and he sighed before rising to get it. "Take a look at what's going on this weekend, then tell me which you'd like to attend," he instructed Cynthia. "Once the weather clears, you should go out and shop for some new dresses. I promised to make up for all the extra hours, so let me show you a good time this weekend, honey."

"You don't have to do that," she said, but he knew he did. She stood and kissed his cheek before taking their daughter upstairs to prepare for the day.

His desire for her would have to wait.

Brennan answered his phone and stared out over the whitecaps of Lake Angelus just beyond the edges of his property.

"Bren, I need your help."

Damnit, Phil. Brennan sighed.

"What now, little brother?"

"Those people. They're coming after me and—"

"So?" Brennan interrupted.

"We're family, ass."

"Watch your tongue with me, little brother."

"They're not just coming for me. They're coming for our entire family."

"Shut up, Phil," Brennan growled low through the phone, then looked around. Once he was sure his wife and daughter had disappeared upstairs, he continued. "You can't say shit like this!"

"But, Bren—"

"You have ninety-nine problems, and all of them are bitches."

"That's not funny."

"Well, it's your own fault."

"You need to—"

"I don't need to do anything," Brennan half-shouted before stopping himself. He rubbed his temple with one hand. "Seriously. Shut up. I already told you I don't want anything to do with the family business. I don't give a shit what happens to you anymore. You brought it on yourself."

"I'm not going to sit around and let them hurt our parents."

"That's not going to happen." Brennan scoffed. Their father's security firm was essentially his own private army. The likelihood of anyone getting near him was slim to nil.

"But they have a cop—"

"You know what your problem is? You don't know when to just sit down and shut the hell up. How many times do I have to say it?"

"Nice, bro. Real funny," Phil deadpanned.

"That's not what I meant," Brennan tried to backpedal his choice of words, but it was too late. Phil had been in a wheelchair ever since he left the hospital. Despite all the money spent on the latest medicine and therapy techniques, no one expected Phil would ever walk again. He was lucky to be alive at all, according to the doctors.

"This little problem with these people needs to be taken care of. If we don't strike first, they're going to hit us hard."

"You messed up, and it's exactly for this reason: you don't think things through." Brennan paused just long enough to let his words settle in. "You shouldn't even be talking about things like this. You're going to get into more trouble if you don't learn to think before you open your big mouth or sic your thugs on random people who don't even pose an actual threat to you."

His brother was an idiot who had spent his entire life getting away with everything. Mommy and Daddy were always there to bail him out. Hell, even Brennan had fought all his brother's battles when Phil didn't want their parents to find out he'd messed up again. Not that their parents were squeaky clean, but the older pair hadn't taught their third child any restraint or reason. Phil was out of control, and he was only going to make everything worse for himself and everyone around him.

Calling and talking about murdering people was exceedingly dangerous. If the phones were tapped—and Brennan would have bet his new Maserati they were—then Phil was only digging himself a deeper hole with the feds.

There was a long silence before his little brother finally spoke again. "I'm scared, Brennan."

Brennan relaxed his shoulders and released a tense breath he hadn't realized he'd been holding. He was a sucker for his family, especially his little brother. Phil always found a way to weasel back into Brennan's bleeding heart. If he was good at anything at all, it was at being a manipulative little bastard.

"How about I come for a visit?" Brennan suggested. "It might be good for you. Then, we can sit down and talk about everything going on. I bet you'll feel a lot better if you have a chance to vent."

"Yeah, I guess."

"This weekend, I'm busy," Brennan said, thinking of the time together he'd promised his wife. "But after I get a few things done in the office this week, I'll drop by for a visit. Maybe even tonight if the weather lets up a little. Would that be good?"

"Fine, bro. I'm counting on you." Phil sounded too firm, as if he already expected Brennan's commitment.

"See you later," Brennan said, hanging up before Phil could find a way to keep him on any longer.

As Brennan headed upstairs to find Cynthia and Lizzie, he chewed on what Phil would try to make him do. He wouldn't, of course. He had too much to lose. He had a wife and daughter he loved more than life itself, a successful business, an expansive home on Lake Angelus, private security, a small army of house help, and private tutoring for his child. He'd never risk his family's safety and their lifestyle to entangle himself in his family's business. It wasn't worth the risk.

When he found Cynthia, she was gently brushing out Lizzie's hair. Lizzie loved to pick her own clothes, and today, she'd chosen a fluffy purple tulle dress. It wouldn't be appropriate if she'd been headed to private school, but she'd be privately tutored until Kindergarten. Besides, it was a snow day. He'd encourage his daughter to let her creativity run wild.

"Who was that?" Cynthia asked when she spotted him.

"Phil," he said softly, leaning against the doorway.

Cynthia said nothing, her gaze focused on Lizzie's hair. Lizzie hardly knew her uncle because Cynthia had always disliked Brennan's brother, and he wasn't allowed to visit without his parents.

"I need to see him and my parents after work. Maybe tonight if the storm ends. Is that all right?"

Cynthia shrugged. "If that's what you feel you need to do, then of course. As long as he isn't coming here."

She used to call Phil names like "creep" and "weirdo," but those little jabs had disappeared since the shooting. Still, Brennan knew it was only out of respect for him and that her feelings toward his brother hadn't changed at all.

Brennan stepped into the room, kissing Lizzie's head before planting a single warm kiss on his wife's soft cheek. "It won't be a big deal, I promise. You focus on parties and dresses. Don't let it sour plans for our big weekend. Deal?"

"Deal," she said with a smile that didn't reach her eyes.

Chapter 7

CHAPTER SEVEN

S am followed Penny as she bounded through the fresh, deep snow, following close until he found where Lucia had fallen. His heart jumped
to his throat, and he dropped to his knees to pull her face from the snow.

"Come on, Lucia," he shouted above the moaning wind. The blizzard
was only getting worse, and the temperature continued to drop. Sam pulled
Lucia into his arms and stood. Gingerly, he stood her up, wrapped an arm
around her shoulders, and half-dragged her back into the house. It was
an odd situation. She'd always been so independent, too much to let him
carry her, even in a playful manner. But today, she faltered. Maybe it was
the exhaustion. Or maybe her will had been broken by the news of Phil's
freedom.

As bad as it had been that he was released to his father's custody and on
house arrest, it was far worse to know that the judge had thrown out all the
charges. A thorough investigation would likely reveal a trail of bribery that
led to the judge's decision, but Sam didn't have the means to initiate such
an operation. Besides, the judge likely had several layers of legal protection
afforded by the very people who'd paid him off.

When he climbed the steps to the front door, it opened before he could
try to reach it. Shelby stood aside and motioned for him to enter. He kept

a tight hold on Lucia. Her body felt weak under his touch. As angry as he was, he was worried now, too.

"Thanks," he said before sitting Lucia on the couch. Her eyes were open, but she stared blankly ahead. "What the hell were you thinking? You can't run out in a blizzard like that—"

"I... I just don't care." She shook her head and squeezed her eyes shut, dropping her head into her hands.

Sam held back a sigh and gritted his teeth.

"She's fine. Just give her a minute," Shelby said, her dark eyes as stone-cold as ever. She took a seat in the recliner and started calmly rocking again. "We have another problem to talk about."

"Damn it. What now?"

"That man—"

"Which man?"

Shelby paused, no emotion on her face. "The one you shot."

Stunned, Sam said nothing. The gravity of what he'd done was only just beginning to sink in.

"He was one of three," she continued. "There are two other men."

"And?" Sam didn't want to have an attitude with Shelby. Frankly, there was something all too eerie in her calm demeanor, reminding him of the special ops guys he'd worked with. She was still but tense, poised to strike when least expected. Whatever her trauma, even he could see it had shaped her into something dangerous and unpredictable. He would always treat her with respect and caution, even if he didn't always trust her.

"And they saw us. Well, at least they saw me. They may have seen Lucia, too."

"You're going to have to add a little more detail because I have no idea what you're referring to at this point."

"We didn't just accidentally find that car, Sam. We found out where that kidnapped girl was being held, and we scouted the place."

"Why the hell wouldn't you just call the cops? I'm sure they have a tip line for this sort of thing."

"They do have a tipline," she said, venom lacing her tone. "And we did call. They couldn't search the place. Not enough evidence for a warrant, and the property owner wouldn't give them permission."

"So what? You can't go around doing this."

"Bullshit, I can't!"

"It's illegal, Shelby!"

"And so is what they're doing." Her voice was steady, and though she did not increase her volume, her commanding tone and steely resolve permeated the air between them. "If the cops can't do anything about it, then I will. No one was there to rescue me, dammit. There were no cops, no good Samaritans, just me. I had to save my damn self! Do you have any idea what that's like? To believe you're going to die? That your life is over? No, you don't. So, I don't need your damn opinions or your permission to do the right thing."

Sam was too stunned to say anything. His guilt over getting her worked up blunted his anger. He simply stared at her, imagining the hell she'd been through last summer. He'd read enough of the reports and heard from Lucia what had happened to Shelby: kidnapped, beaten, raped, starved. And then she had somehow escaped, slipping through the fields and the woods until she found her way to the Michigan State Police post in Pine River. The officer who'd first found her didn't think she'd survive. She not only survived, but she'd thrived.

Shelby was out of the hospital sooner than anyone could have predicted. Her youth, general good health, and mindset all helped her recover quickly. It wasn't long after they'd both left the hospital that she reached out to Lucia. They became fast friends and soon spent far more time together than seemed normal for adult friends. Of course, he'd had friends like that in the Army, but not since he had come home.

"We knew where Kaylie was, so we did what we could, Sam. And no matter the legal consequences, it was the right thing to do."

"We can't change the past. So, what's this problem you're worried about?"

"They saw us, and I'm worried they're going to talk. They also had a security system that probably caught my face."

"So?"

"So, we need to eliminate the traces of our presence at that house. That detective is going to find out about us being at the house. Then, all the weight of our screwed-up legal system will come crashing down on all of us."

As Sam thought about it, he couldn't deny the truth of her assessment. That same system had let Phil off the hook and would hungrily prosecute Sam for pulling the trigger on the man who had pointed his gun at Shelby. Like it or not—and he didn't like it at all—he was now completely roped into the mess these women had dived into headfirst.

"What do you suggest we do?" He absently rubbed his hands together.

"We need to get to the house in Southfield before the cops do," Lucia finally spoke up.

He glanced over and met her gaze, her dark eyes burning into him with fiery resolve.

"And do what, exactly?"

"We need to figure out how to delete the footage from their system. I'm not worried about them mentioning us. Their descriptions would be too vague to track us down, but any pictures or video of us there would be damning."

A fleeting thought tickled his memory. "Southfield? Weren't you looking at a house down there?"

"Well, that was our cover."

It took every ounce of control he had to not react to the way she said "cover." She was a civilian using terms typical for the defense industry.

"Then why are you worried about what the cameras caught? They would actually back up your house-hunting."

"Do you want to take that risk?" Shelby challenged, arching an eyebrow.

"Apparently, you two need a little help with your approach to this stuff. First, stick with your story. If you worked so hard to make a cover story about house hunting, then you preach it until you believe it. Don't go trying to destroy evidence that would support your claims. Besides, if that house is where Kaylie came from, then I'd bet it's already crawling with uniforms."

The sudden idea that he was straying from the blue stabbed at his conscience. Was he working against his fellow LEOs now? No. He could not–he would not–accept that scenario.

But he couldn't deny that he no longer walked the straight and narrow.

His legal and moral ground was shaky at best, but he'd also become deeply disillusioned in the past 24 hours. The man who'd shot him would never be made to pay for his crimes. The scar on Sam's chest would never disappear. It would always be a reminder of the monster who'd tried to kill him and Lucia, the asshole who got off scot-free because a fallible justice system had failed.

He balled his hand into a fist and bit his knuckle. "Dammit."

"There's another problem," Lucia said, her voice returning.

"Of course there is," Sam groaned, but neither woman seemed to notice.

"Natalie said these guys work for a powerful man they call the Fear Doirich."

Sam froze. "I swear I've heard that name before."

"She warned that he'll come after us if they tell him we were involved."

"Fear Doirich is an Irish legend. The Dark Man," Shelby interjected, reading from her phone.

"How could he possibly know to come after us?"

"The security footage." Lucia finally looked at him. "If they send that to their boss and he decides we're the reason why Natalie and Kaylie didn't make it, he'll retaliate. People with this kind of money? They can find us. They can find our families."

"Shit." Sam stood from the couch and began to pace. "Do you realize how deep down the rabbit hole we are now?"

"I'm sorry, Sam," Lucia said, her voice wavering and eyes brimming with tears. "I didn't mean for you to get involved. I didn't want you to know."

"Why?"

"Because. Your job, your life. Your values." She swiped at her falling tears with the back of her hand. "I know how important the law is to you."

It pained him to see her cry, the sight melting his head and wrenching his heart. He thought of the way his heart dropped when he saw the man with the gun. If he'd killed Shelby, he would have turned his gun on Lucia next. "You shouldn't be doing any of this shit. You were right to keep it from me."

He wouldn't let his feelings for her blunt the truth or his anger.

"I'll make it up to you, I swear." Lucia reached for him, but he leaned away from her.

"You two need to put your personal shit aside for a minute. What are we going to do about these other two asshats?" Shelby seemed entirely unaffected by Sam and Lucia's tension.

Sam focused on Lucia. "We have to see this through."

"When do you have to work again?" Shelby asked.

"Today, but I'll use leave. I guess I'm too sick to work," he grumbled. It wasn't too far from the truth, considering his mental state. "I'll get on a telehealth call and get out of work. Shelby, start searching and see what you can find out about the house. Apparently, the two of you have been very good at research, so—"

"They aren't at the house," Lucia interrupted.

Sam turned his gaze on her. She held up a plain black phone he hadn't seen before and turned the screen to him. A dot blinked on a map. "What is that?"

"We put a GPS tracker on their truck." Shelby grinned. "What the hell are they doing all the way up there?"

"Doesn't matter," Sam said, taking the phone from Lucia's hand and studying the map. "Do whatever you need to get ready. I'm going to call my boss, then we're going to have a talk with those two."

"And what?" Shelby prompted. "You're just going to ask nicely, Sam?"

"I guess we'll figure it out on the way, Shelby," he replied cooly.

"What about the roads?" Lucia asked. "The storm is getting worse, not better."

"That's why we got that truck." He said dismissively. "Let's get moving, or the law will find them first."

Chapter 8
CHAPTER EIGHT

Once they'd settled in the cabin and secured Ellie in a bedroom, Tyler and Jeff began cleaning the place up. It'd been a few months since either had visited the cabin, but at least the electricity was still on, ensuring the place was just warm enough to keep the pipes from freezing. They hadn't forgotten to stop and get groceries either, and the rural party store was just how they remembered it: happy for cash payments and camera-free.

It didn't take them long to get the cabin warmed up and clean, briefly wiping a thin layer of dust from the surfaces and bagging up food left in the fridge from the last visit.

As eager as he was to soothe his anxiety with Ellie's help, Tyler knew he needed to check in with the Fear Doirich's men first.

He texted the man known only as "B." Did Derek make it to you last night?

The response was almost immediate. No. Raven and the other are with the police now.

"What?" he half-shouted. What happened?

Interference, the response read. Derek is dead.

"What's wrong?" Jeff asked.

Tyler looked up from his phone, too stunned to speak. He passed the phone to Jeff, who quickly skimmed over the texts.

"No!" Jeff cried out, faltering backward until he fell onto the dusty old couch in the cabin's living room.

While Tyler and Jeff were the closest of the three friends, they still cared for Derek. He'd been like a little brother to them, annoying and stupid. But he was one of them, and they'd looked out for him. Until last night, it seemed, when Tyler had unwittingly sent the youngest of the friends to his death.

A ding broke through the fog of grief, and his numb fingers slipped the phone from Jeff's limp hand.

We need to talk in person. The text read.

Fear washed over Tyler's grief like an icy wave, chilling his blood and clearing his mind. They'd messed up, and if they didn't correct their mistakes, Tyler and Jeff would soon join Derek on the other side.

"Shit," he hissed in a whisper. "They're going to kill us."

The last sentence shook Jeff from his shock. "What?"

"We know too much, and we fucked up. If we can't find a way to make it right, they're going to kill us!"

"Ask him! Ask what we need to do to fix it!"

Tyler fired off a text. I know I messed up. How do I make it right?

We'll talk about that when we meet. Where are you?

With shaking fingers, Tyler tapped out another message. Please, anything. Just tell me what we need to do first.

There was a brief pause, then another ding of doom split the room's heavy silence.

Don't make me track you down.

Tyler immediately powered down the phone and then sat beside Jeff on the couch. "We're fucked. Completely and utterly."

Chapter 9
CHAPTER NINE

Lucia tapped on her wireless mouse, taking screenshots of the popular map service's satellite imagery layer. Occasionally, she'd glance at the GPS tracking indicator on Shelby's burner phone to confirm it was still actively transmitting from the same location. She studied the terrain where the dot had stopped while Shelby showered and Sam called out of work. It was heavily wooded, hiding rolling hills and deep streambeds.

A quick cross-reference between the map and a real estate website showed the property was a three-bedroom cabin with a small barn. There were few pre-sale interior photos, and she was grateful the listing hadn't been removed entirely upon purchase.

The interior was outdated, with 70s wood paneling, Formica countertops, and log cabin-style interior doors throughout.

A hand squeezed Lucia's shoulder, and she started. Turning, she found Sam staring at her through sad green eyes.

"What did you find?"

She wanted to reach out to him, to wrap her arms around his neck and find comfort in his embrace, but she knew he wasn't ready. He'd had to lie to get out of work, and anger burned in his eyes. The way they shined warned Lucia away. Instead of reaching out to him, she pointed at the burner phone. "The tracker is still transmitting from a small property up near West Branch."

"That sounds familiar."

"That's close to I-75, but the cabin is technically in Nester Township north of Gladwin, which is officially in the middle of nowhere. How did your call go?"

He shook his head. "Fine. I'm probably contagious, so I'm out of work for three days. I just have to check in each morning with an update on my symptoms. Let's just hope Dan doesn't try to stop by with soup."

"Unfortunately, he might because we'd do the same for him." Lucia checked her watch. It was already 7 a.m. "So maybe we have twenty-four hours?"

"Not really. At the very least, I have to text Dan tonight to update him on my status. Then, I have to call again in the morning."

"This place is really out there in no man's land. What if we get stuck up there and can't get signal?"

Sam shrugged. "I'll figure it out."

Lucia hesitated and turned her gaze back to the screen. "I don't know what's going to happen when we get there."

"There's no way of knowing. But we've got three capable people here now instead of two. Everyone needs a shower and warm clothing, and we need to gear up."

"Sam," she started, raising her hand.

Clenching his jaw, he stared at her hand and avoided her eyes. "Not yet. Make sure you and Shelby wear something warm." He turned and walked away.

Lucia's eyes stung with tears as she watched him disappear down a hallway toward the room they usually shared. Her office felt cold, empty, and lonely now. Were they back to square one with their relationship?

If they were, it was her own fault. She'd spoken too many lies, carrying the weight of her secrets like a wedge between them.

"What's the plan?" Shelby walked in, stopping in her tracks when she saw Lucia.

Try as she might, Lucia couldn't wipe the tears from her face quickly enough.

"Hey," Shelby whispered as she moved closer, kneeling down next to Lucia's chair. "Do you need me to beat that man's ass?"

"That's not funny," Lucia said, chuckling through her tears anyway.

"I'm sorry, Luce. I know it doesn't seem fair. But it was inevitable. We're just lucky he's not turning us in right now." She rubbed Lucia's back briefly.

"I suppose I should be happy about that."

"Meh. I wouldn't wallow over it. That man loves you. Just give him time. And be totally honest from here on out."

It was a kind gesture, and Lucia appreciated it. "I know. I guess I don't have time to worry about it right now, huh?"

Shelby stared back, her dark eyes glittering with a touch of empathy, but she said nothing.

"I'm going to take a quick shower and get some warm clothes. While I'm doing that, take a look at the images I collected. You're good at planning too, you know?" She forced a smile, still wiping tears as she rose from the chair and strode out of her office.

After a quick shower to remove the past day from her skin–and to prevent cross-contaminating evidence that could connect them to other places–Lucia dressed warmly and collected the best clothes she could find to fit Shelby. She set her friend up with the clothes and gave her a fresh towel for the shower before heading to the basement.

She found Sam filling handgun magazines with ammunition. He faced his workbench, his back to her.

"We'll take two 9 mm's and the 7mm Remington," he said without looking up. "I've already loaded a few mags and–"

Lucia pulled his arm, turning him toward her. She wrapped her arms around his neck and kissed him on his lips.

He was still at first, and her heart skipped a beat as she desperately sought the love he'd always blessed her with. Finally, he relaxed, inhaling sharply before returning her passion. He dropped the ammo and the magazine on the bench behind him before wrapping his arms around her waist. His hands explored her curves, caressed her back, then tangled in her hair.

Sam broke the kiss but didn't push her away. Instead, he pulled her close, and she felt his body tremble. She wished she could know his thoughts.

"Sam, I–"

"Stop, Luce," he whispered into her hair. "I love you, but you have to stop."

She wanted to argue, wanted to explain all the reasons she'd lied and hid this part of her life from him. But the words didn't come. There were no excuses for her terrible choices that had hurt him. They'd endangered his career and his life.

"Are we ready?"

Lucia whirled, breaking from Sam's embrace to find Shelby on the stairs staring at them. Sam turned slowly, coughing as he picked up the magazine to finish filling it.

"Yep," he said, stuffing the magazine in an ammo pouch. "Let's roll before it gets any later. We still have a blizzard to drive through."

Chapter 10
CHAPTER TEN

T he snowfall had lightened, and the fierce winds had died to only a breeze. Mitch pushed through his exhaustion and the chill settling in his bones to watch as paramedics loaded Kaylie and Natalie into an ambulance.

"That body is Derek's," Collins shared, reading from his notes. "He's one of the three young men who lived at the house on Elmwood Street. The other two, Tyler Barnes and Jeff Vandenberg, are nowhere to be found. Their family members claim they haven't seen either of them in weeks, which was normal, apparently."

Mitch nodded. "Seems typical for twenty-somethings, depending on the family traditions."

"Alexis returned to the department after taking care of Jessica for me, and she jumped right back on the case. She searched for any other property records for the suspects but found none."

"Great." Mitch nodded his approval. Alexis was a rising star, one of Southfield Police Department's brightest junior officers. He turned his attention to the barren, snow-covered fields stretching as far as he could see along the horizon. There wasn't a single house in sight.

"I know. But she's combing social media for other close associates they may have run to."

"Let's hope we track them down before the trail goes cold."

"We should have eyes on their financials sometime today. Hopefully, they're using their cards wherever they go."

"I doubt it."

"Nothing left to do right now but see the victims to the hospital. Victim's advocates are waiting to help us take full statements."

Mitch barely heard him. He thought of Derek, his body lying cold in the snow, and remembered hearing how he'd aimed his gun at Shelby. He might have been torn up, but he couldn't imagine what he would have done if Derek had shot her.

"Are you coming? Or are you just going to stand here and turn into a giant grumpy popsicle?"

"I'm exhausted," Mitch said.

"So, you're not going to pull another fast one on me?" Collins eyed him warily.

Mitch sighed, stretching his neck. "It's been a long weekend."

"It's Tuesday, Mitch."

Laughing, Mitch pinched the bridge of his nose. "See what I mean? I'd really like to get some rest. I mean, if you can handle those two at the hospital." He pointed at the ambulance.

"I got them. You go catch some z's, old man."

"Thanks, partner." Mitch began walking to his car, leaving Collins to ride back to Southfield with their boss, Deputy Chief Graves, who was on his way to meet him at the hospital.

"But you best believe I'll be checking up on you!"

Mitch waved a hand without looking back, then stuffed his freezing hands in his coat.

Once in his car, he headed toward the small town of Durand and stopped at the gas station near the freeway to fuel up and grab a cup of coffee. The urge to eat was missing from his body. He felt physically hollow as his thoughts revolved around Shelby and the two missing men.

He didn't want to make Shelby wait to know the truth, but finding the other two men was more important right now. Those monsters needed to be taken off the streets for good.

Letting his coffee cool, Mitch sat in his car in the station's parking lot. He opened the laptop connected to his vehicle's Mobile Data Terminal. Immediately, he emailed Alexis, asking for her to immediately text him with anything that might be helpful. Then, he focused on the social profiles of the three men from the house.

Tyler's was filled with tasteless memes, but Jeff's was a little more interesting. Derek, the young man whose body still lay in the snow, had much more on his public profile than the other two.

Mitch settled in, sipping his coffee as he scrolled through the young man's posts. He scanned each picture, studied every video, and reviewed each friend he tagged.

A picture caught his attention as he fought sleep, struggling to keep his eyes open. Derek stood in the picture with a friend, each of them holding up a largemouth bass for the camera. Beneath clear, bright blue skies, a lake surrounded by dense forest filled the background.

The second man seemed eerily familiar to Mitch.

Scrolling up to read the caption, he found the name Jake Michelson tagged.

Jake. Jake!

That was the man who'd helped deliver unsuspecting women to Tyler, Jeff, and Derek. His real name was Michael Roberts, but he'd used others while scouring local clubs for vulnerable women. He'd turned himself in, confessing his involvement and promising to testify in exchange for protection for his fiancée Sarah.

And here he was, in a picture from a fishing trip with one of the Elmwood house suspects.

Roberts hadn't mentioned being connected to any of the three on social media, and he certainly hadn't brought up any trips.

Best way to spend the first weekend of bass season! with Jake Michelson at Streaked Lake.

Streaked Lake? The location wasn't tagged on the media platform, and a simple map search yielded too many results. Mitch dug into the trip photos, scrolling back and forth until he could determine the area.

One of the earliest posts from their trip showed them smiling in a selfie together while sitting in a truck. This time, it included a tagged location: Gary's Bait, Party, and Pizza Shop.

Typical of remote country stores, they carried a little bit of everything for visitors and residents alike.

This one sat on the western fringes of the vast zip code encompassing the tiny town of Gladwin.

Mitch marked it down on his notepad and began reading through the comments.

Someone had asked "Jake" what he was doing all the way up there.

My friend's cousin has a cabin up here.

Fingers fumbled as he pulled his cell phone from his pocket. He dialed Alexis. She'd been a major help on the case so far, sorting through tips and conducting deep-dive background research.

"Morning," she said, her voice raspy and muffled.

"Are you really sleeping right now?"

"One of us needs to." She grumbled something else he couldn't hear, then yawned. Her voice was clear when she spoke again.

"Come on," Mitch pressed. "It's almost seven! The day's getting away from us."

"Do you know how late I stayed up? We're at a dead end with Barnes and Vandenberg. I didn't lay down until Collins texted and told me you were all right."

"That's sweet and all, but I need your skills."

"Aw, hell. What now?"

"Roberts has a social media profile under an alias. I'm guessing his fiancée has no clue."

"So, what? Did he use it to–"

"It's connected to the suspects from the Elmwood house."

Alexis was silent as she processed his statement.

Mitch continued. "I'm looking at pictures of Roberts with Derek Adams. Roberts wrote that his friend's cousin had a cabin up there."

"That's pretty vague."

"It's the only thing we have."

"You're going up there, aren't you?"

"How long before you can get started? Search for family properties near Gladwin."

"You didn't answer me, detective," Alexis pressed.

Mitch sighed. He hated lying. He hated it more that Alexis already knew him so well. She'd make a great partner for Collins someday. "I'm going to get some shut-eye." It was a compromise. Not a lie, but not entirely the truth either.

"Fine. We'll play that game. Just keep your phone on in case I need to update you. All this sounds like a stretch."

"Yeah, I know. It could be a waste of time. But we have no idea where else they may have gone." Mitch wrapped his fingers around the steering wheel and twisted. "They can't disappear. We have to find them."

"I'm with you all the way," Alexis said through a yawn. "Even for a wild goose chase."

"Thanks." Mitch ended the call and set his GPS destination for the bait, party, and pizza shop.

Chapter 11
CHAPTER ELEVEN

The wind had calmed, and the sun was peeking through the clouds every now and then. A light snowfall still fell from the bright gray skies, adding to the six inches that had accumulated overnight. Sam had slept in the front passenger seat, and Shelby had laid out in the backseat to sleep during the drive.

It was a calm and quiet trip, with music playing inaudibly for background noise so Lucia could focus on the road conditions. With the backroads still slick and packed with snow, Lucia had driven carefully, focusing on safety and control over speed. Even Highway 18 hadn't been cleared by the county's plows and salt trucks yet. If she crashed the truck, then they wouldn't get there at all, and they'd have no chance of accomplishing their mission.

They'd driven for almost two hours by the time they made it to Gladwin–still another twenty snowy miles from their destination–when Lucia stopped for fuel. Sam and Lucia stood together at the gas pumps while Shelby went inside for food and coffee.

When the gas tank was full and Shelby had returned, Sam took over driving so Lucia could rest a little. Shelby took the backseat again without asking, so Lucia leaned the seat back and closed her eyes.

"So, what exactly is the plan, Sam?" Shelby asked.

Lucia groaned inwardly. They were too close to their destination, and now it was time to build some sort of plan. She wouldn't be getting any rest until this was all over. Despite that knowledge, she kept her eyes shut anyway.

"I guess I'll go up there and ask for it."

Her eyes shot open, and she turned to Sam. He didn't bother glancing at her.

"What?" she asked, unsure she'd heard him clearly.

Sam shrugged. "We're not going to sneak around, try to get in undetected to steal the phone. This isn't some spy movie. We don't have a team of hackers who can unlock it and delete all the evidence."

"These men are dangerous," Shelby said slowly. "They will not just give it to you."

"Maybe they will if Lucia is set up with that rifle and can sight in on whoever comes out of that cabin."

"You think so, huh?" Shelby laughed.

"And you," he glanced over his shoulder at Shelby, "you're my wildcard."

"That's the only thing you've said that I could possibly agree with."

"I still don't understand," Lucia interjected. "What the hell is the plan, Sam?"

"You and Shelby spread out, set up to cover the cabin. I'll walk up and strike a deal for the phone."

"Okay, and the backup plan?" Lucia glanced back at Shelby to confirm her worry over the bare-bones, straightforward plan.

"We don't need a backup plan."

"Luce and I always have one," Shelby explained. "Things tend to go sideways, so we need rendezvous points and–"

"That's because you're amateurs."

Lucia felt her mouth fall open, but she was too stunned to control it. Shelby must have also been shocked because she hadn't jumped over the seat and tried to strangle Sam yet.

"Now that you actually have someone with experience here, maybe things won't go 'sideways,' and we can all get in and out without anyone dying today. Wouldn't that be nice for a change?"

"Are you serious?" Shelby glared at Sam, then turned to her friend. "Lucia, is this man serious right now?"

"Oh, I heard all about the bodies they found up by the Manistee National Forest. How many did each of you kill that night? Did you plan to kill them all, or did it just happen after shit went 'sideways'?"

Red filled Lucia's vision, and her face grew hot. "You have no idea all the hell we've been through, what we went through up there to save Miranda and those children!"

"Did you hear that, Sam-the-asshole?" Shelby quipped. "I don't know which Sam you are today, but we saved two babies from being auctioned off to be..." She couldn't speak the words aloud.

Lucia couldn't bear to finish the sentence for her. What the traffickers had intended for those babies was too depraved and monstrous to discuss. But if he knew about the bodies found by law enforcement, then he knew the official conclusion that those infants would have suffered terribly before dying. This part of the market for human flesh had even been briefed by experts to Congress. It was not unknown.

"I have three combat deployments under my belt," Sam said calmly. "Twelve to eighteen months each of almost daily patrols and urban assault. My teams cleared buildings, ran checkpoints, searched civilians, and returned fire in combat engagements. You ain't got shit on that."

Lucia gritted her teeth and nodded. "Sure, Sam. I'll remember that next time we're in Iraq or Afghanistan."

"It's relevant everywhere. Damn it, Lucia! You and your little buddy just can't admit that you don't have it all figured out, huh? You can't handle the idea that I might know more than you about anything tactical."

Her blood boiled in her veins, but she couldn't respond to any of it. Even if she wanted to rebut, Sam wasn't interested in anything she had to say on the matter. And mostly, he was right. She and Shelby were book- and range-trained. They'd only undertaken two 'missions' so far, and both had gone anything but to plan.

"Whatever you say, Sam." Shelby sighed and lay down in the seat again. It was dismissive, but the group was fractured, the air in the cab electrified with tension.

Shame and hurt filled Lucia's thoughts, but she breathed through it, pushing it all to the back of her mind. If she didn't get her head right for what they were about to do, they might not be alive to work through it later.

One step, one minute, one hour at a time, Lucia knew she would get through this. Would her relationship or friendship survive? She couldn't say, and she didn't dare guess on either account.

Chapter 12
CHAPTER TWELVE

The fireplace roared as Jeff added another log, scattering embers and tossing sparks into the air. Tyler watched him stomp out the few embers that had fallen onto the ceramic tiled floor in front of the fireplace. He glanced sideways at his room, wishing he had the energy to play with his new friend. But he didn't have any desire to waste time with her right now.

He had to figure out how they'd live through the day.

There had to be something he could say to convince the boss it wasn't their fault and that they could still be useful.

Jeff seemed to read his mind. "Got any ideas?"

Tyler shook his head, studying the flames as they danced and shifted over the seasoned wood. They fed, hungry, upon the bark and grain, crawling until they'd consumed it all. He usually felt as if he were the flame, but today, he felt like the log. Trapped, succumbing to the heat, consumed by the flame.

"Would it have made a difference if we hadn't left Derek alone yesterday?"

Shrugging, Tyler couldn't tear his gaze from the fire.

"It all started with those stupid bitches." Jeff paced the room in his socks, chewing his fingernails.

Tyler said nothing.

"Why can't we just tell B about them? It's their fault, right?"

"That's weak." Tyler scoffed. He wanted to avoid assassination, too, but excuses never worked with these people. "Excuses are the tools of a coward."

"It's not an excuse! Just tell him."

"No," Tyler said flatly. His fingers tapped the arm of the couch, and his vision blurred as he lost focus.

If a Jeff screams in the forest, Tyler wondered, *and no one is around to hear, does he make a sound?*

"Dude. If they want to kill us anyway, then what does it matter?"

Finally, Tyler looked up. "Why not?"

"Hurry up and send it!" Jeff passed his unlocked phone to Tyler.

Tyler gnawed his top lip as he opened the phone and considered what to send. He tapped the screen, and the cursor blinked.

Finally, he typed a new message in the chat with B. *What if I have information about the people who interrupted the transfer?*

He rose to grab a beer and dropped the phone on the couch. It dinged before he reached the fridge, so he turned back and snapped it up to read the message immediately.

What kind of information?

"What are you waiting for?" Jeff urged, almost shouting now. "Just send it to him!"

Tyler locked eyes with his friend, shaking his head slowly. "No. That's not how this works. We only offer what we have in exchange for something else. Information is power, leverage, or currency. This could pay for our lives. If we give it away without securing some guarantee first, then they could kill us anyway."

Realization dawned on Jeff. His face paled, and he dropped onto the couch, sinking back against the cushions limply.

"I'm going to try and give us a little more time, but that requires patience. If you push me, you'll end up pushing the Fear Doirich's lieutenant. And I'd bet he'd kill us for that alone."

"But–"

"Stay calm," Tyler said, enunciating each word. Jeff nodded, keeping his mouth closed this time.

Returning his attention to the phone, Tyler sent a new message. *Good, clear video.*

They both watched the phone, jumping when it dinged again.

Is that all?

"Damn it!" Jeff jumped up from the couch and began pacing again, dragging his fingers through his hair.

Tyler's stomach sank as he scanned the message over and over again, but he didn't show his fear. He'd always been the leader, and leaders didn't have the luxury of falling apart when it mattered most.

He remembered the footage and what the visitors had left on the Tacoma, then sent another text. *What if I could get them for you?*

Nothing happened for several seconds, then a new message popped up. *I'll ask the boss.*

Tyler released a breath as he dropped the phone on the end table. He stretched his arms, then folded them behind his head and smiled up at Jeff.

The other man's eyes widened. "What?"

"I told you to stay calm."

Maybe he'd live to see tomorrow. And maybe he'd get to enjoy the woman waiting in his room today.

Chapter 13
CHAPTER THIRTEEN

S he hardly recognized her own name anymore. Detective Collins had used it several times when attempting to regain her attention, but it felt like it didn't belong to her anymore.

Natalie wanted to be called by her real name, not the one Tyler and the others had assigned to her. But her old name sounded like it belonged to someone else. There was no denying it now; she wasn't the same person anymore.

Escape and rescue hadn't meant shedding the past six months and returning to her old life as if nothing had happened. While she was gone, the world had moved on without her.

Staring through the glass on the door of her room, she watched as the detective stood just outside her room speaking with his boss, Deputy Chief Graves. With the door closed, she couldn't hear what was being said, but at one point, both cast worried glances her way.

The expression on the detective's face didn't assuage her worries as he opened the door and stepped in. His features were grim, and no smile graced his warm, chestnut visage.

"More questions?" she asked grimly.

"Maybe just a few more, Natalie. Mostly about what happened between when you first disappeared and last night."

She nodded, her gaze locking with his as she waited for the other shoe to drop.

"The doctors tell me that aside from the obvious trauma you've endured, you shouldn't have a problem physically healing." He paused, inviting her to speak, but she allowed silence to fill the void between them. "What do you already know?"

"About what?"

"Did they tell you anything about the outside world?"

"No." She looked down at her hands then, trying to block out the memory of being back in that place. "I was never even sure what month it was."

"You didn't see any clocks or calendars."

Natalie shook her head. "Only the clocks on the stove and microwave. There were no calendars, and they never let me around electronics."

"That's okay. Let's start from the beginning, the night you disappeared in Marquette."

Unwelcome tears fell as she related everything she could remember. He'd previously obtained her permission and started a voice recorder. A summary report would be made later.

Natalie related how they'd taken her at night while she was walking back to her dorm. All the details were blurry, and she could hardly remember anything before that. It all felt like it had happened a lifetime ago. Trying to contain her tears, she recounted how they'd abused her body and tormented her mind, moving her from place to place until she ended up with Tyler, Jeff, and Derek.

"Where was that house?" she asked, wanting to fill the holes in her understanding.

"Southfield."

"Just north of Detroit?"

"That's it."

"Where are they?"

"Who?"

"The other two." She failed to keep the tremor from her voice.

"Derek Ad–"

"He's dead. He was going to kill..." She let the words trail off and swallowed hard.

"Tyler Barnes and Jeff Vandenberg were not at the house when we were searched."

Her heart pounded in her chest. "What? Where, then?"

Collins shook his head. "We're looking."

Natalie's body trembled, and she sucked in a ragged breath as she thought of the men's threats against her father and Kaylie's little sister.

"You have to find them."

"We will."

"Is that a promise?"

Collins didn't answer, and she knew he couldn't swear to it.

"Has anyone called my father?"

"I need to share a few things with you first. "It appears that your brother went missing before you were taken. After you were kidnapped, your father reported Richard–"

"Rich," she corrected. Her brother hated his full name.

"Your father reported Rich missing. But he didn't file a missing person report for you. According to his statements, a man named Phillip Mc-Namara had told him you'd be returned to your dad if he helped Phil get someone else.

"Your father's willingness to testify against McNamara afforded him placement in a witness protection program. Unfortunately, the charges against McNamara were dismissed, so your father is no longer eligible for the program."

"He's not being protected?"

"They're sending him home this morning. I've reached out and asked to have him brought here so he could see you. At one point, your father..." He hesitated and looked at the floor.

"Just say whatever you need to tell me. I have to know."

"Natalie, your father tried to kill himself. Since his arrest for the part he played for McNamara, he's either been explicitly on suicide watch or at least under constant supervision."

"Why would he do that?" She couldn't imagine her father trying to kill himself. It was against his values, against his Christian beliefs.

"He's ashamed of what he's done. He feels terrible. His own guilt over what he's done will punish him for the rest of his life."

"What did he do?"

"There's only so much I can say. You'll need to ask him when you see him."

"Why can't you just tell me?"

"I know the barest of details because it didn't happen in our jurisdiction."

"Oh." Another thought suddenly occurred. "Wait. You said my brother was missing? You used the past tense. Does that mean he's been found?"

Collins nodded slowly, but his expression had only grown more morose. "I'm sorry, Natalie."

"No!"

"He passed away at the end of August."

"Rich!" Sobs racked her body as grief overwhelmed her.

"His funeral was held a few days after his body was found."

"Stop it!" She shrieked. "Get out."

She glanced at Collins, expecting him to look shocked or be angry at her for snapping. But his face showed no emotion. He simply turned away from her and left the room.

Natalie gripped the thin hospital blanket in her hands and pulled it to her face, crying into it as she sobbed. She cried for Rich, her big brother and only sibling. Despite all his problems, she'd loved her brother and always hoped he'd get his life straight. She'd wanted to see him healthy, happy, and making the most of life.

It had always felt like there was more time for him to turn it all around. Until there wasn't.

She cried for her father, too, thinking of the hell he must have gone through. Both of his kids had gone missing, one had died. He'd suffered through not knowing what had happened to his beloved children. And he'd suffered alone.

Natalie needed to see him immediately, and she swore she'd put a smile on when she saw him. She'd do anything to give him a reason to live again.

Chapter 14
CHAPTER FOURTEEN

N ow Brennan was missing dinner with his family. Well, at least the family that he wanted to be with. He downed the rest of the fine bourbon before slamming the tumbler on the counter.

"Phil, if you don't shut the hell up, I'm gonna pop you straight in the mouth." Brennan glared daggers at his little brother. "Everything that has happened is your fault. You fucked up, not me, not Ash, not Dad, not Mom. You!"

Phil's icy blue eyes stared back, unmoving, emotionless. Brennan sometimes wondered if their mother had dropped the kid on his head when he was a baby. Something was missing from him, either emotionally or psychologically. Maybe both.

"I have to go after her," Phil explained. "She's coming after me. After all of our family."

"No," Brennan shook his head before pouring another shot of bourbon. "This Sorenson woman had no clue that she had anything until you started fucking with her. If you would have left her alone, none of this would have happened. And now, I'd bet money she just wants to move on with her life and heal from the shit storm you dropped on her life."

"You're a broken record," Phil snapped as he wheeled himself closer to his brother, apparently unafraid of the eldest's anger. "You've already said that. Probably six times."

"Well, it's true." Brennan shrugged before pouring more bourbon into his glass. The fortune of his family wasn't lost on him as he reflected on how they could speak freely in the bunker-like basement of the expansive Grosse Pointe mansion. "You're such an idiot."

To Brennan's surprise, his little brother flipped open a long, sharp knife and held it up. He was too close for comfort, but Brennan refused to let the little shit intimidate him. He didn't move, didn't even flinch.

"Were you keeping that in your back door just for me?"

"I'd never hurt you, brother," Phil said softly. Brennan couldn't tell whether Phil was being sarcastic or not.

"Then you'd better put it away before I give you another hole to hide stuff in," Brennan warned, keeping his voice calm but deadly serious.

"I won't get caught this time." Phil folded the knife and put it back in his pocket. "I'll die first."

"Stop being so dramatic. And stop calling me and talking all this shit over the phone! Don't you know they're listening to everything? They're tapping you, me, our parents, and maybe even Ash."

"Why do you keep bringing up Ash?" Phil leaned back and drummed the fingers of one hand over the arm of his wheelchair.

"Ash would laugh at all of this." Brennan sipped his whiskey. "And she'd kill you herself if you got our parents wrapped up in your fuckups."

"No—"

"Yes," Brennan cut him off. "You wanna play the big bad and think you're the heartless one, but you ain't shit compared to Ash."

"Ash loves me—" Phil started, but his icy eyes finally belied some emotion: doubt mingled with fear.

"Maybe." Brennan shrugged. "I wouldn't test it, though. So shut your damn mouth about any of this, especially over the phone. Don't talk to me about it, and don't call your buddies. Besides, you don't have real friends anyway. They're all just your goons and 'associates.'" He made air quotes for emphasis.

"Am I supposed to just let everything I've built for the past five years go to shit while Sorenson tries to get revenge?"

"Eureka!" Brennan exclaimed, raising his hands in the air. "The kid finally gets it!"

"You can't be serious," Phil challenged, the icy lack of emotion returning to his eyes. "And how the hell are you blaming me? We're family. You're supposed to stand by your blood. Would you let your own business be destroyed? Allow your family to be targeted by a madwoman?"

"I have private security that will utterly destroy anyone who comes near my family. And considering I didn't build my business around illicit activities, I don't think I have much to worry about. And I didn't start shit with some small-town cowboys. But even if I did, I've built an actual business with structure, organization, and protocols that will keep it running and providing for my family even if I'm not in the picture."

"Aw, look at you," Phil teased. "The big goodie-two-shoes. The first-born, the one who gets to keep his nose clean and build a fortune that the feds won't come for."

"I made a choice, just like you did," Brennan rebutted, taking another swallow of bourbon. Glancing down, he was surprised to find his glass empty already. He thought about pouring himself another but capped the bottle instead. He still had to drive home, and he planned to be fully present to spend the rest of the snow day playing outside with his little girl. "You could have done anything. But you chose to be Daddy's little protege, then buck his authority and start your own shit show."

Phil said nothing for a moment, finally breaking his gaze away from his brother and staring at some imaginary point in his mind.

"Listen, I have a family, a legitimate business, and I've worked my ass off to build a life that breaks the chain. I don't want anything to do with this shit. Not with your 'business,' not with Dad's, and not with Ash's."

"Are you sure you're not adopted?" Phil asked, grinning up at him.

Brennan shrugged. "I'd guess I am, but who knows. Switched at birth, maybe. In this family, I'll happily be the black sheep. I've paid my dues and paid back everything Dad's ever given me. I don't owe anyone anything."

"We're blood," Phil rebutted, emphasizing each word. "That means something."

"Sure. It means when you and Dad fuck up, my phone gets tapped. The feds suddenly get extra interested in my business and my family, too!" Brennan was yelling before he realized it and before he could stop himself.

"Bro, chill," Phil said, raising his hands to his brother.

"Do not tell me to chill," Brennan railed, unable to restrain himself any longer. "Do you even have a soul? What the hell is wrong with you? Fuckin' dead-eye Phil, at it again. Always needs someone to bail him out. If it's not Dad, it's me."

"Dead-eye Phil?" Phil's face fell as he contemplated the moniker.

"Have you looked in a mirror?" Brennan laughed. "Listen, I'm not doing it anymore. I've worked my ass off to build a life I can be proud of, and I'm not risking it for you. None of you!" He pointed up, indicating his parents in the upper levels of the house.

"But what if Sorenson kills me? What if she frames me for something new, and I go to prison?"

Brennan bent down and looked his brother in the eye. "I know you never learned this as a kid, being the baby and all, but there are consequences for your actions. You've never had to deal with consequences, so Mom and

Dad might feel sorry for you, but I don't. It's time to learn. Time to be accountable for your fuckups."

"But I–"

"No more buts!" Brennan shouted. "No more excuses! If you just keep your mouth shut and your nose clean, you'll probably be fine. But leave me the hell out of all of it!"

Brennan's heart thundered in his chest as he stormed out of the basement. He didn't bother looking back at Phil or stopping to speak with either of his parents. The things he'd said about being the black sheep of his criminal family had been buried too long. It felt good to finally say it out loud. As a kid, he knew his father wasn't a normal dad, even among the wealthy. He always had the feeling their family's fortune wasn't entirely legitimate. One day, that hunch was confirmed.

He'd just turned seventeen, and his parents had gifted him a brand-new Corvette. While he was out on the town, driving around, he realized a black sedan had been tailing him for at least three miles. When he stopped to confront the driver, he was held up at gunpoint and kidnapped. They wouldn't tell them who they were or what they wanted, and they beat him every time he opened his mouth.

Brennan's captors had held him in a warehouse until his father came with his own retinue in tow. Apparently, a massive cocaine shipment had gone missing, and his father, Mr. McNamara, was expected to pay restitution. When he didn't, they took Brennan and threatened to kill the firstborn if the father didn't pay up within three hours.

The men who held him had no qualms about beating a tied-up teenager, and Brennan knew they wouldn't hesitate to kill him if they wanted to. Too young, he became all too aware of his own mortality.

No matter how his father apologized and tried to make it up to him, Brennan vowed he would never put his own family through that. When his father had tried to involve him in the "family business," Brennan refused and closed himself off.

All the threats of being financially cut off couldn't change his mind.

Brennan got into college on his own, and he was hired as an executive assistant by a friend's mother at a law firm. That job helped pay for his University of Michigan education. Despite their protests, he returned the Corvette to his parents and bought his own shitty beater car.

He'd done everything possible to make his own way through life.

There was no reason why Brennan should have turned out different than his siblings or his father, but he guessed it had something to do with the summers spent with his maternal grandparents. His siblings hadn't been old enough to remember, but the lessons they taught him had been ingrained in Brennan's heart. He always strove to be as good and as honorable as his grandfather and, like him, to treat the love of his life like a queen. The man had taught him hard work, responsibility, and the importance of the legacy one man left behind him in the world. These were things his father had never discussed or aspired to.

Brennan knew he was the fortunate one of his siblings. Somehow, some seed of goodness had taken root within him, and he'd always guarded and nurtured it.

As he drove slowly home on the slick roads, he reflected on his life's direction and committed to cutting his parents and siblings out of it once and for all.

Chapter 15

CHAPTER FIFTEEN

Mitch could barely keep his eyes open as he neared the bait and pizza shop of Gladwin. He hoped to run in and get a hot slice but expected it to be closed due to the blizzard like most everything else. Although the wind and snow had lightened earlier in the morning, the lull in the storm was ending. The snowy chunks were getting fatter, the wind blasting, and the temperature was expected to drop another ten degrees until it hit the single digits.

The coffee he'd picked up had warmed his body, but he was running on fumes when it came to sleep and food. His Crown Vic's tires crunched through the thick snow as he turned into the bait and pizza shop's parking lot. To his surprise, it had been plowed. An old Chevy with a plow attached to the front was parked near the shop's entrance. The rust bucket was filled with holes and the windshield was cracked, but the driver had still managed to do an excellent job of plowing and clearing the snow so cars could enter.

As he studied the front of the shop, Mitch found a neon open sign glowing back at him from the window.

He smiled as parked and killed the engine. The glass doors were plastered with posters he didn't have time to read while rushing to get out of the wind. Garlic, basil, and oregano filled the warm air, greeting him with the promise of fresh-baked pizza.

"My God that smells good," he said, gaze locking on to the man behind the counter.

"It is good." A man who looked to be about the same age as Mitch glanced up and smiled before turning back to the fishing magazine in his hands. "Better get you a slice before they plow the roads. Everybody all around comes for the pizza. My niece is a wizard with food."

Mitch headed toward the food counter in the back, glancing around as he went. The store was stocked with fishing and hunting supplies on one side and general grocery items on the other side. The prices were high but normal for a small, independently owned store out in the country.

A radio crackled from the tiny kitchen in the back, and Mitch could barely hear the modern country song through the static. He found a woman who appeared to be about thirty years old humming along as she lined up pizza pans and filled the dough with sauce, cheese, and various toppings. Her long dark hair was pulled back in a French braid, and she wore dark mascara and red lipstick. It was all she needed to enhance her natural beauty. She almost looked out of place in the small, dark kitchen.

"Do you have any pizza ready yet?"

She paused what she was doing and glanced up, offering a warm smile. "Sure do. Cheese or pepperoni? I'm making the more interesting stuff now."

"Pepperoni would be great. Two slices, please."

She washed her hands and collected two thick, hot, cheesy slices, settling them side-by-side in a styrofoam container before passing them to Mitch.

"I heard you're a pizza wizard," he said as he accepted the container, excited by the delicious smell.

The woman laughed and shrugged. "If you do something every day for ten years, you better be good at it."

"That's right. Well, thank you. And stay warm."

She smiled politely before returning to her pizzas.

Mitch grabbed a handful of napkins, an energy drink, and two bottles of water before heading to the counter to pay.

He looked around as the man rang up his items, taking note of the wall full of photos. There were people everywhere, some with fish and deer, others toasting cheap beer with friends.

"Do you know all the locals?" Mitch asked on a whim.

"Maybe half." The man shrugged, then input the order into the POS system and pushed forward a card reader.

Mitch paid, then pulled out a paper from his coat pocket.

The man's gaze shot to Mitch's waist, and he knew the man had spotted his duty weapon.

"Have you seen either of these men?" He set the paper on the counter. It had Tyler and Jeff's photos side by side.

While bagging Mitch's things, he glanced from the pictures to Mitch and back again. "Maybe. Why?"

"Who's he asking about?" The woman walked up to the counter and stood next to Mitch, wiping her hands on her apron. She picked up the paper and studied it.

"Have you seen either of these men?"

"Are you a cop?"

"I am." He drew his badge from his pocket and showed it to her. "I just need to ask them a few questions."

One side of her mouth quirked up in a grin, and her dark eyes glittered. "I saw that one this morning." She pointed a finger at Jeff's picture. "He cut the line in front of me at the BP in Gladwin. Had his arms full of groceries."

"When was that?" Mitch asked.

She flipped her wrist over and glanced at her watch. It was a little after seven, I think."

It was almost ten now.

"His friends waited in the car and didn't help him with all them bags. I only got a quick look at him, but I could swear the guy in the truck was the other one in your picture."

"The guy?"

"Yeah. There was a lady in the front seat. She looked to be my age.

"You wouldn't happen to know where they headed, would you?"

She shook her head. "I just know he came in and seemed to be stocking up. He was real nervous, twitchy. Didn't hardly look anybody in the eye."

"Is there anyone you can think of who might know them or where they're going?"

"I'm sorry, officer. There's a lot of property out here that nobody knows about, and we've got a lot of public land, too. If you head into Gladwin, the Sheriff might be able to help you."

"Good to know." He folded the paper and stuffed it back in his coat. "This helps. Thank you."

"I wasn't trying to hold out on you," the man behind the counter said quickly. "Ya just don't ever know who's asking."

"I know," Mitch reassured him. "Have a good day, folks. I'm going to sit in my car and enjoy this and see if maybe the Sheriff can help me."

The pair offered their polite goodbyes, and Mitch shielded his face as he pushed open the door, pizza in one hand and a bag full of drinks in the other.

In his car, Mitch read through his emails while he ate his pizza. He swore it was the best pizza he'd ever had and promised himself he'd have to retire up here just so he could have it every week.

Nothing related to his current case waited for him, so he texted Alexis. Anything?

No, the response came almost immediately.

Mitch sighed as he popped open an energy drink can, swigging the sweet, carbonated liquid between bites.

At some point, he would need sleep, but his mind buzzed at the revelation that Barnes and Vandenberg were here less than two hours before him. He was closer than he thought he'd be, and at least he was on the right track. He dug into social media again, thankful that Roberts had decided he needed a profile for his fake persona.

He hoped he could use the photos from the men's late spring trip to narrow down where Tyler and Jeff might be now.

Chapter 16
CHAPTER SIXTEEN

P hil stared in the mirror as he washed his hands. Everything in the bathroom had been outfitted for his new height. He now had the vaguest sense of his fortune, having watched in wonder at all the renovation work that had to be completed to accommodate his disability. Now he gazed into his own light blue eyes and wondered at his brother's words.

"Dead-eye Phil," he'd called him. And he'd suggested that Ash had used the moniker as well.

His mother had always told him he had the most beautiful eyes, and he'd believed her. Until now. His damned siblings had ruined it for him.

What could be done about the way others perceived a man's eyes?

Phil could change everything cosmetically, but he knew nothing would actually change. Whatever wasn't present in his eyes couldn't be fixed with contacts or surgery. There was something missing in him.

The water began to scald his hands, breaking him from his paralyzing thoughts.

"Time is of the essence," he whispered. He'd begun talking to himself recently, mingling whispered words of comfort and wisdom in the air around him like a sorcerer weaving a spell.

When he emerged from the bathroom, Richard McNamara was half-sitting on the edge of the desk in Phil's study.

"It's not healthy to talk to yourself," the older man grumbled.

Phil blinked and forced a tight smile. "Yes, father."

"I assume the conversation with your brother did not go well. He didn't even bother saying goodbye to your mother before leaving."

Phil shook his head as he settled himself closer to his desk.

Richard sighed. "It's time he learns the importance of loyalty to his blood."

"Should I–"

"No." Richard's gaze pierced through Phil's intentions. "Focus on your current prize. Secure your 'pets' and tie up your loose ends. I'll handle the periphery."

"I might be able to help with–"

Richard shook his head, his expression stern. "This is why you're still an amateur, and it's why you've failed so far. Focus on one thing at a time. One most-important mission must have your full attention until it is achieved. Otherwise, you become stretched too thin. And when you're stretched, you can't catch all the pieces you'll be forced to drop."

"I'll follow your instructions faithfully, father." Phil bowed his head. He didn't want to be seen as an amateur. This was his chance to impress his father, to show he could learn to lead if given a chance. And to demonstrate he was worthy to one day inherit his father's empire.

"I'm sure you will." Richard's tone was less than confident, but Phil knew the only way to change it was to prove himself. And he would do so, no matter the cost.

Chapter 17
CHAPTER SEVENTEEN

T he sound of a plow scraping pavement jolted Mitch from sleep. He hadn't realized he'd fallen asleep and now cursed himself for doing so. After cracking his neck, he stepped out of his car to stretch his body and let the cold air wake him up. A county plow passed by the driveway to the bait and pizza shop, creating a steep snow bank that closed it off from the road.

Mitch shook his head. There was no way around the consequence of clearing the main roads, but the barrier it created was still an annoyance. Especially when there was so much accumulated snow to be moved. Salt spilled from the back of the slow-moving truck as it methodically cleared the roads.

Sitting in the driver's seat of his car, Mitch gave his coffee cup a test sip. To his surprise, it was still warm, so he drank deeply before settling it back in the cupholder and turning on the engine. He turned on the engine to warm up the car just as the door to the pizza shop swung open. The man from behind the counter came out cursing, snow shovel in hand, and nodded at Mitch before heading toward the road to clear the short wall of snow from the driveway entrance.

Mitch grimaced, sympathizing as the man slipped on a slick spot, barely
catching his balance. Turning his attention to his phone, he found a message from Alexis waiting for him. He allowed himself to get excited, but his
hopes were quickly doused. She wasn't finding any property owned in the
area by a cousin of Derek's, although she'd searched property records for
all three of the men's immediate cousins. None of their immediate families
seemed to have homes or connections in Gladwin.

Sighing, he dropped the cell phone and shifted the Vic into drive, turning around in the parking lot. He came to a stop and waited a good distance
away as the man from the shop chipped away at the wall of heavy snow. The
man looked up, and Mitch waved politely as he waited.

He'd finally conceded to asking the local Sheriff for support when a
familiar truck rolled past, heading north on the main road. The driver
looked a lot like the state trooper he'd met the night before.

Mitch thought the man looked pissed. There was also a female in the
front passenger seat and another in the back.

He believed in few things, but this being a coincidence wasn't one of
them.

Rolling down the window, he yelled to the man. "Back up!"

This warning was delivered shortly before Mitch hit the gas and rolled
forward, confident in the tires' grip. The man stumbled backward, falling
butt-first into a thigh-deep snowdrift as Mitch rammed through the bank
of snow across the driveway. His duty car passed through easily, sliding
sideways as he turned left onto the main road to follow the dark blue,
extended cab pickup north from Gladwin.

The area was already beginning to see more traffic. People in SUVs
slowly navigated the rural roads, heading for groceries or fuel for their
generators. Others flew over the frozen fields and the shoulders of the roads
on snowmobiles, either for the same reasons as the SUV drivers or just for
snow day fun.

There wasn't much outside of the town of Gladwin. Even the houses were too far apart to see beyond the interspersed fields and forests. Crossroads came at farther distances, sometimes separated by a mile or more along Highway 18.

It was a far cry from the sprawling metropolitan suburbs Mitch was used to. He'd been born and raised in the cities, living with his father in Royal Oak in the summers. He'd lived most of the time with his mother in Flint the rest of the year, where he met Janie, his high school sweetheart and the mother of his only child.

Mitch shook the memories from his head and focused on keeping his distance from the truck. He drove slowly and let another car get between them. As much as the dark truck stood out in the bright white landscape, so did Mitch's Crown Victoria. It looked out of place on snow-covered roads, and most people would look twice, wondering if it was an active or retired police vehicle.

Despite those factors, no one in the truck seemed to glance back at him. The trio appeared to be talking animatedly, possibly arguing based on the jerking motions of their heads and the number of times they looked at each other. Even after the car between them turned off, they didn't seem to notice Mitch.

When the truck turned onto a crossroad, he was still a safe distance behind, and he didn't take the turn. Instead, he drove past, then found a plowed spot at the next intersection before turning around and heading for the cross street. He braked as he reached it, hesitating in the middle of the snow-packed road. There were no other vehicles on the road as far as he could see. Although a few snowmobiles whined through the crystalline air, they were so far away Mitch had to squint to spot them.

The road he needed to turn down was yet unplowed and thick with snow. As well as he could see, only two vehicles had marred the otherwise unblemished blanket that stretched over the road and its shoulders. Only the forest dared to break the landscape, but even their dark, bare limbs had been wrapped in thick white blankets of snow.

As Mitch stared down the road, he realized he couldn't see the pickup and a low hill had broken his line of sight. Could the old Vic handle the conditions? Or would he quickly be sucked into a ditch?

He glanced at his phone. No signal.

If he did this, he was on his own.

What the hell? He'd come too far to back out now. And if it was the same group from last night, Shelby would be with them. They likely weren't up here for a winter vacation. There were many possibilities but, to his mind, only one probability: the three bystanders who'd saved Kaylie and Natalie the night before were on their way to confront the men responsible for hurting those women.

Chapter 18
CHAPTER EIGHTEEN

S helby couldn't stand to listen to Sam and Lucia bicker anymore. As far as she was concerned, the pair had no business working together, even if they were an excellent pair in every other regard.

"Sam, that's not a plan!" Lucia, the master of planning, was furious now.

"I have to agree," Shelby dared to say, though she kept her voice low. It wouldn't matter. Once they arrived, she'd do her own thing if needed.

"It doesn't matter. We're not going to go in on the offense," he rebutted, his voice confident and unyielding. "Maybe shit always goes sideways because neither of you bothers trying the easy way."

"There is no easy way with these people," Shelby grumbled, exerting every ounce of her self-control to keep from biting Sam's head off.

"I can understand why you feel that way, Shelby," Sam said, his voice softening only a little. "But there's this concept called escalation of force. We start small with an ask, and we escalate through demands, warnings, and finally deadly action. Those rules are usually a solid foundation for getting our people home alive."

"Usually?" Shelby hadn't failed to notice his use of the word.

Sam's jaw clenched, and he ignored the question. "That's what we're doing. You two stay behind and cover me. Lucia, you take the rifle, and

Shelby, you roam. Spread out and try to remain unseen while I do the talking. I'll use my rules to escalate if I have to, but I've got a good chunk of cash here. Most people respond to cash when they see it."

"You're going to get yourself killed," Lucia spat. "I can't let you–"

"You aren't in charge of shit, Lucia," he cut her off. "You don't get to tell me what I can and can't do. The only reason I'm even here in the first place is because you fucked up. You and your friend here have been running around under cover of darkness, playing big boy games and messing with things and people far beyond your understanding. You've been lying to me, keeping me in the dark."

"I'm s–"

"Stop. Don't even. I found your stash of burner phones and GPS trackers. That you have any savvy in this stuff just blows my mind. Everything hidden comes to light eventually. So here we are, me being dragged in to clean up your mess and keep the two of you safe. Do not delude yourself by believing that you can order me around and tell me how anything is going to go."

Lucia had fallen dead silent, staring out the passenger window.

Shelby could see the reflection of her friend's face in the glass. She watched as tears rolled down her face.

"Sam," Shelby said calmly. "You've made your point, and you're right. We screwed up. Now, can we focus on what we need to do right now? I think we're getting close." She tapped Lucia on the shoulder.

Lucia tried to be subtle about wiping the tears from her face. Although Shelby had warned her that everything would catch up to Lucia, she'd never wanted to see her friend in pain.

"Yes," Lucia said softly, her voice even and neutral. "It's on the left in a quarter of a mile. Based on the satellite imagery, it looks like it's pretty far back from the road. The driveway is just a two-track, and the cabin is surrounded by woods."

"Good, maybe we can pull in a little bit." Sam slowed the truck to a crawling pace, and Shelby bent in the seat to tighten her bootlaces and pull her pistol case from beneath the seat. Unbuckling her belt, she also knelt on the floorboards and slid out the hard case holding Lucia's scoped rifle. She felt the truck turn left, then brake suddenly, but she didn't look up, wanting each weapon ready to fire. They might do this Sam's way, but at least they'd be ready to fire if necessary.

"What's wrong?" Lucia asked.

"Cameras." Sam's voice was low as he shifted the truck into reverse and carefully followed his tracks out of the driveway and back onto the road.

"Are they on?" Lucia asked.

Shelby listened quietly to their conversation as she racked the slide of her pistol, loading the first round into the chamber. She double-checked the safety before holstering it on her hip.

"We can't know, so we have to assume they're actively viewing if not recording."

"Damn it."

"We'll park down the road and walk in. If we're lucky, they didn't see us, and even luckier if they're not recording."

Shelby snorted softly, loading Lucia's rifle with a small magazine of 7mm rounds as she joined the conversation. "We've been pretty lucky so far, but never that lucky."

Chapter 19
CHAPTER NINETEEN

Tyler studied the man and the woman in the truck. Was he nervous simply because he was on the run, or was there something to the familiarity he felt when watching them?

A new message dinged his phone, the preview window sliding down from the top of his screen as he reviewed the video recording from the camera at the driveway entrance. The text was from B.

Where are you?

He gritted his teeth and opened up the conversation. While he was considering how to respond, something else in their message history caught his attention. The stills he'd sent from the camera at the house in Southfield almost screamed to him. He scrolled up and tapped on each, and then it hit him. The passenger was one of the women who'd come to his house the day before. More specifically, she was the one who'd attached the GPS tracker to the Tacoma.

Relaxing, he let a grin spread across his face. At least one of those stupid bitches had taken the bait. Tyler hadn't expected either of them to have the balls to follow him, but he was pleasantly surprised. And he couldn't believe the chance he'd taken on the GPS had turned into such a potential bounty. The gamble at keeping the GPS tracker was about to pay off. Whoever these idiots were, they had stepped into his world now.

He doubted any cops would have approached as these two had. If he could have, he'd have bet money that he and the guys had finally pissed off the wrong people, likely another big player in the D. And these people were lackey enforcers.

In the latter case, he could play cat and mouse. Hell, it might even win him points with the Fear Doirich. Tyler needed to find a way back into his good graces anyway.

Currently, there was only one reason "B" wanted to know their location: the boss wanted Tyler and Jeff eliminated. B and the Fear Doirich would be furious if they knew that Tyler hadn't followed their explicit and repeated instructions to delete the text conversations for several months now. He always thought of a backup plan.

Plan A was to hide from Fear Doirich's lieutenant, while plan B was to deliver these people to the lieutenant and save his own skin. Plan C would always be a plea deal and witness protection, and he needed all his texts as evidence to support that potential outcome.

For now, he'd try to get back into the boss's good graces.

Did you ask the boss? Because I know I can get them for you.

He didn't have to wait long for a response:

And how do you think you'll manage that? Do you know where they live? Do you think you can just go and grab either of those women? There are cameras, witnesses, cops, DNA evidence you'd leave at the scene, and many other ways you could be linked back to taking them. You do not have the skill to fulfill any half-witted promise to deliver the two women in the screenshots. Just tell me where you are. I'm supposed to give you some cash so you can lay low until this all blows over.

Tyler's heart pounded in his chest. He recognized the carrot and knew the stick was hiding just behind it. His anxiety threatened to overtake his senses as he thought of the various ways B might kill them and dispose of their corpses.

"Who is it?" Jeff walked into the living room then and handed Tyler a beer.

"It's him," Tyler said, referring to the Fear Doirich's lieutenant.

Jeff said nothing as he sat down on the far end of the couch and sipped from his beer bottle, but his hands trembled.

The phone dinged with another text. *Hurry up and tell me where you are. I don't have all day.*

Tyler flipped back to the recorded event from his driveway camera and took screenshots, carefully finding the clearest picture of the two people in the truck. This had to be what would save them. Whatever he needed to do to earn back his life, he would do it. If he had to kill these trespassers who'd followed him north, he wouldn't hesitate. He'd hate to do it, but he would even kill Jeff, too, if that was the price he needed to pay for his own freedom.

He sent the pictures to B, then typed his next message. *Do you want them dead or alive?*

Chapter 20
CHAPTER TWENTY

S am was unnerved by Lucia's silence as they left the safety of the truck. He hadn't wanted to upset her, but someone had to take control of this trainwreck of a situation before she got herself or Shelby killed.

Life wasn't a game. People didn't respawn.

He wanted to simply be angry at her for all these secret treks and for so arrogantly assuming she could undertake work intended for special teams of law enforcement.

But then he remembered how underfunded those special teams were. The quieter they were about their missions and the people they saved, the less the public knew. It was all for the sake of operational security, but the less the public heard, the less they wanted to fund secretive teams and their operations.

And then, there were cases where the monsters were caught but escaped justice. Like Phil McNamara. His lawyers had twisted the letter of the law to secure their vile client's freedom.

As sticky as Teflon, Sam thought bitterly as he walked up the driveway toward the cabin and an unknown fate.

Sam kept his focus ahead, not letting his worried eyes wander the woods to his right. He didn't want to give away Lucia's presence and location if he could avoid it. He'd feel better if someone covered him in case things went south.

Of course, it would only work if she could actually squeeze the trigger.

Could she kill someone? Sam didn't think so, but he also never imagined she could lie to him like this. Liam had shot Phil McNamara, and Sam had shot a man the night before even though Lucia had him sighted in long enough to fire. She'd had plenty of time, but she hesitated, even though the man could have killed Shelby.

Had Shelby been the only one to pull the trigger during their excursion to the property up by the Manistee National Forest? Or had Lucia taken part but now she was trigger shy?

Regardless of what happened up there, she should have been the one to take the shot last night that saved her friend and ally, but she hadn't.

Sam suddenly felt extremely vulnerable as he approached the cabin, stopping just in front and standing with his hands in his coat pockets. Maybe he couldn't trust Lucia to have his back after all. He hoped at least Shelby would be able to return the favor if someone took aim at him.

He studied the area and the cabin. It was small but looked structurally sound and warm, and he tried not to shiver as he thought of being inside. The winter air was still frigid.

A gray Tacoma sat in front of the cabin, and the now lightly falling snow was beginning to accumulate in a fine layer over it. The men must have arrived this morning, maybe just an hour or two earlier.

***

Lucia had bit her tongue as she followed Sam's lead. He'd parked along the side of the road near the heavily wooded property. Thankfully, the truck wouldn't have trouble getting out of the deep snow, and they had shovels if they did run into any trouble. Of course, that would only help if they had plenty of time to dig themselves out. It wasn't ideal for situations where they might be on the run or dodging bullets.

But Sam had made it clear that it was his rodeo now, and he would handle this with or without her. She'd presented him with the problem, and now he was set on solving it.

After slipping on warm gloves, she stepped out of the truck and took her rifle when Shelby presented it. A momentary flashback reminded her of the previous night's tragedy. Was she ready to possibly kill someone? To take a life?

"Let's go," Sam barked, startling both women. It was a voice she hadn't heard before, and it was distinctly more military than she'd ever heard from him. She wasn't his fiancée right now; she was his soldier. As she nodded, catching his green eyes for only a moment, she knew it was her job to make sure Sam lived through the day. If she hesitated again, it might mean his death.

Lucia swallowed her fear and misgivings and took a path parallel to Sam's as he trekked northward up the driveway. She followed a little behind him and to the east of his path. She turned to say something to Shelby, but her friend had already disappeared into the trees. Even though the branches were bare, the thick snow lining them provided a little more cover, and Lucia could barely see any trace of Shelby. Only the woman's footprints through the snow hinted at her presence.

She returned her gaze forward, finding Sam had kept a slow pace, allowing her the opportunity to move stealthily through the forest. But she could barely see him now, through the dense woods filled with thick patches of undergrowth.

Stepping slowly through the snow and keeping her footfalls close to tree trunks dampened some of the usual crunch. Lucia also matched her pace with Sam's, and it helped her to move as quietly as possible. Recalling the distance between the cabin and the road, she tried to estimate how long it would take at this pace. Although the low-rolling hills wouldn't provide much in the way of landmarks, Lucia was confident in her ability to successfully navigate toward the cabin without seeing it.

Before long, the Tacoma from the house in Southfield took shape through the trees and, beyond that, the small, log cabin-style home. Lucia found a line of sight through the trees as Sam came to a halt nearly forty feet in front of the cabin. She then tried to move back as far as she could without losing sight of Sam and the front door. Staying low, she settled her body in the snow, dug her elbows in, and laid her cheek against the stock.

Sam stood there quietly, gloved hands shoved in his pockets and hot breath fogging in the air as he waited for someone to notice him and come out of the cabin.

Even if it was the whole reason they were there, Lucia didn't want anyone to come out. It was ridiculous, but she hoped they were sleeping or something equally as stupid. Seeing the man she loved through her rifle scope seared pain into her pounding heart and frayed her nerves. She'd already seen him shot once, and it was something she couldn't bear to witness again.

But there he was, standing hard-headed in the face of danger in an attempt to extract her from trouble. Yet again.

The door to the cabin inched open, only cracking at first. Sam held up empty hands, and a man emerged onto the porch steps. It was Tyler, the one who owned the Southfield house. Unlike Sam, he held a pistol, but he kept it at his side, muzzle pointed at the ground.

He said something, but Lucia was too far away to make it out over the wind. She didn't even blink as she trained her aim on Tyler. Watching the scene intently, she studied his face for any sign that he might draw down on Sam.

Laughter broke his face and rose above the ambient noise between them, but Sam did not look amused. Lucia found the next closest tree and crawled through the snow until she was settled behind it. Neither man seemed to notice, unable to hear her gentle movements through the snow or see her at that distance through the forest. At least for this, she was grateful for the distance now between them.

As Sam's face grew more stern, Lucia switched off the safety and readied herself to fire. Light footsteps crunched behind her, and she was thankful that Shelby had returned just in time to back her up. There was likely another man in that house they'd need to deal with, and Shelby could be instrumental in helping capture him alive. If Tyler lifted his pistol toward Sam, Lucia would blow his brains out of his head along with the information they needed to delete the recorded security footage. Hopefully, the other guy, Jeff, would be able to do it.

Another footstep crunched behind her, and Lucia quietly shushed her friend. "Quiet, damn it!" she hissed at her friend.

Something cold and hard pressed against the back of Lucia's skull, and a wave of dread washed through her. She didn't move, praying it was Shelby's version of a sick joke. Movement caught her attention through scope, and she noticed both Sam and Tyler staring straight at her.

"Very slowly now, I want you to switch that safety on," a young man instructed softly, his voice deep.

Lucia did as she was told, switching the safety lever on as the sickness of adrenaline and fear twisted in her gut and raced through her veins. She laid the rifle on its side and slowly spread her hands out to the sides to make it clear she wouldn't put up a fight.

She'd been caught in the worst possible position, and she couldn't dodge bullets, especially from a muzzle remaining in close contact with her skull.

A knee jammed into her back, and she grunted in pain, remembering then what Shelby had told her, how the men who'd hurt her had wanted to hear her agony. They had wanted to hear her scream.

Lucia did not want to give them that pleasure, not if she could help it.

The muzzle of the gun shook and jabbed into her skull as the man's free hand felt down Lucia's body, lingering in her pockets before moving along, clearly searching for something.

"No phone?"

She said nothing, so ground his knee against her spine, making her moan in pain as she fought to control herself even as the breath was pressed from her lungs.

"No," she finally wheezed, digging her fingers into the snow as she fought the pain.

The pressure lifted from her back, but then he grabbed a handful of her hair and pulled, yanking her to her feet.

She looked toward the cabin but couldn't see anything through the forest from this angle. Her fear spiked for Sam, but another yank to her hair twisted her around, and she watched as the barrel of a gun stopped only inches from her nose.

"I don't ever have my safety on," Jeff said.

Her vision focused on him, and she studied his short black hair and blue eyes.

He smirked at her then. "Well, hello to you too. You ain't a bad-lookin' woman."

Lucia shuddered and shook her head.

Jeff nodded his head toward the cabin. "Let's go and get warmed up. Ladies first."

For a split second, Lucia considered her options. She could try to tussle with him, but his hands were steady. All he had to do was pull that trigger, and it would be over for her and probably for Sam too.

No. She needed to comply, at least for now.

Their best hope was Shelby, wherever the hell she was.

Chapter 21
CHAPTER TWENTY-ONE

Shelby watched through the trees as the man with the short black hair searched for Lucia. She wanted to jump in and eliminate him, but she was too far away for a clean shot through the tangled undergrowth. If she gave herself away, it might get both Lucia and Sam killed.

For some reason, the men had seemed satisfied with only having the two, and Shelby wondered why they weren't looking around more. Had they not seen all three of them in the truck from the driveway's camera?

She brushed her questions aside. None of it mattered. If they didn't know she was here, it might give her a slight advantage. Any advantage was welcome on someone else's home turf.

Remaining perfectly still, she studied the surroundings as the dark-haired man pushed Lucia through the snow and toward the cabin. She didn't move a muscle until she heard the door to the cabin slam shut.

Nothing but the breeze made a sound, and Shelby listened as it howled long and lonely over the treetops. The storm had ended this morning, but it sounded like another was on the way.

Carefully, Shelby crawled forward through the snow, her fingers freezing in the thin gloves she'd found in Lucia's closet. She wasn't dressed to be out here long, and the cold was already getting to her. The brown leather jacket Lucia had given her was more fashionable than functional, and the long-sleeved turtle neck sweater was too thin for the dead of winter.

Whatever she was going to do, she needed to do it fast before she froze and became useless to her friends.

She pulled her phone from her coat pocket and glanced at it, though she didn't turn it on.

Who could she call to save them?

Not the cops. None of them were supposed to be here or should have known where these men on the lam would be. Calling 9-1-1 could only be a last resort.

But she couldn't call Lee, either. He wasn't equipped with the skills or manpower to ride to the rescue and save them. Hell, he didn't even have a car or a driver's license.

Ginger was out of the question, too.

Matt. The name bobbed to the surface of the ocean of her thoughts no matter how hard she'd tried to keep it away. No. She couldn't call him. He might like her, but she didn't know him well enough to trust him with something like this. Logically, that was the right answer, and she knew it. But something else within her rebutted with an unspeakable trust and faith.

He's important, it argued. He's part of our fate.

"Stop it," she hissed through clenched teeth. This was it. She was finally losing her damn mind.

Closing her eyes, she counted to six as she inhaled, then counted to six again as she controlled her exhalation. Repeating this pattern several times, she calmed her racing heart and cleared the racing thoughts from her mind.

She rose to her feet then and thrust the phone back into her pocket, its screen still dark. Breathing into her fingers, she warmed them first, then slowly, carefully, made her way to the rear of the cabin as quietly as possible while keeping an eye out for any more trail cameras.

Chapter 22

CHAPTER TWENTY-TWO

M itch drove the Vic slowly over the unplowed road, squinting in the bright morning light as he passed between open, snow-covered fields and through overgrown patches of forest. A sharp pain throbbed above his left eye, and he recognized the threat of the migraine creeping into his brain.

Two sets of tire tracks from trucks bore through the snow, guiding him down the hidden road. He didn't dare stray from the tracks lest he drive into a ditch and get stuck. He'd probably have to wait hours for a tow truck to come get his car out, and he didn't need any more delays.

Despite following the tracks, he didn't see anything ahead of him on the open road, and there was no cloud of kicked-up snow dust to indicate the vehicle he followed was somewhere ahead of him.

Just as he was beginning to wonder if he'd waited too long to follow them, Mitch rounded a slight curve and saw his quarry parked on the shoulder of the road just beyond a driveway flanked by dense woods. He also noticed the camera mounted on a tree and pointed at the driveway entrance. Mitch kept driving, and as he passed the truck, he drove into a perfect blanket of untouched snow. He could guess where the road was, but it wasn't safe for him, especially as he was intent on following the people he'd met at the scene of the shooting the night before.

He still couldn't believe it would be a coincidence, and now he wondered if he'd helped the wrong people. Had Natalie and Kaylie lied about the involvement of the other three people? Was his own daughter...

Mitch braked, gently bringing the car to a stop before reversing carefully and taking a three-point turn to change direction. He pulled up behind the truck and parked his car, though he didn't dare to edge the Vic off the shoulder as much as the truck had.

He stared at the blue 4x4 truck for a moment while he considered his next steps, then took out his notebook and pen to write down the license plate. If he didn't need to do anything with this information, that would be great. But if he'd been wrong and let a pack of monsters walk away from a shooting, he needed to make it right. For now, that meant collecting every piece of information possible that would let him track them down later or keep tabs on them.

After taking down the plate number and the truck's make and model, Mitch killed the Vic's engine and bundled up. When he stepped out, the icy breeze swept his cheeks with an unwelcome caress.

He checked his pistol in his shoulder holster, then unbuttoned the strap to more quickly retrieve it if necessary before zipping up his parka. It was too cold to walk around with it open. Right now, he had to stay warm enough to focus.

Mitch needed to find out why the trio were here, in the area where he'd tracked the men from Southfield. One way or another, hell was bound to be unleashed today. He prayed today's Lone Ranger act wouldn't land him six feet under, robbing him of the chance to tell his daughter the truth.

Chapter 23

CHAPTER TWENTY-THREE

Lucia flexed the muscles in her arms and legs as Jeff secured her to a hard, wooden dining table chair with zip ties. He lashed each of her wrists to the back legs of the chair and her ankles to the front legs. The air smelled of wood smoke, pizza, and cheap beer.

The space where Jeff now secured her was a small bedroom holding only a ratty, old brown dresser and a twin bed loaded with a pile of unfolded blankets.

"What did you do to Sam?" she demanded, her voice hoarse as she fought to keep it strong.

He snorted a laugh. "Is that your boyfriend?"

She realized too late that she shouldn't have revealed Sam's name.

"You're kinda cute," Jeff said as he stood back to survey his work. He leaned forward and pulled at her arms, then her legs. Lucia kept her muscles tight in hopes he wouldn't yank at them again.

But he did. He yanked hard, and Lucia barely kept herself from crying out, gritting her teeth against the sharp pain of the hard plastic now digging into her flesh.

"I'm sorry." He caressed her cheek with his long, thick fingers. "Did that hurt?"

He stared at her, but she refused to make eye contact, unflinching as she stared at the wall instead.

"Look at me!" Jeff grabbed her chin roughly and pulled her face toward him, but she closed her eyes and kept her mouth shut. "I'm gonna make you talk." The menace in his voice sent a chill through her, but she held it back and kept her eyes closed.

Before he could say or do anything else, the door creaked.

Lucia relaxed her eyes, opening them to find Tyler, the registered sex offender and murderer, standing in the threshold. He stared back at her, their gazes locking for the briefest moment before she glanced away again.

"What kind of man brings his woman along?" he asked as he stepped into the room.

"She ain't talking," Jeff said, his voice tinged with disgust.

"Awful pretty though, ain't she?"

"I sure thought so. Prettier than the other one, for sure. But they both look like they're a sure bet for a good time."

Lucia's heart dropped. The other one? How had they caught Shelby so soon?

"Don't you touch her," she growled, glaring at Tyler.

He stared at her, eyes wide and mouth agape for a few seconds. Then the corners of his mouth crooked upward in a sadistic smile, his eyes alight. With more speed than she expected, he closed the distance between them and loomed over her. Grabbing a handful of her hair, he yanked her head back and smiled down at her.

"I'll touch you and her as much as I want. What the hell are you going to do about it?"

Jeff snickered beside him, but it didn't last long.

Lucia tilted her chin up and spat directly in Tyler's face. "Fuck you, asshole."

Tyler froze, and Jeff's jaw dropped, his eyes wide in shock or fear. He slowly took two steps back, getting out of the way just before Tyler exploded.

He hauled his arm back and slapped Lucia across the face, hitting her so hard that stars filled her vision even before she fell backward. Her chair slammed against the floor so violently that it bounced, causing her head to hit twice against the floor.

Lucia desperately struggled for consciousness, caught between being dazed from the hit and instinctively fighting for survival.

Tyler dropped and straddled her stomach, raising his arm to hit her again. Before he could strike, she bucked her hips and slammed her knees into his ass, pushing as hard as she could. He flew over her head, sprawling and grasping at her as he went.

"I'm going to kill you!" he screamed as he scrambled to his feet. He lifted his foot, ready to kick her in the face, but Jeff pulled him back at the last minute.

"Stop!"

"What the hell?!"

"Tyler! We need her alive, or the deal's off!"

Lucia felt like her head was underwater, but she heard him clearly enough. As dazed as she was, she knew the words meant something bad for her.

"What deal?" she mumbled the question, her bottom lip stinging as she spoke.

"Shut your damn mouth!" Tyler's fists clenched at his sides, and Jeff pulled him toward the door.

"Calm down, man, or you're going to screw us!"

Tyler spun on his heel and flung the door open before storming out of the room. Jeff followed closely behind, leaving Lucia on the floor, still strapped to her chair. When their voices faded away to another part of the cabin, she relaxed and let out a groan for her aching muscles and her throbbing head. She wiggled her hands and ankles against her restraints only briefly before giving up.

She was exhausted, and she was in so much more pain as the adrenaline wore off. As a wave of dizziness rolled through her, she wondered if Tyler had given her a concussion. As long as he left Shelby alone, Lucia would gladly take any punishment he wanted to deal out.

Shelby couldn't be made to go through that again. The rape. Abuse. Torment. Imprisonment.

And now she was at risk of suffering it all again because they'd come into this without a clear plan. Lucia loved Sam, but she shouldn't have let him come. But no, she'd not only let him come, she'd kept her mouth shut while he took the lead. She could have ditched him, dropped him at a gas station, anything but this. His audacious, half-assed plan had proven to be exactly that.

Despite her anger, she still worried for him. If Tyler had used Lucia as leverage to ensure Sam's compliance, he could be in danger too. It was exactly the kind of situation she'd hoped to avoid. Now, they had no sure way out of it.

Chapter 24

CHAPTER TWENTY-FOUR

T he snow was less frigid as Shelby rounded the cabin and headed deeper into the more densely clustered trees. She wondered if the snow was softer here because of how little sunshine broke through the tangle of branches even when they were leafless in the dead of winter. This area didn't have a chance to begin melting before freezing over again.

Birds chirped busily from the trees as she changed direction. Now that she believed she'd flanked the cabin, she made a beeline for the rear of the building, staying close to the trees for cover and taking her time to make sure she hadn't been spotted. The last thing she needed to do was walk into a trap or have them out hunting for her.

If neither Sam nor Lucia said anything, then the men might not know she was there at all.

Her fingers slipped over the handle of the knife sheathed on her belt. It always brought her comfort, and she felt naked without it. Between that and her pistol, she thought she might have a fighting chance–even if she was outnumbered.

Once she could see the rear of the cabin clearly, she studied it carefully. There were two windows on either side of the rear door. It was a battered-looking thing, sitting waterlogged in a weathered frame, but appeared sturdy enough. Would they leave it unlocked?

Shelby waited for several minutes, studying the house for any sign of movement. She saw none, but she did hear shouting from inside. Her gut twisted, and she feared then for the lives of the people closest to her.

Even if Shelby wasn't the warmest, brightest ball of sunshine on her best days, she did love Lucia and Sam like family. It had only been a few months, but she felt closer to them than to anyone else, especially not her own mother. She'd never known a huggy, lovey kind of family as a kid, and she didn't see how that would ever change. But she understood loyalty now, and she believed that these two people had given it to her. They had no desire to hurt her or use her, and they wanted her to heal and be happy, regardless of how her trust issues formed her defensive attitude.

Everyone's idea of normalcy was different, and for her, normal meant pain, loneliness, distrust, and keeping oneself distanced from others. To show emotion was to show weakness, and when one showed weakness, that vulnerability would be exploited. Her stepfather took joy in her tears when he'd hurt her or her mother. She hoped he would live long enough to become frail, small, and defenseless, so he could experience the kind of helplessness he'd put others through.

Shelby would never return to her mother and stepfather. There would be no calls, no letters, no reconciliation, no holiday parties with the old family.

Sam, Lucia, and Lee were her family now, and a better family than she'd ever dreamed she might have.

And now, she had to act fast to save two-thirds of her claimed family.

Staring at the back door, she had just psyched herself up to bolt across the twenty feet of open space when a hand grabbed her by the shoulder.

Shelby did not scream.

She reached for her knife, unsheathing it and slashing outward in a matter of seconds as she spun toward the person who'd surprised her.

He jumped back, pulling his face just out of reach of the blade. As he put his hands up, Shelby recognized him, but she didn't drop her knife.

"Detective?"

"Careful," he whispered. "You almost hurt yourself. He held up his hands defensively and nodded toward the ground.

Shelby tried to look using her peripheral vision, not wanting to take her focus off him. "What are you doing here?"

"Police business. What about you?"

"My own business."

"We can't sit here in a standoff, Shelby."

The way he said her name, as if he already knew her, grated at her nerves. "You must be good with names."

He nodded. "Call me Mitch. Where are your friends?"

"Okay. What are you talking about? How did I almost hurt myself?"

Mitch sighed, skirted her personal space, pulled her away, and kicked at the spot where she'd almost stepped.

A metal trap snapped shut, its thick metal edges clapping together so loudly it echoed through the trees. Shelby pressed herself against the tree and gestured for Mitch to do the same, hiding in case the men looked out for what creature had fallen victim to their trap. If they poked their heads out or looked through the windows, Shelby couldn't tell. She waited several minutes, glancing around and at Mitch, before daring a look toward the cabin.

No one stared back at her from the windows or the doorway, and she could no longer hear shouting from within.

"Thanks," she whispered as Mitch returned to her.

"I need to know what you're doing," he said plainly, his gaze piercing her.

Shelby shrugged. Maybe the old man would help her even out the odds a little. "Came here to talk. But the assholes in that house got the jump on my friends and took them inside. At gunpoint," she added for emphasis.

"What would you say if I guessed the men in that house were from Southfield and had something to do with hurting the women you helped last night?"

Shelby almost withered beneath his burning gaze, but she resisted, breathing deeply and setting her resolve.

Show no weakness.

"Sounds like you have a hunch."

"Sure," Mitch deadpanned. "I've been trying to track them down all morning. Came this way on a hunch. Then I saw your friend's truck."

"So, what now, Detective?" She emphasized the last word, its sour taste sticking to the roof of her mouth.

"Well, I was just going to call for backup, but you being here throws a wrench in my plans."

"How so? Why don't you just call them before these fuckers kill two good people?"

Mitch studied her in silence for several seconds, his eyes scanning her face. "Your presence last night and this morning will raise too many questions, and I won't be able to keep you all out of trouble. I have an idea about what is going on here, but I'd prefer plausible deniability. I'd also prefer to make sure you and those other two good people get out of here alive and without becoming persons of interest in the investigations of multiple agencies."

"Point taken." Shelby nodded. The last thing she needed was a rusty old cop on her heels, but she knew she didn't have a choice. What she didn't understand was why he was intent on making sure she and her friends didn't get caught up in the investigation.

She turned her gaze back on the house. Shouting reached her ears again. Two men's muffled voices rang through the walls, although no one could be seen in the windows. "I think this is as good a chance as any other. They sound pissed. And I don't see any cameras." She pointed toward the back of the house, her fingers clenching into fists.

"Wait." Mitch surveyed the clearing between them and the house, then nodded.

Shelby led the way, sprinting from the trees, crossing the clearing in seconds. It was not a silent movement, but she hoped the men's shouting would prevent them from hearing her.

The detective followed, but he half-ran, half-limped through the snow.

"Are you hurt?" she whispered when he pressed himself against the side of the house next to her.

He shook his head. "Just a bad knee."

Shelby wanted to ask what the hell he was doing out here alone, but she bit her tongue. It didn't matter. She stared at him a moment longer, and he stared back. Something about his eyes unnerved her.

"See anything out of place?"

"No," he said, keeping his voice low as he scanned the unblemished snow surrounding the backdoor. "But we still need to be careful."

She stared at the entrance. The muffled shouts faded as tempers calmed, and the men moved farther toward the front of the house. After a moment's hesitation, she reached for the doorknob.

Chapter 25

CHAPTER TWENTY-FIVE

Collins checked his phone for the ninth time in as many minutes. No new text messages, no missed calls. He grumbled in frustration. His intuition flared as he tapped Mitch's number and let it ring over his phone speaker once more. The older man wasn't at home, he wasn't at the office, and he wasn't in between.

He wasn't where he was supposed to be.

"Damnit." Collins ended the call as Mitch's generic voice message began. The roads were still bad in most places, and with so many accidents and buried cars on the freeway, it would take a few hours to clear the most important roadways. Secondary roads would be cleared afterward.

Anything could have happened to Mitch after he left the scene. His car could have slid off the road, a tire gone flat, or the engine died. But he should have had some way to communicate, and he should have been answering his phone. In his gut, Collins knew his partner hadn't obeyed the order to go home and rest.

Collins was nearly back to Southfield when he pulled over at a gas station, grabbed a fresh cup of coffee, and dialed the Southfield Police Department dispatch.

"Southfield–"

"Good morning," he interrupted the male voice that answered. "Detective Gabriel Collins here. I need immediate support."

"Officer Stephens. What can I do for you, Detective?"

"I need to know the location of my partner's car."

"Sounds serious. Is everything okay?" The clacking of computer keys beat out a steady rhythm in the background.

"I won't know until I can track him down. Look for Detective Mitch Ward."

"Hold."

Collins ground his teeth and cursed the low buzzing coming through the line.

"Detective, I have a location."

"Great. Where is he?"

"The GPS is transmitting from a rural location. The nearest town is..." Stephens' words trailed off as his keyboard clacked in the background. "Knowland."

"Knowland? Where the hell is that?"

Stephens ignored him. "I'm forwarding the coordinates to you now. Is there anything else, Detective?"

"Not right now."

"Sure. Stay safe out there. The roads are a disaster."

"Thanks." Collins ended the call and pulled the coordinates into his map program from his email. Knowland, a tiny village on the northern edge of Gladwin County, was a two-and-a-half-hour drive from Southfield in the best weather and would likely be a four-hour drive in the current conditions.

"Meaning the asshole never went home like he was supposed to," Collins snapped before pounding the bottom of his fist against the steering wheel. He dialed Mitch's number again and sighed when it went straight to voicemail. "He had one damn job today. A single, easy order. Head home, and get some sleep. But no, not him. He's an old dog with a new bone and just can't let it go."

After chewing on his options, Collins called back to the department and asked to be forwarded to the Gladwin County dispatch. Despite having such a relatively sparse population, the county was busy with its limited Sheriff resources. Too busy, in fact, to go check on his partner unless Collins had a reason to believe there was danger. For now, all first responders were focused on welfare checks in areas without power, checking on vehicles that had slid off the road or become stranded in deep snow. Tragic, preventable deaths happen every year from carbon monoxide poisoning due to blocked tailpipes and people trying to stay warm in their cars while stuck in a snowbank.

The State Police didn't have a post in Gladwin County but had others in nearby counties, so he called around next. All were sympathetic, at least, but the answer was nearly the same: they couldn't dedicate the resources without knowing Mitch was in danger. But they bent a little, taking the coordinates and promising to send someone over that way as soon as they could, which would probably be in a few hours. Collins thanked them and hung up, cursing once he knew the line was dead.

He was exhausted. The last 24 hours had been wild, and he hadn't slept yet since catching up with Mitch at the scene of the car fire.

The way he saw it, two choices stood before him, and he didn't like either: he could head up to Gladwin County and hope Mitch was still there when he arrived, or he could head home and get some rest while assuming Mitch was fine and would return on his own without incident. The latter outcome was just as likely as the former, and he wasn't keen on waiting for the State Police to make time to check on Mitch.

Collins would simply have to wait it out. It would be embarrassing to go all the way up there after Mitch if he was only visiting family–or

God-forbid a girlfriend. Keeping that final scenario in the forefront of his thoughts, Collins headed home to get a little rest so he'd be fresh to wrap up the case of Kaylie's disappearance and recovery.

Chapter 26

CHAPTER TWENTY-SIX

S am winced as he regained consciousness, a splitting headache filling his awareness before the pain around his wrists or sounds from the other room.

"That was fucking unnecessary," he grumbled, remembering the buttstroke to the head he'd been given by one of the men. He had no choice but to comply once he saw they'd found Lucia. The other bastard had pointed his gun at the back of her skull.

As lucidity returned, his thoughts exploded in a whirlwind.

He quickly reined them in and honed in on his first objective: situational awareness.

After blinking a few times to clear his blurred vision, Sam found himself staring at a cheap wooden door. It looked flimsy and cheap, something from the late seventies that could be easily broken or go up in smoke if exposed to a little heat.

He surveyed his environment slowly, recognizing the small area he was in as a bedroom, complete with a twin bed covered in a messy pile of crumpled blankets, a nightstand, a dresser, and a single square window covered with a deteriorating red and blue curtain.

Muffled voices rose from somewhere in the cabin. A man screamed with rage, and another yelled at him. Sam hoped there were only the two men he'd already seen, and the sounds were coming from both of them.

He stilled as a thought suddenly struck him. Why were they pissed off and screaming?

Lucia!

His attempt to rise from his sitting position was immediately halted. Glancing down, he realized he'd been zip-tied to a wooden dining chair. "Damn it!"

The shouting stopped, but the lowered voices became more audible as they moved closer. Sam stilled, listening closely as he could finally make out their words.

"I don't care how much she pisses you off, you cannot touch her, Tyler," the first man half-shouted.

"Oh, I'm going to touch her, alright," Tyler shot back. "Just you wait, Jeff, I'll—"

"Shut up! Now. Where's your phone? Call that asshole back and tell him we got them."

Tyler sighed, and several seconds of silence followed before he spoke again. "Hey man, I told you. I can deliver the woman who kicked all this shit off. How? Because I've got her and another guy zip-tied to chairs right now. Hell, I could even take her and the guy out if you want."

Sickness threatened Sam's silence at those words.

"What's he saying?" Jeff asked. Tyler activated the speaker function, and goosebumps rose on Sam's skin as a deep, gravelly voice echoed through the phone.

"How the hell did you get her? It doesn't matter. Now, you just need to tell me where you are."

"No," Tyler said firmly, firmly. "I need a guarantee that this gets us back in. That if we hand her over to you, you're not going to smoke both of us when you get here."

Silence.

"Hello?" Tyler pressed.

"I'll call the boss and see what he wants to do. In the meantime, don't touch a hair on her head—"

"Too late," Tyler muttered.

"What did you do?"

"The bitch spit on me, so I lost my temper."

Sam's stomach twisted, and he prayed she was okay.

"You clearly have a death wish. If she's not okay, you're not okay," the mysterious man stated as a matter of fact.

"She's fine." Tyler tried to backtrack, softening his voice. "Maybe a bruise or two, but—"

"For every bruise she has, you'll get three."

Silence.

"She can piss on your grave for all I care, but unless I tell you to touch her, you better smile and turn the other cheek, or I'll do more than just put a bullet in your brain."

Whoever the voice belonged to was undoubtedly a seasoned killer, and Sam had no intention of being here when the man tracked down Dumb and Dumber. He tugged at his hands and legs, but they were tied so tightly to the chair that they were beginning to go numb.

"Understood," Tyler finally replied, his voice now bereft of any edge. "I'll send you pictures of the woman and the man we've got so you can pass them on to the boss. We'll do whatever we can to serve the Fear Doirich and get back on his good side."

Sam didn't know who this "Fear Doirich" was, but by the change in Tyler's tone, he must have been terrifying.

"I'll get your answer from the boss about your status within five minutes. Six minutes from now, send me the address even if I haven't called. If you don't, you won't be pardoned, and I'll leave pieces of your rotting corpses strewn all over the backcountry."

Oh, hell no. It was time to get out of Dodge.

"Six minutes," Tyler affirmed.

"Good boy," the man mocked before the line went dead.

"We need a backup plan," the first man stated.

"No shit, Sherlock," Tyler said. Footsteps warned Sam, but he didn't have the time or ability to do anything before the door burst inward.

"Hey, asshole," Tyler said, taking a picture as soon as Sam lifted his head. He turned and left the room as quickly as he'd entered, closing the door behind him.

Footsteps thudded through the house, and Jeff said something hastily, reminding Tyler to keep his temper in check.

"Lucia," Sam grumbled quietly, but he wasn't angry with her. He was pissed at himself. This escalated so much more quickly and went so much farther sideways than he could have imagined.

He thought he could handle this better than she and Shelby, but he was wrong.

This wasn't the battlefield he was used to. Hell, it wasn't even supposed to be one. This was his homeland, and they all should have been safe here.

But safety and the reign of law and order were grand illusions for the naive. The law could only reach so far, and Shelby and Lucia had been handling it while he still pretended he was doing the best he could. And it had landed himself and Lucia in grave peril.

This was not Iraq or Afghanistan. He didn't have the upper hand as part of a superior military force, and he didn't have a platoon, squad, or division of people to back him up. He also wasn't on the side of the law in this case.

There was no legitimate reason for him to be tied up in some criminal's cabin, about to be traded off to God only knew what fate.

Sam let his chin drop to his chest, focusing on his breath and devising a way to get them out of this mess he'd walked right into. Maybe he didn't have it all figured out, and he needed to at least hear out Lucia and Shelby's ideas next time rather than going in blind and overconfident.

Like the asshole he'd been all morning.

His world had slowly been twisting and turning itself inside out, and he couldn't ignore it anymore. Whether she knew it or not, Sam believed in his soul that Lucia was the one for him. Come hell or high water, he'd fight to protect her from the law and the lawless.

For now, though, as he tugged again at his numb limbs, he prayed Shelby was working on a plan to get them out of this before the professional came.

He closed his eyes, resigning to his capture.

A rustling sound caught his attention. He opened one eye and surveyed the room.

The sound continued as the pile of blankets moved.

"Who's there?" he hissed the question in a whisper.

The pile undulated faster until the blankets fell away from a pale face framed by long dark hair.

Frightened eyes pleaded with him, but no words fell from lips covered in duct tape.

Sam's stomach twisted in horror as he realized he was looking at another captive.

A solitary tear trailed across her face until it disappeared into the blankets beneath her.

Tyler's voice caught Sam's ears, growing louder as he approached the room.

"If I can't touch that bitch, I'm gonna touch the new girl. Gotta get in one last good time just in case he decides to kill us."

"Whoa, dammit, just wait. Can't we bail?" Jeff protested. They stood and talked just outside the bedroom door now.

"No. If we run, they'll eventually catch us, and then it's lights out for good. But if this works, we have a chance at getting back in the FD's good graces. Then we have jobs again, protection, and a network. Without him, we ain't got a chance. Now let's have a little fun just in case this really is the end of the world."

The knob twisted, and the door swung open, Tyler leading the way in and grinning at Sam.

"You good and awake? You must be Sam. Am I right? Well, you lucky bastard, you're about to get a helluva show."

Jeff said nothing, his expression grim, and he ignored Sam altogether. "Let's take her out there." He threw a thumb over his shoulder toward the living room. "I want to be able to hear if anyone else drives up."

"Fine," Tyler agreed as he pulled the blanket off the woman. She wore jeans and a blouse, but her hands and feet were duct-taped.

"You're a piece of shit," Sam spat.

Tyler froze, his hand outstretched toward the woman. His head turned slowly, his eyes boring into Sam's.

Sam tried not to smile, knowing that he was about to put himself in a world of pain.

"That's right, you sick fuck. I've seen plenty like you. All jacked up in your head, too pathetic to get a willing woman."

Tyler's jaw clenched, and he shook his head before turning his attention back to the woman, grabbing the duct tape around her ankles and yanking her to the edge of the bed.

"Get your hands off her," Sam snapped. But Tyler didn't look at him again.

"Maybe I should stay in here and let you watch." Tyler grinned at Sam, pulling a knife from his back pocket and cutting the duct tape around her feet. "Then you can see a real man in action."

"You're nothing but a little bitch pretending to be a man."

Tyler froze again, his knife hand falling to his side.

"Say it again, asshole." His bright eyes shone madly. "Say. It. Again."

"You ain't nothin' but a bitch." Sam let a wild grin spread across his face as Tyler trembled, their eyes locked.

Finally, he moved again. He folded the pocket knife and clutched it in his hand, flexing his knuckles before swinging his fist into Sam's face.

Chapter 27
CHAPTER TWENTY-SEVEN

Lucia fought to stay calm as she listened to the commotion, listened as Jeff failed to keep Tyler from beating Sam. She'd heard three male voices and knew it was him. Her heart thudded in her chest as she struggled against her bonds, cursing the zip ties holding her limbs tight to the chair.

Wiggling in her seat, she tried to build momentum to move the legs, hoping the old, creaking wood dining chair would break if given enough pressure.

The sound of the door knob turning stilled Lucia immediately, and she faced the door, gritting her teeth and ready to spit fiery insults again if it meant she might save Sam from any more pain. But the glittering dark eyes that greeted her didn't belong to either of the men.

Shelby held a gloved finger to her lips, motioning for silence as she slipped into the room. That had been surprising enough, but Lucia was shocked further when an older man walked in behind her and closed the door.

He stared into her eyes and remained silent until recognition dawned in her mind. She hardly noticed as Shelby cut the zip ties and freed her.

"What the hell..." she started in a whisper, but words failed her. There were too many questions, and both Shelby and the detective shook their heads at her.

But she couldn't be quiet, as noise from the other end of the house reminded her that someone she loved dearly might be getting the beating of his life right now.

"Sam!" she hissed quietly, her eyes stinging with the threat of tears as she stood from the chair.

Shelby nodded, and Detective Ward moved closer before speaking. He kept his voice low and his hands at his sides. "We'll get Sam, but we have to be careful in case one or both are armed."

Lucia focused on her breath to regain her composure. "Both have weapons," she confirmed, "either on their persons or nearby."

The detective's eyes hardened, but he tipped his head in acknowledgment as Shelby took out a knife cut the zip ties binding Lucia to the chair.

An idea dawned in Lucia's mind then, and she dared to trust herself to save Sam.

"Stay here."

Lucia opened the door before they could argue, but neither Shelby nor the detective moved to stop her. Steeling herself, she stepped into the shadowed hallway.

Jeff reeled backward as Tyler swung at him again. He hadn't meant to incur Tyler's wrath, but his friend was blinded by fury.

"You can't kill him!" Jeff argued as Tyler punched Sam again, opening a cut above his eye. Blood poured down the man's face, and Tyler grinned wickedly.

"Then the bastard better live. I'm just gonna make sure he keeps his mouth shut from now on!" Tyler leaned back and kicked his foot into the Sam's chest, forcing the chair backward. The man grunted as he hit the floor.

His captive gasped for air as Tyler, still seething with anger, stared down at him with clenched fists, ready to strike again. "Are you gonna shut your mouth, or do we need to keep playing this game?"

From the floor, Sam turned his head and spit blood onto the dusty old planks, then caught his breath before speaking again. "Me being tied up is the only way you could ever kick my ass, you pu—"

"You're dead!" Tyler roared, his pupils so dilated his eyes looked as black as midnight. Jeff tackled him, pushing with every ounce of muscle in his eyes until he slammed Tyler backward into the wall.

"Stop!" He stared into Tyler's eyes. "Remember what that man said?! He's going to put bullets in our brains if we fuck this up! Bullets in our BRAINS!"

Tyler relaxed only a little under Jeff's grip, his eyes started returning to normal, and his breath slowed.

"Calm down, and get him cleaned up. We can tell the dude that he tried to escape or some shit. Just don't prove him right about us being idiots, please!"

Tyler spun and punched the wall, burying his fist into the aged wood paneling.

"Can you handle this, or should I? I don't know about you, but I need a damn drink."

"Get the whiskey. I'll clean this shithead up and get the girl out of here."

The man on the floor laughed, occasionally choking on his own blood and spitting it out onto the carpet.

"Are you sure?" Jeff asked, studying Tyler carefully. "I'm not dying for your temper."

Tyler's menacing gaze turned to Jeff, and he knew then that his only friend would probably kill him if he thought it necessary.

Jeff slowly backed himself out of the room and turned toward the tiny kitchen that was open to the living room area. Beyond it was the dark hallway, and something glittered within it.

He squinted, stepping toward the darkness until he made it out.

A pair of dark eyes set in a beautiful but bruised face.

Shit!

Jeff hesitated. He could call for Tyler, but Tyler already walked the edge of madness, and he might kill the only person who could keep them from being murdered. No. He wouldn't call Tyler and risk him murdering this woman that the Fear Doirich's man wanted alive and unharmed.

He straightened and grabbed the rifle leaning against the cabinets as he passed the kitchenette.

She backed up one step for each of his steps forward until disappearing into the room where he'd last seen her zip-tied to the chair. How the hell had she gotten free?

He held up the rifle, ready to threaten her, but he kept the safety on, knowing that accidentally shooting her would be the same as intentionally shooting her—either way, the action would sign his death warrant. With or without Tyler, he'd fight tooth or nail to walk out of this cabin alive.

Chapter 28

CHAPTER TWENTY-EIGHT

Mitch backed up against the wall farthest from the door and raised his weapon as soon as Lucia cleared the door. Only steps behind her, one of the men from the house in Southfield entered. A name rose to mind: Jeff Vandenberg. Not the young man Mitch had spoken to, but one of the three known to live in the house. One of the two who'd fled the house while their roommate Derek met his fate out in the bleak, wind-whipped countryside of Shiawassee County.

Did either of them know yet?

There wasn't time to wonder. They'd find out sooner or later, and Mitch needed to keep all information closely guarded.

"Drop your weapon, son," Mitch commanded as their eyes locked.

Jeff's wild eyes flitted between Mitch, Lucia, and Shelby, all with weapons pointed at him.

"Fuck." He groaned but put one hand up and allowed the rifle's butt-stock to swing toward the floor. "Who the hell are you?"

"You don't remember?" Mitch said, keeping his voice low.

"I don't have time for this shit. You better let me go and just walk away from this, old man."

"That's not going to happen."

Jeff, still scowling, dipped his head in resignation. "It'll be your funeral and mine," he muttered.

Shelby silently stepped forward and slipped the rifle out of his hands before stepping out of arm's length and quietly opening the bolt to eject the live round. As she released the hinged floor plate and emptied the rest of the rounds to clear the rifle, Mitch motioned for Jeff to sit in the chair where Lucia had been restrained. The tables had turned, or so he hoped.

"Have any of those zip ties handy in here?"

Jeff shook his head, glaring at Mitch and holding eye contact. If not for Mitch's pistol, he was sure he'd be brawling with the younger man. Until he was neutralized, he was dangerous.

"Fine. We'll do it the old-fashioned way." Mitch shrugged. Once Shelby joined Lucia in covering him and keeping an eye on the door, he took a set of cuffs from an interior pocket in his coat and secured Jeff's hands behind the back of the chair. He wasn't cuffed to the chair because Mitch wanted to be able to move him quickly if needed. "If you move, I'll allow one of these lovely young women to shoot you as many times as they'd like."

"Stuff him in the closet," Lucia suggested, her voice as cold as steel. "We need to get to Sam now."

"Is that his name?" Jeff grinned. "Tyler's tuning him up real good. You may not have much of a man left by now."

Before Mitch could stop her, Lucia hauled her free hand back, curled her fist, and swung a left hook that knocked Jeff out of the chair and onto the floor.

Mitch rushed forward, stopping Lucia just as she swung her leg back, her kick aimed at the dazed man's face.

"Stop!" he commanded. "He's playing you. Just ignore him."

He ushered her toward the door where Shelby waited, keeping a lookout for the other man.

"What about him?" she asked, tipping her head toward Jeff.

"Leave him there. Your friend has a mean left, so I don't think he'll be getting up right away. We need to stop the other one from laying the beat down on your man." He glanced at Lucia, hoping she could get her impulses under control. "Do you want to stay here and watch this one?"

"Hell no," she growled. "Let's go get Sam now!"

She headed for the hallway, a pistol gripped tightly in her hands and ready to aim. He knew a person out for blood when he saw one.

He readied his pistol and calmed his breath.

A flash of pain sliced through his head, and his vision went white. He was only vaguely aware as the sensation of falling overcame him. Scrambling feet thudded over the thick carpet, voices mingled, rising and falling until silence reigned.

Mitch's vision cleared only slightly. His blurry sight settled on a large blob, but he couldn't make it out. He blinked several times, willing his vision to clear. Though he tried to rub his eyes, his limbs refused to obey his commands.

His sight cleared just enough to make out the figure hovering above him.

Jeff stood behind Lucia, his hands still cuffed but now in front of him. The chain links stretched under Lucia's chin, half-choking her. With his right hand, Jeff held Lucia's pistol pointed at her head. The fingers of his other hand were outstretched over the other side of her head, clawing into her skin and squeezing her face.

"Drop it," Jeff commanded. "You know I'll kill her."

Mitch willed his legs to move, but nothing happened. He had to move. He had to stop this.

"Calm down," Shelby said. Mitch tilted his head just enough to see her. She held her pistol pointed toward the ceiling in one hand and her other hand palm out in surrender.

"That's what I thought." Jeff's growing fury was unmistakable, and he would make them all pay for getting the drop on him. "First things first."

Mitch's gaze finally returned to Jeff, only to find himself staring down the barrel of a pistol.

Everything slowed at that moment. He thought of everything he'd done in his life and, more so, of all the things he'd never had a chance to do. The things he still wanted to do.

Like meeting his daughter to apologize for not being there while she was growing up. Admit that he could have fought harder for partial custody. Take responsibility for letting it go when he shouldn't have.

He wanted to finally give her the teddy bear he'd kept in his desk drawer after all these years.

But he'd waited too long. And the thing her mother had feared most, her reason for cutting him off, was coming true. Mitch knew he was about to die in the line of duty, fighting for other people, following his heart and his instincts.

Closing his eyes, he imagined the disappointment he'd cause his peers and his chief. Gabriel Collins and his wife Jessica. Would they forgive him?

He hoped he'd get to meet them and his daughter in the next life. Maybe he'd do better next time.

Accepting his inevitable fate, he waited for the shot that would bring the darkness and imagined the flag-covered coffin his body would be laid to rest in.

Chapter 29

CHAPTER TWENTY-NINE

A shot rang out in the small room, but the end did not come for Mitch. His ears hurt, and all sound was muffled, but there was no more pain than what he'd already been enduring. Two bodies fell to the floor beside him.

With great effort and determination, he rolled over and pushed his hands against the floor, raising his chest up and getting his feet beneath him. Slender fingers grasped him by the arm and helped him to the bed. He sat, holding his aching head in his hands, desperate for his vision to clear.

"Luce, are you okay?" Shelby said, her voice clear and calm as she let him go and tended to Lucia.

"Okay? You could have killed me!"

"But I didn't. You're fine."

"Damn it, Shelby."

"I couldn't let him shoot the detective. I'm not going to let these bastards kill any more innocent people."

"You're right, but another two inches to the left, and you'd be cleaning my brains off the wall too!"

"I hit what I aim at." Shelby shrugged, and Mitch watched her in wonder. "And he never saw it coming."

A chill crawled down Mitch's spine. He tried to stand but fell back onto the bed again.

"Don't," Lucia protested. "He hit you with that monstrosity." She pointed at a marble-based lamp topped with a ceramic buffalo and a faux leather shade. The cord had been torn out of the wall, and the corner of the white base was covered in a red smear. Mitch guessed it was his blood.

He turned to look at Jeff. Jeff's body, rather. There was no chance he survived that headshot. Only the occasional muscle spasm.

"Holy shit," Mitch muttered.

"Detective? Stay here." Shelby fixed her dark eyes on him until he nodded in reluctant acknowledgment. He was well aware that the concussion he likely had made him more of a liability than an asset. As soon as they left the room, he planned to do something—anything—useful, yet for the moment, he could barely grasp the fact that he was still breathing. His heart still pumped blood through his aching body. And Shelby, clearly a vigilante, had saved his life.

While he knew he couldn't keep them out of the reports this time, he wouldn't let anything happen to any of them. Especially not to her.

He also wouldn't be able to hide from the truth anymore. From what he had to do. From the right thing.

"Try not to kill the other one," Mitch said as the women readied themselves to leave the room. "If we don't have one alive, the group of you will be three and oh for run-ins with suspects."

"I'll try—" Lucia started.

"You'll keep him alive, or you'll end up in jail. Are we clear?"

"We'll keep him alive then, boss." Shelby gave Mitch a mock salute before raising her weapon, slicing the corner, and clearing the hallway before moving carefully into it.

The house was quiet aside from light groaning. Her stomach tightened, and she knew they needed to move fast to get to Sam. Regardless of what shape he was in physically, any expression of his pain would send Lucia into a frenzy, and Shelby didn't want this situation to go any further sideways than it already had.

As she approached the end of the hallway where it opened into the kitchenette and living room, a hand swiped down on her muzzle, and she unintentionally squeezed the trigger, firing a shot into the floor. She flicked the safety on as Tyler tried to pull the gun from her hands. She sprawled forward from the momentum but never lost her grip on the pistol, pulling Tyler with her.

They scuffled, his nails scratching at her fingers, but she rolled, twisting it out of his reach. He was on her in a flash, straddling her back as she stretched her arms away. He punched her once in the back of the head. The strike didn't have enough momentum to hurt much, so she twisted her body, maneuvering out from under him. Before she could point her weapon at him, Lucia lunged forward and pistol-whipped him across his brow.

A sick thud signaled the blow had struck its target, and Tyler stumbled backward, dazed. He grasped for a pocket knife that had fallen on the floor, but it was at least a foot out of his reach.

"Concussions for everyone," Shelby muttered as she rose to her feet. She kicked the knife away and grabbed Lucia before she could aim her pistol at the incapacitated man. "Hurry and get to Sam. I'll handle this one."

"But he—"

"He'll pay, Lucia. But there's a cop in the other room, and we don't want to get on his bad side. You heard what he said. And we're certainly not going to start eliminating witnesses at this point. Then we'd be no better than these monsters." She spotted movement in her peripheral vision and looked away just long enough to jab the steel toe of her winter boot into Tyler's shin, causing him to cry out and grab the affected area with both hands.

"Bitch!"

Shelby snorted and returned her gaze to Lucia, whose face softened a little. Finally, she spun on her heel and stalked toward the other bedroom.

"Do you like bondage?" Lucia dug through the kitchen drawers until she found Tyler's stash of black zip ties.

Chapter 30
CHAPTER THIRTY

The sounds of a scuffle erupted somewhere in the house, and Sam knew he could use the noise to cover his attempts to free himself. Rocking forward, he lifted the chair off the floor and shifted his weight to the balls of his feet. With his wrists secured to the arms of the chair, he was stuck hunched over, but he suspected he had enough leverage for what he intended to do.

Once he had his balance, Sam pushed off the balls of his feet and spun 180 degrees. He slammed the chair on his back against the solid wood dresser. Broken pieces were scattered across the minimal floor space. His head pounded, his face throbbed, and his body ached with every movement, but he'd never underestimate what Tyler might do to Lucia if given enough time to think about it.

Especially after the sound of the gunshot.

Sam scrambled to his feet, his head swimming with dizziness, and listened carefully. It was quiet for a moment, then he heard another shot and muffled voices. His stomach tightened with worry, and prayed the shots had nothing to do with Lucia.

If he didn't have an innocent woman to protect, he'd have already bolted out of the bedroom and attacked the men head-on.

Most of the chair had fallen to pieces, but the chair arms and splinters of its legs were still attached to him. He searched the room, opening the closet to find a wood axe leaning against the wall. Rubbing the zip ties over the blade, he quickly freed himself of the chair's remnants and then turned his attention to the woman on the bed. She sobbed after he pulled the duct tape from her wrists and mouth, but he quickly hushed her.

Lifting her into a sitting position, he hastily whispered words of comfort. "I won't hurt you. I'm an officer."

She finally turned her blue eyes to meet his before looking him up and down. "You don't look like a cop." She didn't whisper but still kept her voice low.

He put a finger over his lips and tipped his head toward the door.

She nodded and swiped the back of her hand over the tears trailing down her cheeks.

"What's your name?"

"Ellie," she answered, her voice trembling.

"I'm Sam. I want you to sit tight, Ellie, but get ready to run. Just stay calm, and I'll get you out of here."

"Okay." She looked a little more confident now, crawling to the far corner of the bed and wrapping her arms around her knees.

Sam hefted the axe and flattened himself to the wall near the door, slowing his breath and preparing to attack whichever of the men walked through the door first.

Minutes crawled by, and nothing happened.

"Hey," the woman hissed in a whisper. He turned his head slightly to find her pointing at the window. "Let's just get out!"

For a fraction of a second, he almost agreed. He considered getting this poor woman out of this hell hole and to safety, then coming back to take down these bastards.

He eyed the single-twist lock on the inside of the window and listened to the stillness in the house.

The woman waved toward the window again, but he shook his head. Footsteps thudded over the creaky floorboards and toward the bedroom. He could sprint for the window and climb through it after Ellie, but once he was out, he didn't know if he could safely find a way back in to get Lucia.

And Sam refused to leave without her.

The footsteps reached the door to the bedroom and quieted. Sam readied himself, gripping the axe handle and raising it overhead.

In two more breaths, the squeaky knob turned, and the door cracked open.

Chapter 31
CHAPTER THIRTY-ONE

Lucia teetered backward just in time as the blade of an axe passed within inches of her face. The draft caused by its passing caressed the backs of her hands. She fell and scrambled backward, reaching to take her pistol out of its holster once more.

Was there a third man?

"Sam?" She raised her pistol, pointing it at the door.

"Luce? That you?"

"Damn it, Sam! You almost killed me."

"Shit!"

She reholstered her pistol as the door flung open. Sam glanced around before striding toward her with an awkward limp.

Lucia studied his face as she got to her feet. She swallowed her immediate thoughts as well as the lump that formed in her throat. Blood from multiple cuts had dried over his bruised, swollen face, and ligature marks dug deeply into his wrists.

Before she could say anything, he pulled her into a tight embrace, burying his fingers through the tangles of her dark hair. He kissed her cheek, breathing hard and squeezing her body close to his.

Hugging him back just as fiercely, she wove her arms around his neck and let her fingers travel over his scalp, searching for any other wounds. He'd been badly beaten, but she could find no more damage to his head than what was apparent on his face.

"Are you okay?" she whispered in his ear.

"I'd like to say I've seen worse." He pulled back from her embrace and stared at her. "But I already feel like I've been hit by a truck. What about you?"

"I'm okay," she said, even though she didn't feel it.

"It's safe now, Ellie," Sam called, turning his head back toward the room he'd come from. "Come out here when you're ready."

"Ellie?"

"Yeah. Those monsters had a woman tied up on the bed in there."

His green eyes focused on her, falling dark as his thumb traced over the welts and bruises on her face. She tried not to flinch, relaxing to let his gentle fingers lift her chin. His face twisted with fury when he spotted the finger-shaped bruises stretched across her throat.

"I'm going to kill him," he growled. He spun to survey the room, and his eyes fell on Tyler, who grinned up at him maliciously.

"I could teach you a thing or two, Sam."

Before Sam could get close, Shelby stepped between them. "Nope. Don't even think about it."

"Are you joking right now, Shelby? I can't believe you weren't the first to string him up!"

She shook her head. "The detective is here. And he wants this shitbag alive." Bending down, she yanked Tyler to his feet and shuffled him toward the front of the cabin.

"What do you think you're do—" Tyler's complaint was cut short when Shelby pushed him face down onto the musty carpet.

"What detective?"

"Nice to see you again," a man called from the darkened hallway.

Lucia stepped close to Sam and held his arm. "The one we met last night." She watched his face closely, and it only took a few moments longer before he seemed to recognize the older man.

Sam opened his mouth to say something, but no words came.

Mitch waved a hand dismissively as he walked past them to sit on a chair at the small round table between the kitchenette and the living room. "Don't bother lying or trying to come up with excuses." He pointed at Shelby, who rested a boot on Tyler's face. With his hands zip-tied behind his back and his ankles hooked together with a few more, he wouldn't get far without help. The older cop lowered his voice, forcing them to come closer so Tyler wouldn't hear them on the other side of the room. "This young woman saved my life. None of you will end up in jail. At least not this time."

"How did you know we were here?"

Mitch motioned for them to keep their voices down. "Immediately after I left the scene where I met you three last night, I went searching for Barnes and his friend. I was stuck in Knowland and out of leads when I saw your truck roll by. Thought it was a little odd to see you again so soon, so I followed you."

Lucia's stomach twisted. She hadn't noticed they'd been followed. She hadn't even considered the possibility.

As she kicked herself for her complacency, she noticed Shelby rummaging through a coat closet near the front door. She pulled a pair of tan marksmanship ear muffs from a shelf in the top of the closet.

Shelby tried them on, watching Mitch as he spoke, then bent down and snugged them over Tyler's ears before rejoining the group. He yelled an incoherent string of expletives toward Shelby as she walked away, but she ignored him. Judging by his slurred words, the ear muffs worked.

"So where do we go from here?" Sam asked.

"Just follow my lead. Your phones have probably all been pinging towers right about the same schedule as mine, so we'll just say that I accidentally grabbed one of your phones when we parted ways last night. Then you followed it using that find function. When you saw my car on the road and heard gunshots, you came running to help."

"You sure seem to have this all figured out already." Sam crossed his arms over his chest, and Lucia poked him in the ribs, wishing he'd save his macho bullshit for another day.

"Sounds good to me," Shelby said.

"Since when do you ever agree to anything so easily?" Sam challenged.

"When it's coming from the man in charge. The one who has our fate securely in his hands."

"Fair point," Lucia interjected. "What then? We got ambushed?"

"Yes. You were ambushed trying to help me, but Shelby was never captured, so she was able to help me free the rest of you."

The familiar way in which he spoke Shelby's name caught Lucia's attention. What was that about?

"We'll stick to the truth after the point when we freed Lucia," he continued, turning his gaze to Shelby. "The truth is easier, so keep your statements to a bare minimum and only repeat what I've instructed."

"Fine," Sam muttered, limping over to the table to sit down across from Mitch.

"I've already made the calls." Mitch sighed, glanced at Shelby again, then returned his gaze to Sam. "They'll be on scene any second now. Does anyone have any questions before this kicks off?"

"They said something about a man they called the 'Fear Doirich'. Do you know what that means?"

Lucia thought about it, but it didn't sound familiar to her, so she kept quiet. Shelby didn't say anything, either.

Mitch nodded. "I've heard that name coming up quite a bit lately. Big bad boss down in the Metro. He's making waves, and he's the one responsible for capturing and holding the two women you saved last night."

"They said something about that. Not him," Lucia nodded toward Tyler, "but the other one. He said they had to keep me alive."

"I heard them talking with another guy who sounded like he worked for this boss of theirs. He ordered them to give him this address so he could collect. Threatened to kill both of them if they messed this up."

"Well, the other one is already dead." Mitch turned tired eyes toward Shelby. She didn't move, didn't speak, only studied the imaginary dirt under her nails. "He would have killed me if not for her."

"How did it get so far?" Sam asked, letting his face fall into his hands. "Ow!" He jerked his head up.

Lucia searched the drawers until she found a washcloth. She ran water in the sink until it turned cold, then soaked the rag and hurried back to gently clean the cuts and bruises on his face.

"Do we have to worry about this boss or his men?" she asked, grateful Sam wasn't fighting her attempts to tend to his wounds.

Mitch shrugged. "Can't say for certain. Sounds like he's got money and power, but I have no idea the extent to which that's true. At least at this point. Just stay vigilant."

Sam scoffed.

Lucia knew what he was thinking. "We're tired of being vigilant."

The questioning look on Mitch's face invited an explanation, and she might have given him one, but a woman appeared in the doorway of the bedroom where Sam had been held.

"Another time," she said.

"Are you sure it's safe now?" Ellie asked. They studied the young woman who looked as haggard as the rest of them.

"It's safe, ma'am." Mitch fumbled through his interior coat pockets before sliding out his badge and holding it out for her inspection. She didn't spend much time studying it before tears filled her eyes, and she leaned against the kitchen sink. Her fingers trembled as she tucked the loose strands of hair behind her ears.

Before Lucia could try to comfort the woman, she was halted by the chirp of a police siren as vehicles rumbled up the driveway.

"I wan' a lawya!" Tyler shouted the garbled words from his position face-down on the floor.

Chapter 32

CHAPTER THIRTY-TWO

M itch listened carefully as each of the vigilante trio recited the story as he'd instructed; short on details, straight to the point, and exactly as he'd intended. Although he couldn't keep them fully out of the official reports this time, he at least had a plan to ensure they wouldn't become the subject of any criminal investigations. Instead, they'd be hailed as heroes, especially Sam. There was something almost mythological about an off-duty state trooper coming to the rescue of a fellow law enforcement officer.

If Mitch was a betting man, he'd put money on Sam receiving some kind of award at the state level. And if he didn't get it there, Mitch would make sure the young LEO received something from the Southfield Police Department.

It wasn't just for appearances either, although the lack of award recommendations would certainly raise eyebrows. Aside from that, Mitch knew Sam was in a tough spot, and no matter the circumstances, he'd still managed to do the morally correct thing, and he'd goaded Tyler into viciously beating him instead of hurting Ellie again. The self-sacrifice was admirable enough, but in the face of an inestimable enemy with unknown motives, it was genuinely heroic.

Tyler could have killed Sam, might have killed him if he hadn't heard the gunshot that had killed Jeff.

Whatever bad man they'd been scared of had never shown up, but that wasn't surprising given the overwhelming police presence that had arrived after he'd called. Apparently, a deputy sheriff's car had already been on its way to him after Collins had called in and asked for a welfare check.

Mitch knew he would be in serious trouble with his partner when they spoke again, so he silenced all of Collins's calls and texts until he was done working with the local and state units to finalize the interviews and begin processing the crime scene.

Tyler kept his mouth shut other than reiterating his desire to contact his lawyer. Not just any lawyer, and especially not a public defender, but some fancy Macomb County lawyer well-known for his work as a criminal defender.

Struggling against dizziness and nausea, Mitch struggled to move around the house and converse without attracting attention to himself. The Gladwin County Sheriff himself was on the scene, overseeing the investigation from his officers and coordinating with the state police for support with their wealth of resources. He pulled Mitch aside at one point, stepping with him out into the fresh air.

"You need to go to the hospital," Sheriff Timothy Anson stated plainly, holding eye contact with Mitch as he shoved his hands in his coat pockets.

The fiercest part of the blizzard had finally passed, but the wind was still strong, dropping the windchill to the low single digits.

"As soon as I'm done here–"

Anson raised a hand to cut him off. "I have your report, we have our interviews of the victim and passersby, and I've got the remaining suspect under control. Your work is done for now."

Mitch shook his head. "Respectfully, I've busted my ass working this case and tracking these guys down. I need custody of Barnes. I'm aiming for a perp walk."

The sheriff raised his eyebrows. "Bold of you."

Mitch held his ground, knowing there were a few ways to go about getting what he wanted, but his preferred method was to work with the man in charge.

"Fine," Anson grumbled. "But you're in no shape to handle a suspect. Go get your head checked at the hospital first, then work with your department on the transfer. I promise I'll make it as fast and smooth as possible from my end.

"I appreciate that, Sheriff, truly."

"Maybe I just want to get back to my fireplace, and the venison stew my wife started this morning." Anson coughed and shrugged. "I'll just be relieved to focus on digging out all the people foolish enough to have to drive around in the blizzard. I got a couple of reservists that can take you to the hospital, and I'll have one of 'em drive your car so you don't have to come all the way back out here to get it."

Mitch thanked him again, satisfied with the outcome despite not wanting to bother with the hospital. He knew he had a concussion, but he didn't have time for doctors, tests, and waiting endlessly for results, especially if they said he couldn't drive.

Still, he'd agreed to Anson's requirements, and he wouldn't do anything to earn his ire.

It was finally over, and he could finally slow down and take care of himself a little better.

Ellie, Lucia, and Sam had already been taken by the paramedics to the local hospital. Shelby had followed in Lucia's truck, promising she'd wait around until they were all cleared to go home. Ellie's fiancé and parents would probably be waiting at the hospital by the time she arrived, and he was thankful they'd found Tyler and Jeff before they could inflict a lifelong wound upon yet another family.

Her car had been found on the freeway, stuck in a snowbank just as she'd described.

It was simply bad luck that the first people to stop and offer help were two men already on the run from the law and persons of interest in the disappearance of Kaylie Nielsen. Even worse luck that she'd wanted to surprise her fiancé and hadn't told him—or anyone else—that she was heading out to meet him ahead of schedule. No one even knew she was missing until after she'd been rescued.

Anson headed back in, but Mitch didn't follow. He wandered toward the road where most of the police and responder vehicles were parked and made a call while he waited for the escorts Anson would assign to him.

"Where the hell are you?" Collins answered after the first ring.

"Bum-fuck-nowhere, Gladwin County."

"And why are you up there?"

"I found them, Gabe."

"What do you mean?"

"I found the other two men from the house in Southfield."

"Jesus, Mitch."

"One dead, one in custody. We need to start the transfer request right away. Can you help me get it started? The sheriff up here is willing to hand him over, but made it clear he expected me to go directly to the hospital. Even has a couple of his guys taking me there in a minute."

"Shit. Of course you got banged up. What happened?"

"Hit with a lamp. Damn thing had a marble base, too."

"You're lucky you're not dead."

"I know, I know."

"You're gonna have a lot of paperwork to do, and the DC will have your ass! Plus, you've got a pissed-off partner. Are you happy now?"

Mitch nodded as he stared into the quiet woods surrounding the cabin.
He thought of Kaylie, Ellie, Lucia, and Sam. All safe.

And he thought of Shelby.

"You know what? I really am."

Chapter 33

CHAPTER
THIRTY-THREE

Lucia relaxed her arm as the nurse ripped the tape off the IV from the back of her hand and slid the needle out. The woman was probably ten years older than Lucia and adept at her work. With one hand, she held the swab against Lucia's skin while the other hand discarded the needle in the sharps container. She taped the swab and glanced up, catching Lucia's gaze.

"Do you have any questions about the doctor's discharge instructions?"

Lucia shook her head. "Rest, hot and cold compresses, and lots of fluids."

"The strong stuff runs out pretty fast," the nurse noted, referring to the painkillers prescribed to Lucia, "but they last a little longer if you only take them as needed."

"I'll try to make them last," Lucia reassured her.

The nurse nodded. "All right. You take it easy."

"Thanks. You too." Lucia flashed a glance at Shelby, sitting still as a statue in a chair between the bed and the room's only window.

After she'd left, Shelby broke the silence. "Sam's okay."

Tears stung the backs of Lucia's eyelids, so she squeezed them shut and sucked in a breath, desperate to hold back the wave of emotion threatening to overwhelm her now.

"You're okay too." Shelby stood and slid her hand between the curtains, peering through the window. The snow-covered landscape blinded the world as it reflected a sun that hadn't been seen in at least three days.

"I don't know how." Lucia rose, untied the hospital gown, and let it fall to the floor. "But you're right. I am. We are. I can't believe we lived through this." The lump tightened in her throat.

"Because we're not as bad as Sam thought."

Lucia ignored the comment. She knew it had been made partly out of spite and partly because Shelby was restless and eager to get home to Lee, Ginger, and the pub.

"What do you think about that cop?"

The question caught Lucia off-guard. She'd hardly been able to think about anything but Sam's well-being and Ellie's.

"I don't know. It seems like he's interested in keeping our hands clean, so what does it matter?"

"Something is off about that man," Shelby grumbled.

"As long as he keeps his word and keeps us on the right side of things, I'm not really worried. Maybe he gets it."

Shelby turned and glared, tipping her head toward the doorway as Lucia slid her pants on.

"Ugh." Lucia rolled her eyes. "Let's see if we can wait with Sam."

She picked up her things, and they left the room together.

They were not allowed to wait in Sam's room. Instead, they alternated between the waiting room and the sidewalk in front of the hospital's emergency room entrance.

The cold air chilled Lucia's anxiety and calmed her nerves, but it heightened the pain she was already in. Welts and bruises covered her face, shoulders, chest, and thighs. Her throat still ached, black and blue where Tyler's fingers had squeezed so hard she thought he would kill her.

Standing in the snow, shivering against the cold and the aching of her body, Lucia wished she hadn't quit smoking. She'd about kill to have a cigarette just then.

Before she could hunt down the inevitable smoke area in the designated spots away from the entrance, Shelby found her and dragged her by the arm back into the hospital.

A blast of heat warmed her skin, Lucia limping as they entered through the sliding doors and headed for the waiting room again.

"Sit," Shelby commanded, as if Lucia needed another person besides Sam to order her around.

"Stop it."

Shelby's flat stare met her, and she held out a styrofoam container and a bottle of water. "Time to eat, Luce."

"Where'd you get that?"

"The cafeteria. Where else?"

Lucia accepted both, uncapping the bottle and sipping at first. It wasn't until the water hit her lips that she realized just how thirsty she was. The IV hydration hadn't even penetrated the true depth of her thirst.

She drank half of it before Shelby stopped her.

"Slow down. Eat something."

Her thirst quenched for the moment, Lucia opened the container to find a plain burger and steamed vegetables. She knew it wouldn't be the best thing she'd ever tasted, but once the smell hit her nostrils, her stomach growled, and her hunger overwhelmed her hesitation.

She did her best to eat slowly, chewing carefully before swallowing to spare her sore throat, but she managed to eat it quickly.

As she finished, Shelby opened the orange bottle that contained her no-refill painkiller prescription and handed Lucia a single pill.

"Take this with the rest of your water."

As much as she'd initially resisted Shelby's mothering, Lucia didn't mind as much now. She needed food and drink, and now it was time to take something to relieve the pain.

She almost feared those little white pills, feared what they could do to her body and brain. It wasn't just the potential for addiction that made her hesitate, but the knowledge that her senses would be dulled by the medicine. She wanted to know Sam was okay before she relieved her pain.

But she didn't know how long she'd have to wait. No matter how she positioned her body, the aching, stabbing pain radiated through her muscles and seeped into her bones.

Tossing the pill into the back of her throat, Lucia followed it with the rest of her water.

Shelby took the bottle, tossing it into the nearest trash can while Lucia leaned back in her chair and waited for relief to kick in.

After a few minutes, her mind loosened and her body relaxed. The fuzzy feeling settled over Lucia like a haze, and she embraced the experience and the way it dulled her pain.

Time blurred, and the room spun even when she closed her eyes.

Meaningless visions fluttered behind her eyelids until a gentle hand shook her shoulder.

Lucia fought to the surface of consciousness, opening her eyes to find a doctor staring at her.

A man's voice finally broke through the muffled fog. "Miss Sorensen? Can you understand me?"

"Yes," she said, but it sounded slurred.

"I'm taking care of both of them," Shelby said, stepping in.

Lucia nodded before the doctor could ask. "Shelby's in charge."

"Sam is in a lot of pain. He has a concussion, three cracked ribs, and a couple of loose teeth. I've already spoken with his post commander, and he'll be off duty until he's medically cleared." He handed Shelby an orange pill bottle and a handful of freshly printed paperwork.

"Instructions?"

"Yes. He can take one of these," he shook the bottle before handing it to Shelby, "every six hours as needed, not to exceed four doses in a twenty-four-hour period."

Shelby nodded, accepting the bottle and paperwork.

"Detailed care instructions are there," he gestured toward the papers now in Shelby's hands, "but the main thing he needs is rest and hydration. He should move as little as possible for the next week if you and Miss Sorensen can help take care of him."

"Understood," Shelby said.

"I'll take care of him," Lucia interrupted, fighting to speak coherently. "I won't leave his side."

Shelby and the doctor both glanced at her briefly before returning to their conversation.

"There is someone who can take care of them, right?"

"Yes. I'll make sure someone is with them when I can't be."

"Good." The doctor nodded. "I have a nurse bringing him down now if you want to drive your vehicle to the entrance to pick him up."

"Of course. Thank you so much for your help."

"Just keep these two out of trouble, will you?" He grinned at Shelby. "And yourself."

Lucia pushed herself to her feet and steadied herself once the doctor had excused himself.

"Come on, Loopy." Shelby patted Lucia's shoulder, guiding her out of the hospital and into the parking lot again.

Lucia, her senses too dull to protest or even care, followed obediently, climbing in the back of the truck and lying down. The motion of the truck made her nauseous as Shelby drove to the Emergency Room entrance.

But as soon as the passenger door opened, she bolted upright, ignoring the pinches of pain crawling like lighting through her body as she did so. She flinched, but she pushed through it, eager to see Sam.

One eye was swollen shut, and the cut above it was stitched and bandaged. His battered, pale face tilted up as a nurse rolled him close and engaged the brakes on the wheelchair.

His gaze met Lucia's, waiting for him, and his bruised lips quirked up.

Even in her fuzzy state, her heart melted, and she released all her remaining tension into a smile of her own.

Shelby helped Sam climb into the back seat of the truck to sit next to Lucia. They found positions as comfortable as they could while holding each other for the drive home.

All that had come before and all that would come after didn't matter in that moment as Lucia gingerly lay her head against Sam's chest. She snuggled her body close to his, cursing every bump just as he did.

But a new warmth coursed through her as he began to twine his fingers through her hair. Sam was alive, he was going to be okay, and she no longer doubted that he still loved her.

He gently kissed the back of her hand, solidifying her belief in the heart of the man who now wrapped his arm around her shoulders.

Chapter 34

CHAPTER
THIRTY-FOUR

S helby settled Sam and Lucia on the couches in their living room, then walked and fed Penny before leaving.

After reminding them at least four times that she had taken care of Penny, she locked the house behind her and drove the truck back home to Merrill. Although she knew neither of them would mind, she wanted to do her best to make sure they didn't wake up surprised and thinking that their truck had been stolen.

As an extra precaution, she left a note on the counter near their pain meds and used Lucia's phone to text Sam's friend, Joe Guzman. She shared a brief rundown of all the details in her text—at least the ones the detective had cleared them to share. Joe texted back immediately to let her know he'd check on them first thing in the morning.

Before getting back on the road, Shelby texted Lee to let him know she'd be in for work after a shower. Then she turned up the radio and switched to a classic rock station, glancing at the time as she pulled the truck onto M46 and headed east. It was already past seven.

Lee and Ginger would probably both insist she sleep, and she knew she could use it. She'd gotten very little in the past 48 hours, but her thoughts still buzzed with worry as she tried to untangle all the mysteries beneath the placid surface of her mind. Exhaustion ached in her muscles and occasionally blurred her vision, but she fought it out of spite.

Shelby needed time to unwind and settle back into a bit of normalcy before she'd be able to relax and rest. If she laid down in bed now, she'd lay there staring at the ceiling, the endless thoughts tearing at the fragile edges of her sanity all the while. Keeping herself busy kept the madness from a lifetime of trauma at bay.

It was a short drive home from Sam and Lucia's place, and it gave her little time to think. She still couldn't put a finger on what had bothered her so deeply about Detective Ward. The problem swirled just beneath the surface of her mind throughout the drive. She chewed on it as she parked in front of the stairs up to her apartment, jogged up them, and took a quick, hot shower.

Swiping the fog from the mirror with her hand, her reflection stared back at her, and something clicked. It was in the shape of her eyes, the slant of her nose, the bow of her lips. The warm sepia of her skin was only half as rich and deep as her mother's.

She'd always known why but not who.

Someone else stared back at her from that mirror now, a traitor, an imposter. Somehow familiar, but someone she didn't know at all.

"No," she muttered, breathless, her gaze locked on the reflection of her almost-black eyes. "Stop looking for ghosts, Shelby, or you'll find them."

Kicking the vanity cabinets, she broke the spell and turned her attention to her clothes. She dressed quickly, muttering curses even as she applied light makeup for work. After pulling on the fitted black t-shirt and dark blue jeans as quickly as she could, she hurried out, slowing only to lock her apartment door before hurrying down to the pub.

Denial consumed Shelby's mind, holding the truth of what she'd seen in the mirror on just the other side of an actual epiphany. Once she allowed that realization to eclipse her mind, there would be no coming back to blissful ignorance. She hoped it was all a simple delusion brought on by stress and lack of sleep over the past few days. It was the answer to a question she'd ruminated over her whole life. And it was an answer she desperately needed to avoid as long as possible right now.

Shelby turned her focus to the parking lot instead, noting with a grimace that it was nearly full already. She sighed, and her steps slowed. While the ever-growing popularity of their little pub was good for Lee's pride in his menu and Ginger's bottom line, it grated at Shelby. The place had barely been surviving month to month when she'd been hired. As much as she wanted Ginger and Lee to be successful, she also wanted quiet anonymity to go with her minimal paycheck.

When she pushed through the doors of the pub, she was not prepared to bump face first into Matt's chest. His strong hands caught her before she could fall backward.

"Shelby!"

"DD?" she asked, half-dazed as he righted her.

"Are you okay?"

"No," she grumbled, twisting out of his grasp and sliding past him. She didn't want to look directly into anyone's eyes right now, especially not his. They were attractive and, more importantly, always and unexplainably filled with concern for her. She heard his heavy footsteps follow her despite the low rumble of the growing dinner crowd.

"Hey," he called. "Did I mess up? Is this my answer?"

Shelby stopped in her tracks, blowing out a breath and squeezing her eyes shut briefly. "No," she turned to face him, "it's not. You didn't do anything wrong. I'm just... I have a lot going on right now."

He nodded solemnly for a moment, his gaze falling only slightly before he offered a sad half-smile, his happy demeanor deflating by the second. "I understand. I won't bother you anymore."

Damnit. She couldn't stand to see him like that and hated that she didn't know why. Or, at least, she didn't want to admit why.

Matt turned to leave, but she grabbed his arm to stop him, stepping closer so she could turn his face back to hers. "Don't be so dramatic." She tried to force a smile. "If you've figured out anything about me by this point, you should know I'm not going to play with you. I'm going to tell you exactly how I feel. And, at least right now, I feel like you shouldn't head out just yet."

"Are you sure? You don't have to pretend—"

"Stop it. I'll be busy, as usual, but it'd be nice to have your company whenever I get a break." It was a little too honest for Shelby, and she cringed inwardly at how pathetic it sounded. "I mean, if you don't have anything better to do tonight."

He laughed, shaking his head, but his blue eyes brightened, and his shoulders relaxed. "Nothing at all, especially when I'm off-duty."

While Matt settled himself at the bar, Shelby checked in with Ginger, then clocked in and began taking orders. Starting with Matt's.

Chapter 35
CHAPTER THIRTY-FIVE

Wednesday, December 7th

M itch woke late the next morning, his tired eyes opening to sunlight streaming past the edges of the curtains. It had been years since he'd last slept past dawn, and he felt more refreshed and energized than he could remember despite the ache of bruised and exhausted muscles. Although he'd been through a whirlwind of action over the past week, his successes in finding three victims alive closed enough open loops in his brain to let him relax and sleep. It also helped that he'd found the three men responsible for kidnapping Kaylie.

He'd ride this high for a few days —or even a couple of weeks, if he was lucky. The energy gained from his wins would feed into open cases and, hopefully, reinvigorate his investigations. Embracing that anticipation of solving more cases, Mitch got himself ready for work quickly. The drive was easier now that the storm had passed and the roads were plowed and salted. Everything was looking up. He pulled his car into the lot behind the Southfield Police Department and hurried to the entrance, allowing the ghost of a smile to lift his lips as the mid-morning winter sun glared down on him.

Mitch didn't even fear the reprimands he knew would be heading his way for all the ways he'd deliberately ignored standard procedures and regulations. The risk had been worth the reward in the end, and he'd do it over again a thousand times.

Because each of those "wrong" decisions had led him to find the victims. And Shelby.

"Well, hallelujah," Collins said from Mitch's desk as he approached. "Mitchell Ward lives." He half-sat, half-leaned on the corner of the desk, shaking his head at his partner. In spite of his disapproving expression, his eyes were soft, and the lines around his eyes belied his worry.

"Yep." Mitch nodded as he took his seat and tapped his keyboard. "I'm still on this side of the grave. For now."

"You got anything for me, partner?" Collins laid bitter emphasis on the last word. "Or are you just gonna keep leaving me in the dark?"

"No," Mitch sat back and shook his head, giving his undivided attention to Collins. "You're right. I'm a shit partner, and you deserve better."

"Stop it."

"I'm serious. I didn't want you to get hurt. I felt it in my gut. I knew shit would go sideways, and I didn't want your family to suffer if something happened to you."

"And what about you?"

Mitch shrugged. "What about me?"

"Don't play that game with me. What if something happens to you?"

"I don't have anything to lose, and there's no one to lose me. No one suffers if I die."

"You better drop that act right now—"

"What act? It's the simple truth. My only child doesn't know me. I have no wife. My parents are already gone. And my siblings... well, they barely know me. I might as well be a ghost already."

"Wow. That's such a healthy and positive attitude."

Mitch ignored the comment and turned his attention to his computer screen. "What matters is that I make things right with you. At least you understand why I made the choices I did, right?"

Collins sighed and scratched absently at the stubble on his chin. "Sure, man. Just know that Jess and I care about you. The kids... well, you're their favorite uncle."

The sincerity of his words and the thought of hurting the kids fell on Mitch like a brick, but he didn't let himself flinch.

"Look, I'm not going to kill myself or anything. I'm actually feeling pretty good right now. And I'll try not to purposely take on any more suicide missions."

"That's a good start. Now, what about your daughter?"

Mitch froze, turning his gaze slowly toward Collins.

"Got you, sucker. You leave me in the lurch, act like a glory hound, and try to be this self-deprecating antihero, but I got your number. So, it's time to pull the trigger and stop hiding. Look her up and reach out to her."

He'd thought on that exact topic the whole way home from the hospital the night before and until he'd crashed into his bed. He wanted so badly to do just that: to call her up and tell her, to offer her the chance to get to know each other.

"What if she doesn't want to know me?" He barely finished his sentence, faltering at the thought and suddenly embarrassed at how soft his voice had become.

"If she doesn't, then you back off and let her go," Collins replied quickly, seizing the moment. "But you can't know what she wants until you ask her. You might be the missing part of her history that she needs to know so she can feel whole and ready to take on the world."

Mitch shook his head, but Collins didn't let him interrupt.

"Don't argue. She's a young woman now, exploring her life and her identity, the big wide world, and finding herself. Our history helps shape

our future, especially when we're uncovering the pieces we've been searching for our whole lives."

"Sure, but is it right to jump into her life without any warning? Maybe
it's better I wait until—"

"No," Collins said firmly. "You know who she is, but I'd bet money she
doesn't have a clue who her biological father is. You hold all the cards, and
it's unfair to her if you keep them to yourself."

"You really believe that?"

Collins nodded. "Show your cards, man."

Mitch nodded and cleared his throat, blinking against the stinging in his
eyes.

Reaching down, he pulled open the bottom right drawer of his desk and
stared into it. He hesitated, frozen in fear of what might come, then broke
the spell and stuck his hand in the drawer.

He grabbed the old teddy bear, the object of his fear and adoration, and
lifted it gently before setting it on his desk. Then he opened up the database
he most often turned to and typed her name in the search. He needed to
be sure.

"It's a start," Collins said. "Call first, but you may want to meet her for
coffee or something and break the news in person. It'd be more respectful
that way."

"How long do you think before I'm off for the day?"

Collins shrugged, staring at the decades-old toy Mitch had set on the
desk. "Fill out that mountain of paperwork waiting in your inbox, and then
you'll be placed on administrative leave for at least a week, maybe two, until
it's all sorted out and you're cleared from shooting one suspect on Monday
and... whatever happened to the other one yesterday.

"Right. I'll get all that done, then I'll call her. Figure out a time to meet
up, and..."

"And tell her the truth."

"Of course," Mitch said flatly, and he let his gaze rest once more on the gift he'd saved for her from all those years ago. The teddy bear rested on the corner of his desk, its glassy black eyes staring back sadly through its matted polyester fur.

Chapter 36
CHAPTER THIRTY-SIX

Lucia's muscles ached as she regained consciousness. She was vaguely aware of Penny whining and licking her hand.

"It's okay, girl," she muttered. Her throat was dry, and the words stuck in her mouth, but she rolled herself off the couch. She stood, teetered, then limped toward the door, her bruised body aching with every step, every breath.

Unfortunately for Penny, Lucia wasn't in any shape to go for long walks today, but with the deep snow covering the land, the Rottie wouldn't want to be out long anyway. She opened the door, and Penny ran out, circling a bit before doing her business and running back into the house.

"Good girl." Lucia rubbed Penny's soft ears before limping toward the kitchen. She found her phone and Sam's phone next to each other and charging on the countertop next to the coffeemaker. Beside them, a sticky note with familiar handwriting scrawled across it. Leaning her weight against the counter for support, she focused her muddled brain on the words.

I drove your truck home. Don't call the cops on me. Joe said he'd check on you two in the morning. – Shelby

Lucia snorted and started the coffee before grabbing the orange prescription bottle with her name on the label and reading the instructions. One dose by oral route every 4-6 hours as needed. It had been at least 12 hours, and she desperately needed it. She took the medication, settled herself on one of the counter stools, and rested her head on the cool surface. The meds didn't kick in until she'd finished making a pot of coffee.

Sam still slept, his deep breaths quiet in the stillness of the room. They had both opted to sleep on the couches instead of their bed so they could be closer to the kitchen to take their meds. She silently limped back to her couch and set her freshly poured mug on the coffee table.

Lucia sipped her coffee for a few minutes, letting herself sink further into the fuzz of the painkillers, then carefully laid down on the couch and pulled the blanket over herself again until the jingle of Penny's tags rang through the mire in her brain.

Fuck. Lucia didn't have the energy or lucidity to say it out loud, but she would have if she could.

She let herself come slowly back to consciousness, huffing as she opened her eyes and turned her gaze to the door. Three light knocks sounded, and then a key slid into the lock. Joe Guzman, Sam's best friend, let himself in, keys in one hand and a drink carrier in the other. A plastic bag hung from his wrist.

"You have a key?" she asked, slurring her words.

"Of course." The keys, the drink carrier, and the bag were all dropped onto the entry table, then his boots thunked on the floor after he took them off. "You didn't know I was coming?"

Lucia recalled Shelby's note. "I knew. I'm just...in a lot of pain right now."

Joe gave a muted chuckle as he brought the drink carrier and the plastic bag to the kitchen counter. "I can't wait to hear this story. But first, come eat."

She squeezed her eyes shut and groaned. "Do I have to?"

A pill bottle rattled in the kitchen. "According to the label, you're supposed to take your dose with a meal. Have you eaten yet?"

"No."

"Have you taken a dose yet?"

"Yes."

"Get your ass up here before I wake up Sam and tell on you."

"Shut up." Lucia sat up too quickly, forcing her to wait until her vision settled before rising from the couch once more.

"Such a lady," he teased.

"Such a gentleman." She stuck out her tongue at him as she eased onto a stool. Despite their banter, she was thankful he'd come. She and Sam were too beat up to handle making meals right now.

"I see you already made coffee."

"Barely."

"Well, I brought you fresh coffee plus breakfast sandwiches from your favorite local shop. Not to mention hash browns and extra bacon."

"Okay, you win. I'm the asshole." She didn't think she could feel hungry until the moment she smelled the food, watching hungrily as he put it on a plate for her. He slid it across the counter with a handful of napkins, then passed her a to-go cup of coffee.

"What is that smell?" Sam asked, half-muttering the words. "Is that food?"

"That's right," Lucia said. "Our favorite boyfriend brought us breakfast."

Joe ignored her as he filled a glass with tap water and prepared a dose of Sam's painkillers for him. "Come on up here, buddy. How are you feeling?"

"Like I've been hit by a Mack truck." Sam stood from the couch he'd been lying on and limped over to the counter, gingerly taking the seat next to Lucia. He rubbed her shoulder, then reached for the water and the pill.

"From the rumors I've heard, it was more like two Mack trucks."

Sam paused, his painkiller only inches from his mouth. "You're not going to interrogate us while we're fucked up on opioids, are you?"

Joe shook his head. "No. I'm only messing with you. Well, there are some rumors flying around. But the post commander isn't sharing what's in the reports he received from Genessee and..." he paused dramatically, "the Southfield Police Department."

"Shit." Lucia sighed before taking a bite of her breakfast sandwich.

"I don't know," Joe continued. "Sounds like Sam is up for a pretty big award, maybe two."

She froze and met Joe's gaze, who then turned to Sam. "How many people did you save up in the middle of nowhere?"

Sam shook his head, took his medicine, and gulped down his glass of water. He looked at Joe and motioned for him to pass a sandwich. "I did what I thought was right.You know how it is."

Even Lucia raised an eyebrow at that.

"No." Joe stared hard at Sam. "I don't know. Tell me, Sam. Tell me how it is."

"Can we just eat?" Sam pleaded. "I need food and coffee before these meds kick in."

"Sure, man."

"When does he have to be back in?" Lucia asked, breaking the growing tension gathering over them.

"The Post Commander is going to come visit, and he'll talk to Sam about all that."

Lucia shrugged, feigning nonchalance, but it pricked her pride to be reminded that she was an outsider. It shouldn't have bothered her since she wasn't an officer, but for some reason, it did. Maybe because his friends and coworkers were the only people she really saw in her day-to-day life anymore.

Another thought pricked her mind, heightening the sensation of exclusion: Sam had been with her, and he'd involved himself in her "extracurricular" activities. If he was caught, there would be hell to pay for both of them.

Lucia gritted her teeth at the thought of them being separated at any point, but she kept her cool on the surface. It wouldn't do either of them any good if she became suspiciously defensive.

Joe turned the conversation to the only thing they could agree on anymore: the horrendous blizzard that had blown through over the weekend. In many places, the power had been knocked out, and some rural towns were still snowed in. Although, in those places, most Michiganders simply got around on their snowmobiles.

Need groceries? Take your snowmobile. Want to enjoy the winter wonderland? Perfect for a snowmobile ride. Got to get out of the house and away from your family? Head to the local bar on your snowmobile.

Many of Lucia's childhood friends and their families were probably riding their horses into town. She wished she could do that too, but it wasn't part of her life anymore, as much as it ached.

For now, she'd settle for coming out of facing human traffickers alive.

Joe cleaned up the breakfast mess, walked Penny, and made sure Lucia and Sam were settled before he headed back to the Michigan State Police post in Pine River.

Lucia waited until she couldn't hear his engine anymore before turning her full attention to Sam. He was lying face-up on his couch, his eyes closed, one arm resting over his head, and one leg bent. There were so many things she wanted to say. So many things she needed to say.

She didn't even know where to start.

Words failed her, forming in her mind only to die on the tip of her tongue. So she started simple.

"Are you in a lot of pain?"

Sam opened one eye and peered at her. "I'm floating. It's not so bad right now." He shut his eye again.

Minutes of silence passed between them, with only the rattle of Penny's collar to disturb it.

Lucia sighed and squeezed her eyes shut. She knew exactly what she had to say, no matter how hard it was.

"I'm sorry, Sam. Again."

"Why?"

Her eyes popped open, and she sat up on the couch and faced him. "Huh?"

"What do you think apologizing is going to do? Is it going to un-bruise my ribs?"

Lucia's heart sank, and she bit her bottom lip. "No, I–"

"Will it erase my black eye and instantly heal my limp from my fucked up knee?"

She shook her head and closed her eyes again.

"You don't have to apologize. I know what you mean, but it doesn't matter."

"Why?" she asked, her voice barely a whisper.

"Because I chose you."

Lucia's breath caught in her throat. Had she heard him right?

"I chose to follow the path you set before me, no matter what hell it led into."

He got up and limped over, settling himself on the couch next to her. She pushed herself up, hesitating only briefly before reaching out for his hand.

"The entire situation sucks, but I love you. I've always loved you, and I'll always choose you, Lucia."

Tears burned in her eyes, and she threw herself into his arms. He groaned and winced when she hugged him too hard, but he didn't let her pull away. Instead, he pulled her closer.

"It's okay. It's worth all the pain just to be with you."

Chapter 37

CHAPTER THIRTY-SEVEN

L ee stared at Shelby over their early lunch, a smirk on his boyish face. She tried to ignore him, but his smirk soon turned into a wide smile as the news reporter continued her story on the TV over the bar.

"Multiple victims were rescued, along with an unidentified officer. Authorities are withholding the names of those involved pending completion of their investigation."

"Where did you say you went again?" Lee asked.

She stared back at him and took an exaggerated bite of her steak, chewing noisily before mumbling as if she were trying to speak with a full mouth.

He shook his head and chuckled. "How the hell did I get so lucky when you found me?"

"Ha!" It was Shelby's turn to laugh. She knew her friends liked her, but it was still a sentiment she struggled to accept. Her mother and stepfather never wanted her, and she'd never known the sperm donor who'd walked out on her family when she was just a baby. Why would anyone else want her around?

It continually surprised her that, for some reason, these people in her life now really did seem to want her around.

"Well," he said as he stood up from the bar stool, "I hope you like your lunch. I have a lot to prep for dinner. Ginger put out the word about some special tonight and a free meal for anyone who lost power, so it's going to be a lot busier than usual."

Shelby groaned, chewing slowly. She wanted to savor her meal and her solitude before the rush started. In just forty-five minutes, they'd open the doors for lunch. Some people were still buried in by the snow, but most of the major roads had been plowed and salted, and the pub sat on a corner along the main highway. She hoped the afternoon wouldn't be as busy as she feared.

Unfortunately for Shelby, patrons were waiting when she unlocked the doors, and the steady stream of people kept the pub at least half-full. She hustled, taking orders, serving food and drinks, and bussing. Before she knew it, it was time to take a break before the dinner rush started.

Shelby was leaning against the brick facade near the front entrance and wishing for a cigarette when a familiar truck pulled into the parking lot. Matt stepped out, locked his truck, and smiled broadly as he walked toward her.

She had to force back the urge to smile back at him. It hadn't actually been that long since they'd last seen each other—only a few days—but it felt like it had been weeks.

That couldn't be a good sign, surely, but then again, she'd just been through hell with Lucia and Sam. Who knew how long the calm would last before the devil came calling again?

As he approached, she let her guard down and let her face light up. He was easy on the eyes, and his presence comforted her too. On top of all that, he had a great sense of humor and a level-headed demeanor. He was the rock shielding her from the chaos crashing like waves over her complicated life. When she rested in his shadow, she felt like she could finally relax a little.

"What are you doing here?"

He shrugged. "I hate cooking. Why are you standing out here? Are you smoking again?"

"No. But I shouldn't have to smoke to get a break." She tipped her head toward the door. "Looks like it'll be busy in there tonight."

"That's good, though, right?"

It was her turn to shrug. "I like when it's quiet."

"So do I."

"Do you ever work anymore, Deputy?" She winked and tapped the toe of his boot with her own.

"I should have been on tonight, but I got a couple more days off. Another deputy had something come up with family this weekend, so I volunteered to switch with her."

"Are you always such a good guy?" she teased.

"You kidding? Didn't you notice my shining armor?"

Shelby chortled. "You're right!" She headed for the pub door, allowing him to open it for her this time.

"What the hell else am I going to do?" He chuckled and ran nervous fingers over his short hair. "I get bored on the weekends anyway."

"Well, you could take me on that date you've been practically begging me for."

He stopped behind her, momentarily frozen in his tracks, so she turned to face him and beamed a sly grin at him.

"You really thought I was going to leave you hangin'?"

His face turned red, and a dimple formed on his cheek, but he couldn't hide his happy grin. "Maybe. But now you can just tell me when and where."

"I'll tell you when," she said, pulling him along by the arm as she stepped around tables and continued to the bar. "But you can decide where. I think you know enough about me to pick something just right for us to do."

"No. You're the quietest woman I've ever met, and–"

"Shh." She held a finger to her lips and stared up into his excited blue eyes. "It's not that serious. Just trust your gut, and I bet we'll have a great time."

He nodded. "I'll do my best."

"Now, I have to get back to work."

"Great. That'll give me time to Google 'best date ideas for scary women' while I eat dinner."

She lightly punched his bicep and pointed her finger at him in warning, then burst out laughing. It felt good to laugh, she realized as she walked behind the bar to start taking orders. Maybe life could be a little more like this from now on.

Chapter 38

CHAPTER THIRTY-EIGHT

Phil pinched the bridge of his nose and squeezed his eyes shut as Bran explained the course of events of the past week over the phone's speaker. Again. He still couldn't believe he'd been foolish to hope the idiot Tyler and his remaining lackey friend could handle a simple task like keeping two people tied up.

Bran had forwarded the pictures to Phil: Lucia and her cop boyfriend, zip-tied to chairs and kept in separate rooms.

How could anyone mess that up?

To his surprise, Phil's father, Richard, was even more pissed than he was.

"Explain to me exactly how they went from having those two thorns in my side captive and zip-tied to chairs, to one now being in police custody and the other dead?"

"Sir," Bran started, then cleared his throat. "From what I learned, there was another cop on site that they didn't know about, and he worked with another woman, Shelby Ford. This is the same woman your son had his... 'interactions' with late last year. Before his accident."

The accident Bran referred to was the day Phil had been teaching Lucia a good lesson when Liam Thompson had snuck up and shot him in the back. That memory was the only thing that burned worse than his desire to wrap his fingers around Shelby's perfect neck and squeeze until she choked and begged with her eyes for him to stop. He could see it in his mind, feel her warm skin on his fingers.

"Are you just going to sit there like an invalid?"

Phil opened his eyes and glared at his father. "Is that supposed to be funny?"

"This is no time for weakness, son."

"I'm not weak, I'm a paraplegic. Do we really have to do this again?"

"Watch your tone, or I'll knock your teeth out," the old man growled.

Phil tossed his hands up in a gesture of surrender. "Forgive me my sins, Father."

"Sir," Bran interrupted the squabble. "What are your next instructions?"

Phil propped his elbow on the arm of his wheelchair and rested his chin in his hand. "What else is there to do?" He chewed his lip and stared out over the frozen lake, its icy cover glittering in the evening light just beyond his window.

"It's time to rid our family of these vermin," Richard grumbled as he pulled out his phone and began scrolling through his contacts.

"Father?" It was always Father, never "Dad."

"What?"

"You aren't usually so hasty."

"I tire of cleaning up your ridiculous messes. It's time to end it and move on with our lives."

"You don't understand," Phil started, stunned at the resolve in his father's voice.

"Oh, I understand far better than you. These people no longer waited for you to come for them. They are not only interfering with your operations, they're also taking out your pawns."

"But this isn't chess."

"Why not? They're all pieces on the board, and those pests are pieces we need to remove from play."

"It's not that simple. In chess, you can't account for the one thing that these people have in spades."

Richard sighed, looking up from his phone to stare expectantly at his youngest son. "Don't mix analogies. What do you believe they have that I cannot account for?"

"Luck. Fate. Fortune. Whatever you want to call it, they have it, and I've lost it. Lady Luck no longer smiles on me."

Richard shook his head and returned his attention to his phone. "You can feel sorry for yourself if you must, God knows I would, but I don't need your superstition. Say your prayers, repent for your sins, and stave off your trip to hell, but save the fortune-telling for your mother."

Phil shrugged. "At the very least, I wouldn't underestimate them."

"Unlike you, I run no such risk. I have their estimation, and I know where they're found wanting. My men will exploit every weakness and any misstep or mistake."

"I expect you'll count me among your men," Bran interjected over the phone's speaker.

"You sound awfully confident," Richard said.

"I am, sir."

"Then count yourself in. Sit tight while I map out a strategy and put the right pieces in play."

"What can we actually do to turn this in our favor?" Phil asked, intrigued at his father's determination.

"Simple," his father responded nonchalantly as he scribbled across the thick, creme-colored paper. "We target the most important pieces and throw everything at them until they're off the board."

"I guess your metaphors–I'm sorry, 'analogies'–are beyond my dull in-
tellect, Father." He tried half-heartedly to keep his mocking tone from
being obvious. "Where are we supposed to start?"

"With their queen, of course."

Chapter 39

CHAPTER THIRTY-NINE

Mitch clutched the steering wheel in a white-knuckled grip as he took the freeway off-ramp. His GPS fed him instructions in its monotone female voice, and he hardly heard them. He stopped, looked both ways, then turned left onto M46. It would only be about ten minutes now, and he'd arrive at his destination.

But this would be so much more than simply a physical destination.

He'd been running from this for over twenty years now. These days, he could only be honest with himself. If only he had been braver as a young man, he would have fought tooth and nail for his daughter. But he hadn't. Not until now.

Once the department had officially placed him on administrative leave, Mitch had headed home to start his research. What he found when he dug into his daughter's recent background disturbed him, to put it mildly. She had been kidnapped by suspected human traffickers during the past summer but escaped. Pain tightened his chest in a vice-like grip as he read through the detailed reports filed after her escape.

Worry gripped him. It only took him a few hours, but he'd been able to build out her network of known connections and a series of loosely linked news reports. It almost appeared that she was connected to cases where other trafficking victims were mysteriously rescued. Was she a...a vigilante?

Of course, the indicators were all circumstantial, but they were there nonetheless. It wouldn't take a genius to put it all together, and he couldn't imagine how she hadn't been caught yet.

He was both thrilled and devastated as he considered his suspicions; devastated by the knowledge of the horrors she'd suffered, thrilled by her ability to survive and escape, but also worried about what she might be involved in now. Worse, he considered how long she could keep it up before she got caught, especially now that she was on an official report after the incident in Gladwin County.

Obviously, they hadn't been up there by coincidence, but he was glad they'd done it because they'd caught the two fugitives he'd been chasing and saved another of their unfortunate victims. He'd known it since the first time he spotted Shelby after the crash in Durand, but he had hoped it was a coincidence.

Mitch had never thought he would have the chance to meet his daughter under normal circumstances, and he couldn't have guessed they'd meet trying to save the same person.

He'd faced her twice now, and he'd kept his secret all the while.

While he told himself that it had never been the right time, he knew it was just an easy excuse. He shouldn't have to meet her like this at all, but this was the hand he'd been dealt. Although Collins had suggested Mitch call first, he didn't have the balls to do it. Nothing terrified him more than the possibility of her outright rejection.

Meeting her in person had only solidified her hard demeanor in his imagination. She didn't seem as extroverted, carefree, and playful as her mother always had. Thinking of the kind of hardships she must have endured as a child set his jaw to clenching, and his stomach tightened painfully.

All he could do was tell her the truth and hope she'd give him a chance to do right by her going forward. Nothing could ever make up for the fact that he'd never been there, but maybe a proper introduction would make for a decent start between them.

The only thing he had left now was hope, however infinitesimal it felt.

Mitch pulled his car into the parking lot in front of Ginger's Pub and Grill and painfully peeled his aching fingers from the steering wheel before putting it in park and killing the engine.

Twilight had fallen, and the underbelly of the night sky glowed gently in orange from the city lights of nearby Saginaw. He stared at the entrance, steadily building up the nerve to walk in. He gripped his keys in one hand and opened his door with the other, welcoming the chill that quickly sucked away the warm air.

It would snow again soon. The smell was thick in the air. He breathed it deep into his lungs as he walked slowly toward the pub. Would it be a gentle snow, or were they in for another storm?

Chapter 40
CHAPTER FORTY

M att's eyes sparkled as he stared into Shelby's, and she wasn't even trying to keep a smile from her face anymore. Was she actually having... fun?

"Come on," he said. "Let's do a shot together."

She glanced around at the few tables with customers. The dinner rush seemed to be over now, and the night was turning out quieter than she expected. Her prediction had been wrong, and it shouldn't have bothered her as much as it did. But something in her mind was off-kilter tonight.

And it had been at least six months since she'd last had a drink. Since before she'd been kidnapped...

Matt rested a gentle hand on hers. "Are you okay? I'm not trying to pressure you."

She realized she was frowning, and her vision had lost focus. Shaking her head, she forced the thoughts away. "Sorry. You didn't. I just—"

"For heaven's sake," Ginger interrupted. Her thick, curly red hair hung loosely down her back, and she wore a green turtleneck, dark blue jeans, and black boots that accentuated her curvy, middle-aged body. Having always taken good care of herself, she took pride in her appearance and leaned into the cougar stereotype. "We're slow. If you don't have fun with him, I will!"

"Save me, Shelby!" Matt played along.

Ginger laughed heartily. She always enjoyed flirting with the customers, especially the Sheriff and his deputies. They'd been good to her, and to all of them.

"Why the hell not?" Shelby sighed dramatically, then poured two shots of bourbon and passed one to Matt. Ginger went out on the floor to check the tables, shooting her a wink along the way. They tossed back the shots, and she waited, grimacing as the liquid burned its way down.

"You really don't drink, do you?" Matt asked, watching her with a smirk on his face.

She shook her head. "I'm too busy, and it's too expensive." But she knew it was more than that.

Shelby had watched her mother battle the bottle her entire childhood. As far as she knew, the woman was still battling it. She'd never been able to resist the call of the drink and pry herself from its life-numbing grasp. Those memories had always unnerved Shelby, so she usually stayed away from the stuff and never drank enough to truly get drunk. Even a buzz had scared her in the past. What if she ended up just like her mother? Passed out on the couch, an empty bottle lying nearby, while a sadistic boyfriend abused her child?

No. That wouldn't happen. Because Shelby wouldn't be having any children, not with her self-selected life's purpose, and she sure as hell wouldn't let that devil in the bottle steal her life away and rob her of the ability to protect others.

Matt nudged his shot glass across the bar and gently squeezed her fingers, pulling Shelby from her dark reverie once more. "It's nice to let go once in a while, though, and a few drinks help most people do that. We don't need to, though."

"We can indulge for one night," she reassured him as she poured them both another round. "Before Ginger cop-naps you."

They both laughed and took the second shot. Her inhibitions loosening, Shelby rounded the bar and sat on a stool next to him. By the third round, they were shoulder to shoulder, and her head tingled as her walls steadily fell. She was too buzzed to be scared anymore, and her muscles melted with relaxation. Admittedly, she liked how it was already taking the edge off her tired, worried mind.

"Ginger," she called across the pub to a corner table where Ginger sat working on her laptop. "Do you need any help?"

The older woman glanced over her shoulder at the nearly empty dining room. "You're kidding, right?"

Shelby snickered and rounded the bar to grab her jacket, and Matt stood to join her. "I'm taking my not-a-smoke-break."

Ginger rolled her eyes and waved dismissively at her before returning her attention to her laptop.

Matt offered his arm, and Shelby only hesitated for a second before looping her arm through his. His warmth radiated even through his thick Carhartt coat, and she'd had just enough alcohol to let herself lean against him instead of keeping her distance.

Maybe tonight, she'd finally let go and pretend to be normal. Just enough to enjoy her time with this man that she could no longer deny her attraction to. He was gentle, kind, and honest, and he was bringing out a side of her she didn't think existed. She wanted this, she admitted to herself as she let him lead her toward the door.

She wanted his attention, his smile, his closeness.

They walked across the pub floor, and he opened the door for her, placing a firm hand against the small of her back as she passed through first.

She'd been focused on the sensation of butterflies in her stomach and the overwhelming warmth in her cheeks as her eyes adjusted to the darkness outside. Then she started to see the shape of a person walking toward her, so she stepped aside, expecting them to walk past her and head into the pub.

But they mirrored her actions and stepped to the same side.

Shelby sucked in a breath as her vision sharpened and his face became clear. "Detective Ward?"

"Good evening," he said simply, then nodded to Matt before returning his gaze to her. "Can we talk?"

Her heart pounded in her chest, and her breath came fast and shallow. She willed her body to calm down. Surely, he wouldn't say anything in front of Matt.

"Sure," she answered in a whisper, her voice lost. This couldn't be good. And it certainly wouldn't be anything Matt needed to hear. She turned to him. "Can you ask Ginger for a cigarette?"

He stared into her eyes briefly, asking nonverbally if she was okay, and she nodded.

"No problem," he answered after a moment, apparently satisfied with her silent response.

Once he'd disappeared back into the pub, Shelby motioned for the detective to follow her as she moved away from the entrance and around the side of the building. She stopped near the stairs that led to her apartment.

"What's wrong?"

"Wrong?"

"I can't assume you would drive all the way up here to see me unless something had gone wrong with one of the victims, the reports, or our official version of the story."

"Nothing's wrong. Everything is, essentially, where we left it. Actually," he dropped his gaze to the snow and shifted his feet, then met her gaze again, "I'm not here about any of that."

Her mind whirred with myriad thoughts, all vying impossibly for her undivided attention, but she maintained a thin facade of quiet confidence. "What are you here for then?"

Shelby hoped he would say he'd gotten her number wrong, insist on getting her some kind of award for her help, or even ask her to come in and give her statement again. But some small part of her knew he wasn't here about any of that.

"It's hard to tell you this, but..." He swallowed and paused. The orange lamp over the pub cast his face in a warm glow, and the wrinkles on his face tightened as his glassy eyes narrowed.

Were those tears brimming in his eyes?

"I'm your father, Shelby."

The air left Shelby's lungs, and her heart seemed to stop. Her mouth didn't move, her gaze didn't leave him. A memory of her reflection in the mirror the day before flashed through her mind, and the truth stung her heart like a wasp. Somewhere deep in her subconscious, she had known the truth. She'd known it since the moment he'd stared at her too long on the side of the road in Durand.

Silence hung heavy in the air between them until it snapped like a tightly stretched thread beneath the weight of more words.

"I'm sorry I didn't tell you sooner. It was never the right time."

"Excuse me?" She finally forced words out of her mouth, though her voice rasped as they squeezed past the growing lump in her throat. "How do you know?"

"I wouldn't have come all the way up here unless I was sure. Your mother is Janie Ford, and she was my high school sweetheart." His own voice cracked now, and he shoved his hands deep into the pockets of his coat. But he never took his eyes off her.

·

"Why..." Shelby couldn't think, couldn't hear, couldn't see through the tears blurring her vision and threatening to fall. "I don't know... I can't process this. You knew all this time, and you didn't tell me?"

"I'm sorry for that. I'm here now because I thought you deserved to know the truth. And if there's anything you want to know, anything at all, just ask. I'll tell you everything."

That sparked a bonfire inside Shelby's heart.

Her vision sharpened suddenly, and everything around them snapped into laser focus. The light breeze teasing the branches of the elm tree near the street, the snowflakes drifting lazily down from the sky, the tremble of Mitch's body as he shivered. She didn't know if it was from the cold or fear, but she didn't feel sorry for him.

She focused her pain-fueled glare fully on him and found her voice again. "Anything?"

He nodded.

"Where the hell have you been all my life?" Shelby screamed at him. "Why don't we start there, Detective?" She added a mocking emphasis on the last word, watching with bitter satisfaction as he flinched and the hope alight in his eyes flickered and died. "Why did you abandon your fiancé and baby? How can they let shit-bag sperm donors like you be cops and never pay a dime in child support?"

Mitch shook his head, finally breaking eye contact with her. "That's not the way it happened. I never got a chance—"

"You?! YOU never got a chance?" Her voice rose again, and she didn't have the clarity of mind to even consider controlling it. "What about me? What about the little girl you left behind? How many other kids do you have out there growing up without a decent father in their lives?"

"You're right, I should have—"

"You should have been there for me!" Shelby screamed, fists clenched at her sides.

Chapter 41
CHAPTER FORTY-ONE

The pub door flew open, and Matt raced toward Mitch and Shelby.

"Please, Shelby. Just give me a chance to explain—"

"You don't deserve a snowball's chance in hell!" Shelby stepped within swinging distance.

"Hey!" Matt jumped between them and held up his arms to keep Shelby back. "What's going on?"

"Get him out of here! You hear me, asshole?" Shelby shouted, angling around Matt's shoulder to make eye contact with the detective. "Leave! Go, and don't even look back. You can't just walk into my life and drop that on me."

"I'd do anything—" Mitch's plea was cut short.

"All this time, all these years, you never had a daughter. And now you still don't have one, and you never will!"

Matt turned to the detective, herding Shelby behind him with one hand. "I don't know what's going on," he said. That had to be a lie. Shelby hadn't left out any of the important details. "But I think you need to leave."

Shelby glared at Mitch, wanting her words and anger to bear down on his soul the way his absence had bore down on hers for more than two decades.

Somehow, the pain on his face and the lone tear trailing down his cheek and freezing in the icy air didn't give her the satisfaction she thought it would. Instead, it added another deep cut to her battered heart. This pain was a double-edged sword only she could wield.

"Leave!" Shelby cried, her fierce bravado crumbling as tears spilled from her eyes. She turned then, unable to look at him anymore, and ran up the stairs, taking two at a time and digging her keys out of her jacket pocket.

Her hands shook violently as she fumbled to unlock the door. She cursed as she dropped them, then stooped to pick them up. Using both hands to steady herself, she slid the right key into the lock. After turning back the bolt, she pushed her way inside. Matt's voice faded as she closed the door and pressed her back against it, sliding down until she hit the floor. She curled her knees to her chest and held her head in her hands, sobbing under the weight of the emotions that flooded her broken mind.

All the abuse she'd suffered as a child, the unaddressed trauma from being kidnapped and raped, and the humanity she'd stuffed away when she'd been killing the worst of men roared to the surface as if a great dam had broken. Every painful memory spilled forth, each one connected to the others in an infinite chain of fate.

If he had been there... If her father had been there when she was a helpless little girl, before she'd been hurt by the first of her mother's boyfriends, could he have protected her?

Could he have saved her from all of this?

For the first time since she was ten years old, Shelby surrendered to her pain. Sobs wracked her body, and her tears fell freely.

Chapter 42
CHAPTER FORTY-TWO

M att glanced over his shoulder as Shelby finally disappeared into her apartment, then returned his attention to the man she'd been hollering at.

"I'm Matt Douglas, Sheriff's Deputy." He offered out his hand, but Mitch didn't shake it. "At least when I'm on duty."

"Detective Mitch Ward, Southfield Police. But I'm not here on official business, and it looks like you aren't either."

"Why exactly are you here?" Matt asked. It probably came off a little aggressive, but that was okay. After the way the stranger had upset Shelby, Matt felt compelled to defend her.

Mitch pinched the bridge of his nose, sniffed harshly, then shook his head. "I guess I was just trying to do the right thing." His voice trembled, but he met Matt's eyes. "Are you the boyfriend?"

Matt didn't answer.

"Doesn't matter, I guess. Here." He pulled a card from his jacket and held it out. "If she ever changes her mind... If she needs me..." Mitch let the words trail off.

Matt accepted the card and inspected it in the glow of the streetlights.

As soon as the card left his fingertips, Mitch turned away. He pulled something else from his pocket and set it on the hood of Lucia's blue truck. Then he strode to his car, jumped in, and spun his tires as he rolled out east on M46.

The card he'd handed Matt was his official information, but it included his cell phone number.

Matt stuffed it in his pocket, looked up at the apartment door, and sighed heavily.

It should have been a fun night. His beautiful mystery woman was filled with all sorts of secret twists and turns, and he was well aware that he was probably in over his head with this one.

But that was okay.

He'd never taken the easy path before, and he wasn't about to start now.

Matt jogged up the stairs and knocked lightly on the door before letting himself in. He'd never been in her apartment before. It was close to what he'd imagined, being clean and meticulously organized, but a bit more spartan.

"You put my mother on the phone, or I'll come down there and strangle you with your own intestines!"

He froze. Well, that was creative. Was she good for a threat like that?

A brief silence, and he closed the door softly behind him.

"Don't give me that shit, Janie. I'm not calling to pretend that I miss your drunk ass."

He could almost make out the words sputtering out from a frantic voice on the other end of the line.

"Why didn't you tell me about him? You never even told me who he was!" A pause. "Yes, my father! Well, I just met the bastard, and I was completely blindsided thanks to you."

Matt didn't think it was right to eavesdrop, so he turned, thinking to let himself out, but she came around the corner of the kitchen wall and grabbed him by the arm. Her eyes were red, and her face puffy from crying, but she pulled him toward the living room while the voice on the phone shrieked at her. She motioned for him to sit on the couch, then disappeared down the hallway and into a bedroom. Although she shut the door, the walls were thin, and he heard every word.

"I'll never call you 'mom' because you don't deserve it. You were a glorified legal guardian and a shitty excuse even for that. Why couldn't you tell me the truth about anything? You should have at least told me his name!"

Shelby appeared again, fresh tears flowing down her cheeks. She sat next to Matt and dropped her phone on the table. It was completely off.

"Thank you for coming to my rescue," she said when she finally broke the silence. Her voice was low, and she trembled as she clasped her hands together and leaned forward to prop her elbows on her knees. A curtain of soft, wavy black hair hid her face.

Matt couldn't help himself. He reached over and pulled her close. Her body stiffened at first, but then she relaxed against him, shuddering with muffled sobs.

"That detective... That's your dad?"

She nodded.

"And you didn't know? Never met him until now?"

Shelby sat up, wiped the tears from her face, and pushed her hair behind her ears. "I never knew." Her voice was only a whisper.

"I'm so sorry, Shelby."

She jumped from the couch and strode into the kitchen. Matt followed close on her heels. Realization sparked as she pulled a full bottle of whiskey from an upper cabinet and spun the cap off. It clattered onto the counter and rolled off to the floor, but she didn't spare it a glance.

Matt watched, hurting for her, as she swallowed a giant gulp of the whiskey. She cringed as it went down, took a ragged breath, then raised the bottle again.

He wrapped his hand around the glass, halting her. She turned a wide-eyed death stare toward him and tried to rip the bottle from his hand. But he didn't let go, twisting it from her grasp and spilling a few drops in the process.

"What the hell are you doing?" she hissed her words through gritted teeth. It hurt him to hear the pain in her voice. He knew if she raised her voice, she'd break down again.

"This isn't the answer."

"It's the answer for everyone else, damn it." She reached for the bottle, but he jerked it back, keeping it well out of her reach.

"So?"

"So why not me, Matt? I need it!"

She lunged for it, grasping him by the shirt and moving with him as he stepped backward.

"Stop it!" He reached his free arm around her back, pulled her against his chest, and spun her with him in the tight galley kitchen until he could turn the bottle upside down in the sink.

"No!" She tried to push away, but he held her tight as the bottle emptied down the drain.

Shelby melted against him, hitting his chest weakly with her balled fists, sobbing her protests as she watched her poison disappear.

"You're going to be okay, and you don't need this to get there."

"I don't want this," she cried.

"What?"

"I don't want to feel any of this. God, Matt. It hurts to fucking breathe!"

As the last drops of whiskey trickled into the sink drain, Matt swept Shelby into his arms and walked back to the couch. He lowered himself into it and held her close. It felt natural to be so close to her, and there was nothing more he wanted at that moment than to take her pain away, to shoulder it for her, to add it to his own scars if only to spare her suffering.

"I don't want to live," Shelby managed through exhausted sobs.

"You have to," Matt said as he stroked her hair. "Too many people need you."

"I can't take this pain," she muttered, her words muffled against his coat.

"You're not alone."

Shelby stiffened, then pushed herself until she was sitting upright in his lap, and her tortured gaze honed in on him. "What the hell do you care?"

He couldn't deny that it hurt to hear her say those words, but he stayed calm. "You know I care."

She rose off the couch, then clenched her fists and railed at him. "Why? What do you want from me? I can't give you anything. I'm nobody!"

"I don't know what I want. I just want to be here with you right now."

"For what? What the hell is your obsession? You're just going to take what you want and leave me."

He stared at her a moment, his body tense, then stood and stepped closer to her. He leaned down and spoke softly in her ear. "Then tell me to leave."

She growled, feral, primal, then pushed his chest. To his surprise, he stumbled back, and he hardly recognized the open palm flying toward his face.

He barely caught her by the wrist in time, then caught her other hand as she tried again to slap him. "Stop doing that," he demanded in a low growl.

"Hurt me," Shelby said, dark eyes glittering with tears as she glared up at him, face twisted with pain and fury. "You want me so bad? Hurt me, break me, scatter the pieces—"

Matt released her wrists, then wrapped one arm around her body to hug her close and used his other hand to wipe the tears from her face. "I could never hurt you," he said, his lips only inches from hers as he gazed down into her stormy, dark eyes.

Shelby bit her lip, twisting his jacket in her fingers as the tears continued to fall.

"Push me away if you want, but I will never hurt you, and I won't leave unless you ask me to."

"Damn you," she cried, but her maelstrom had already lost its power and was rapidly deflating.

"Tell me to leave." He stared at her, waiting for the words to pass her lips.

She hesitated, saying nothing though her tears still fell. So he caressed her cheek, let her go, and headed for the door.

"Stay with me," she pleaded softly, pulling him by the arm.

He turned toward her, but before he could speak, she rose on her tiptoes and kissed him. It was timid at first, and he almost pushed her away. Then she threw her arms around his neck and kissed him with a fire and fervor he'd never experienced. Fearful, hungry, desperate, longing.

Then she nipped his lip and pressed her nails into the back of his neck. Almost goading him into being rough with her, but he wouldn't take the bait. He'd been through worse, and he knew he could take whatever this little firecracker had to give him.

Shelby needed someone who could take it, and he was that man.

However long this lasted, Matt knew it was right. They were right. She could pour all of her pain into him, and he'd take every ounce and still beg for more. If he had believed in fate, then this beautiful, broken soul was the missing half of his own. And he would kill to hold her as long as this cruel, hard world would let him.

Chapter 43

CHAPTER
FORTY-THREE

Mitch kept the radio off as he drove east. His vision blurred, eyes straining against the dark of night and the blinding lights of cars ahead and behind. Whether his body ached from the physical pain or the mental, he didn't know. He couldn't think. Didn't want to.

None of it really mattered anymore.

He didn't make it far on M46, though he'd intended to go back home to Southfield.

Home.

The word felt odd to him as he thought of it now. He mulled it over while pulling into the first motel he spotted as he entered the outer edge of Saginaw. He decided it wasn't important to make it back to Southfield.

Mitch parked in front of the motel's office in the center of the long building, its neon vacancy sign buzzing and flickering in the window. He sat there, leaning back in his seat and letting his eyes wander over the misshapen blobs of darkness in the poorly lit lot. Looking at them through his rearview mirror, he mused over their fuzzy edges, carved out by the weak glow of the motel's lights.

He squinted at the covered sconces in front of each door and muttered a curse under his breath. It fogged in the frigid air, then disappeared, and he realized he'd been sitting idle long enough for the car to get cold.

Finally, Mitch dragged himself out, slammed the driver's door behind him, and walked into the motel office. The stink of lemon cleaner and cigarettes immediately assailed him, and he wrinkled his nose as he approached the counter and pulled his wallet from his pocket.

The man on the other side of the corner had pale skin, dark eyes, and thin, jet-black hair combed over his balding scalp. He was wiry and thin, looked to be in his mid-fifties, and dressed simply in a gray hoodie and blue jeans. A name tag pinned to his chest read "Carl."

"Need a room?"

Mitch nodded. "One night should do."

Carl pulled a registration card and a pen from the desk on his side of the counter and slid them toward Mitch.

"In town on business?"

Mitch ignored him and filled out the card, keeping the details as vague as possible.

"You're a cop, ain't ya?"

"Now, why would you think that, Carl?"

Carl flinched, and he looked taken aback at the use of his name. Funny how people reacted to hearing their name.

"It wouldn't matter if I was, would it?"

"No, sir. Not at all." Carl took the completed registration, driver's license, and credit card when Mitch offered them.

It only took a minute for the man to process all the pieces. He handed back Mitch's driver's license and a room key.

"Number 14," he said as he sat back down in his chair. "I'm closing up the office at ten, but I'll be back here at seven tomorrow morning if you need anything."

"Great." Mitch had no desire to wake up and see Carl at breakfast. "Where's the nearest liquor store?"

⸺⸻❖⸻⸺

When Mitch returned to the motel with a fifth of whiskey in hand, he stepped out of his car and into the cold without fighting the frigid wind that bit at his neck. It was almost painful, and he welcomed that feeling now. He wanted to hurt, to suppress that survival instinct that compelled him to cover his bare skin.

He unlocked the door to Number 14 and walked into a drab, lifeless motel room. Although the signs on the door clearly warned of the fines for lighting up in the rooms, the room smelt of stale cigarette smoke and something... else.

Something acrid and sharp and chemical.

Likely the type of thing one smoked and would sell off the entirety of their possessions to get more of.

Mitch locked the deadbolt and set his keys and whiskey on the narrow desk. Without turning on the lights, he dropped heavily onto the edge of the bed and stared at the black, dead screen of cheap television.

After several minutes of staring into the darkest shadows in the room, Mitch loosened the tie he wore into work earlier that day–before they'd put him on administrative leave. Before he'd practically run through the parking lot to his car, anxious to get out of work so he could go see his daughter. He hadn't wanted to waste time changing, so he had gone home first, researched Shelby to find her address, then drove straight to Merrill.

But it had all been a waste of time. He was worse off now than before he'd made the foolish assumption that he mattered to a child he'd never known.

And she was right. He'd never been there for her, and so, he'd never really had a daughter. Revealing the truth about his biological contribution to her existence hadn't changed that fact.

The teddy bear he'd brought came to mind as he let the tie slide from around his neck.

Mitch couldn't explain why he'd bothered leaving the old stuffed bear on the hood of Lucia's truck. He knew that truck now, knew it was hers, and that Shelby must have driven it. But he didn't know why he'd taken the trouble to set the toy on it before driving away.

He wanted to mull it over, to thoroughly analyze his own thoughts and actions as he would with any other subject, but he was too tired for that. Too hurt.

Too empty.

A glint of ambient light reflected off the thick glass of the whiskey bottle, catching his eye. He didn't want it, but he needed it. There was no desire left to consume. Only the desire to be consumed by oblivion itself.

Back in Southfield, his Deputy Chief would probably fast-track him to retirement at this point and keep him on desk duty until then. He probably wouldn't even let him touch any more tough cases because they knew he'd rather croak on the job than not chase every possible lead.

And what would he do after they booted him?

Mitch surveyed the dark, unfamiliar corners of his room and scoffed. They reminded him of his drab old apartment. He certainly couldn't just sit at his desk until he expired.

Try as he might, he couldn't think of how he imagined life would be if Shelby had rejected him. That's because he hadn't counted on it. Couldn't have predicted it, as likely as it had been.

As much as his partner might consider him a cynic, he'd been hopeful. That flickering candle of hope that he could reconcile with his only child had kept him going all these years, kept him alive and fighting.

But that fragile flame had been snuffed out, and all he could see now was the sweet, silent embrace of darkness beckoning to him.

There was nothing else, no one waiting for him on the other side of this night.

All that remained was to decide how to end it.

He glanced at the tie lying in his lap. That was one option. Cremation was something he thought he'd prefer, but he would never endanger anyone else who might be in the building tonight.

The icy, polluted waters of the Saginaw River would gladly take him, but so would Lake Huron, if he had enough energy to drive up to Bay City.

And then, there was the pistol resting heavy in his hand. How had it gotten there from his holster?

If he didn't fuck it up, it could be quick.

"Decisions, decisions," he muttered ruefully, setting the pistol down next to the whiskey bottle.

Sighing heavily, he drew his phone from his coat pocket and unlocked the screen. His fingers hovered over the message until he decided what to say, hoping it wouldn't raise his only friend's suspicions.

Promise me you'll look after Shelby Ford.

Mitch squeezed his eyes shut when his phone dinged almost immediately.

He shrugged. It didn't matter.

Bullets were faster than cars anyway.

The woman who saved you in Gladwin? Why?

Carelessly, he tapped out his final message to Collins.

She's my daughter.

A gun was the only logical way Mitch could see to help him out of this world. He had known this was the surest way to end his painful, lonely, empty existence, but it took a lot of energy and balls to pull that trigger.

So he picked up the bottle of whiskey from the desk and started drinking it, slowly at first, then as much as he could gulp. He drank until all the pain in his heart was numbed. It didn't take much to get him there since he usually only drank beer.

It wasn't long before he had to stop and piss. His lifeless corpse would already be a mess when they found him, but if he could minimize any of the gore for those people who had to clean him up, it was a decent thing to try to do. But he was unsteady on his feet, and he was already seeing double.

He managed to make it to the narrow bathroom and piss in the toilet instead of on the floor. Leaning on the sink, he snorted a laugh as he washed his hands, and it quickly turned to a choked sob. With his hands wet, he pushed himself through the doorway, stumbled toward the desk, and grabbed the gun.

Mitch struggled to tighten his fingers around the grip and bumped into the bed, falling onto it. He barely held onto the pistol, but was still in his palm when landed facedown on the stale-smelling bedspread. He hated to wonder about the last time it had been cleaned. His movements were as sloppy as his brain, but after some fumbling around, he finally felt the cold of the muzzle pressed against his temple.

"Shelby," he muttered into the disgusting bedspread before releasing a long breath.

Chapter 44
CHAPTER FORTY-FOUR

Thursday, December 8th

An endless offensive of snow pellets pinged against the double-paned glass of the single window in Shelby's bedroom. She slowly became aware of the almost soothing noise as she woke from a deep, restful slumber to the still darkness of early morning.

First, she recognized the endless tapping as the wind drove the graupel against the glass. Then, the gentle breathing of Matt lying on his back next to her. Bits and pieces came to her out of order, but she gradually fit the puzzle of the previous evening's events together.

Had they slept together? Literally, yes, but they hadn't had sex.

Shelby had been exhausted to begin with, but the explosive encounter with her father and the first contact in six months with her mother had drained every last ounce of her mental and physical energy. She never could have predicted that she'd meet her father without knowing him first, without some kind of warning. It hurt to think she'd been completely oblivious when they'd first spoken, when she had stood eye to eye with him, and when they'd saved her friends together. He had known while Shelby hadn't, and she couldn't pin down why that made her so angry.

But she'd always hated being in the dark. He had knowledge then that she didn't, knowledge he wouldn't share or...

She hated to admit it. Knowledge that he *couldn't* share with her.

Shelby rolled over and stared at Matt's calm face and short-cropped blonde hair in the ambient light. She paused to study this man who had been there to catch her as she crumbled, one who seemed to have been waiting all along to do just that. She was at once both tempted to return to sleep nestled in his embrace and worried about his true intentions. Could she really trust him? He'd stuck around ever since they'd met, getting closer each week.

Close enough now to kill her if he wanted.

Shelby thought she'd built up her resilience, strength, and stamina to a degree greater than what she'd displayed the night before, but she ended up paying for her hubris in tears. Her complete emotional breakdown was humiliating, and she'd put herself at Matt's mercy. She liked him, but she didn't truly know him all that well.

Lucky for her, he hadn't turned out to be a wolf in sheep's clothing.

He lay sleeping in her bed now after spending his night comforting her, literally sweeping her off her feet and holding her through her darkest hours. Was it real, or was it all an act?

Shaking her head to clear the paranoid thoughts, she knew she was the one awake and staring at him in the dark. He'd had the chance all night while she was broken and vulnerable, and she'd fallen asleep in his embrace.

He was not the enemy.

Only her deep-rooted fears, insecurity, and trauma threatened her now.

Even with that knowledge, she had too many other worries on her mind to go back to bed.

In the span of a few hours, she'd gained a father and possibly a boyfriend too.

She sighed softly before rolling over. Matt didn't wake, surprisingly. The old-school radio alarm clock on her nightstand read 2:00 a.m. Too early to go anywhere or do anything useful, but she couldn't just lay here. She was awake now and distinctly aware of the emotional hangover from the previous evening's unexpected events. It was so much to take in, too much to process.

Most of her life had been spent in flux between two states of being: wondering if she would ever meet her father or not thinking of him at all. His absence from her life had left a painfully empty place in her heart, a chasm that couldn't be filled by any addiction or the presence of other people or healed by simply running away.

Her memory of the pain in Mitch's eyes flashed through her mind, and a lump grew in her throat. Her fingers grasped the sheets, and her body tensed. She felt like she couldn't breathe.

Slipping out from under Matt's embrace and the covers, she navigated her room in the ambient glow of the streetlights outside her window. She started to open her dresser but then realized she'd fallen asleep in her clothes.

Who knew a couple of drinks and meeting her long-lost father for the first time could end in complete and absolute exhaustion mentally, physically, and spiritually?

Not to mention, she'd hardly slept since she and Mitch had rescued Sam and Lucia and Tyler's newest victim at the cabin up in Butman.

After slipping on her boots, grabbing a jacket, and stuffing her phone in her pocket, she stepped out into the frigid night air.

Stars glittered high above, bright and crisp against the dark velvet of deep space, despite the light pollution from Flint and Detroit. Her breath fogged in the cold, still air as she studied the wonders of the heavens.

The steps were salted, so she had no trouble making her way to ground level. Too late, she realized she'd left her gloves upstairs. Instead of going back up to get them, she shoved her hands in her pockets and made a beeline toward the main road. Looking left then right, she finally turned and walked east without knowing why. It was the direction she fought so hard to avoid since she'd left her mother's house, but now she was inexplicably drawn that way. Maybe it wasn't for her mother, whom she detested.

If Shelby wanted to go to, say, Southfield, she'd also have to head east. She lifted the hood of her jacket and picked up her pace. It felt good to walk in the quiet of the night. A few cars passed going in either direction, but on a weeknight, even M46 was relatively slow at two in the morning.

The light breeze created by her pace nipped at her cheeks and nose, and she started to shiver as the cold seeped into her bones. Her jacket was too light for a walk like this, but she knew she wouldn't be out for long. She just needed a little time to stretch her legs beneath the stars. A little time to think by herself.

About Matt. Mitch. Did it mean anything that both were cops and their names were so damn similar, or was it all part of some divine joke?

Such surface matters were only avoiding the most important topic: her father.

Sure, she'd been awful to him the night before. Unnecessarily but understandably so. Now, with a little rest, she was rethinking her hostile, explosive reaction. He hadn't done anything to hurt her, and he'd come hours out of his way to share the truth with her. And she had to admit that there hadn't been a better time to tell her before, not while they were trying to save lives or when other officers were around.

Why had he come at all, if not to connect with the daughter he'd never known?

Shelby wanted desperately to maintain the anger she'd felt the night before, even feed it, but the flames had died to embers now. Curiosity increasingly replaced that fast-dying fury, and she wondered about him as she walked beyond the weak lights of Merrill and into the dark countryside.

She didn't know how long she'd been walking, her mind so entrenched in untangling her thoughts and feelings that she'd only now noticed it was snowing again. A slight pause to study the darkness around her, to be in this silent, dark, comforting moment between the outposts of small-town civilization, then she turned and headed back toward town and her apartment.

Lights from the small group of buildings flickered as the snow fell faster. A few flakes collected on Shelby's eyelashes only to melt within seconds. The snow fell straight down as the wind hadn't picked up yet, but she knew that could change at any moment, and the last thing she needed was to get caught in a blizzard. Now that she'd had some time to cool off—literally—she was ready to confront all that awaited her in the warmth of her apartment: a very difficult call to her newly-found father and figuring out whatever relationship territory she'd probably entered with Matt.

It was too much to do on her own, and she needed the support of her best friend. Taking her phone from her pocket with trembling fingers, she tapped out the words in a text. A single tear fell, freezing on her cheek.

I think I need help.

Shelby returned the phone to her jacket pocket and considered the whirlwind of faces and voices vying for space in her mind as she walked back the short distance toward Merrill. Complex conversations raged in her head, ones that might never play out in real life. As she entered the area warmly brightened by the soft orange streetlights, she picked up her pace, undeniably cold now and ready to warm up in her apartment.

The pub quickly came into view in the tiny town, with Lucia's truck that Shelby had borrowed in front of it. Something sat on the hood of the truck, and she focused on it, trying to make out what the little lump was on as she walked closer.

She grabbed the stuffed bear and dusted the snow from its soft brown face. Its glassy black eyes stared up at her, worn and sorrowful. Somehow, she knew instinctively the bear had been meant for her. Before she could make the conscious acknowledgment and whisper any gratitude into the wind, the sound of an engine down-shifting caught her attention.

The speed limit in Merrill slowed from 55 to 45 MPH, but this sounded slower. There were no traffic lights or stop signs, so no one needed to slow down unless they were turning off the main road, which rarely happened this early in the morning.

Shelby turned to face the sound, and her heart jumped into her throat when she found two men in ski masks leaping toward her from the open side door of a white van.

Chapter 45
CHAPTER FORTY-FIVE

L ucia opened her eyes and stared at the wall until her vision adjusted to the darkness. She turned over and glanced at Sam sleeping peacefully with his arm around her. Smiling to herself, she thought back to their evening spent "making up" despite their various injuries. Somewhere between words and tangled bodies, they'd managed to mend what she worried had been irreparably broken.

Her conscious smile melted as she checked her watch. It was almost three in the morning. She should have been too tired to be awake and so alert, especially after all the painkillers. But something niggled at her mind from the core of her being, buzzing in her head.

Something wasn't right. She slid out from under Sam's arm, thanking the drugs for keeping him asleep, and dropped her feet onto the rug, then spotted Penny's sleeping form lying near the foot of the bed. The dog's steady, whistling breath paused as she picked up her head from her paws and turned to stare at Lucia. Penny wagged her stubby tail softly in expectation and yawned widely.

Sam was fine, and so was Penny. The power was still on, so the security system was still functioning, and all was quiet. Everything seemed all right.

But even as Lucia thought it, a shiver rolled through her aching body. It was probably time for her and Sam's next dose of painkillers.

She reached for her phone on the nightstand and unlocked the screen to find a single text message waiting for her from Shelby.

I think I need help.

A wave of goosebumps pricked her skin, and she stared at the message, frozen in surprise at the peculiarity of it. Logically, she wanted to take her time, analyze the message, and calmly call her friend. Instinctively, she already knew she was running out of time.

Lucia dialed Shelby's number, held the phone to her ear, and listened as it rang until the voicemail message played.

She cursed under her breath and dialed again, then hit the speakerphone button and tossed it onto the bed next to Sam. Her trembling fingers fumbled over the light switch as the first ring sounded over the speaker, and it startled Sam awake.

"What's wrong?" he mumbled, groggy as he blinked away the sleep.

"Shelby," Lucia managed hoarsely, her throat already tight with anxiety. "Something's wrong." She limped to the dresser and pulled clothes from her drawers. The ring rattled over the speaker again. "Are you with me?"

Sam fell back into the pillows and rubbed his eyes. "Why exactly are you worried?" He picked up the phone and glanced at the screen as it rang again. "It's barely three o'clock. Nobody should be answering their phone this early. Come back to bed."

Lucia gingerly snugged her legs into black winter leggings and yanked a t-shirt on before climbing onto the bed and taking the phone from him. She ended the call and opened Shelby's last message before putting it back in his hand.

"She only sent it ten minutes ago."

"Did you hear this text come in?"

"No. The ringer was off, so it didn't even vibrate. I just woke up, checked my phone, and then I found it." She took a hair tie from the nightstand and loosely braided her hair, watching his eyes widen as he read the message.

"Okay. That's not right." He flipped back the covers and started getting dressed while Lucia put on a pair of boot socks. She climbed onto the bed and grabbed her phone, then slipped it into her back pocket before heading for the door.

In mere minutes, they'd locked up the house, holstered their pistols, and gotten Sam's truck on the road. On a normal day, they probably would have packed a backup firearm for one or both of them and let the truck warm up before they took off. But this wasn't a wait-and-see situation, not with a text like that from someone as proud, unemotional, and guarded as Shelby. It wasn't at all like her.

The fifteen-minute drive seemed to take twice as long as they sped anxiously toward Shelby's place above Ginger's pub. Neither Sam nor Lucia spoke, too tired and numb as their meds wore off. Although the radio had jolted to life with the truck, the volume was too low for either of them to hear it well. And they were too deep in thought with their worries to be distracted by it. Lucia could hardly tear her gaze away from her screen when she wasn't actively trying to call Shelby.

When they reached the pub, Sam started to pull into the parking lot in front of the stairs that led up to Shelby's apartment but slammed the brakes suddenly. The truck skidded to a stop over the center line, then he put it in reverse and backed up until his headlights pointed toward Lucia's truck. "Look at that," he said, nodding his head toward it.

Lucia stared, trying to figure out what he was looking at, but all she saw was her truck quickly being covered in fresh snow. And...

"Is that a toy?"

"What? I mean the tire tracks, Luce."

She pretended not to notice the irritation in his voice. "Not until you pointed it out."

Sam backed up the truck until he could pull over on the shoulder. He jumped out, and Lucia followed after him. "Give me your phone."

Lucia handed it over and watched intently as he started taking pictures of the tire tracks that would be made invisible by fresh snow in another ten minutes. The warm glow of the streetlights was plenty to light the scene, despite the early hour. He took photo after photo, angle after angle, with and without flash, of the tire tracks as they veered off the main road and into the parking lot, and the flurry of footsteps pressed into the thin layer of older snow near her truck and the stuffed bear lying next to the front tire.

"What do you see, Lucia?" He quizzed as he snapped photos of the surrounding area.

Her mouth was dry, and she nervously glanced at the oncoming car, watching silently until it passed them and continued down the highway. "It doesn't look good. It looks like..."

"She fought back," he said grimly, finishing for her.

"No," Lucia muttered, her voice shaking. "That's jumping to conclusions, Sam. She could be upstairs right now and—"

"How many times have you called her?" He stopped snapping new pictures to review the ones he'd taken.

"But she could have her ringer off like I did."

Sam shrugged, then gestured toward the stairs that led to Shelby's apartment. "We better find out. Fast."

Lucia jogged across the tiny parking lot and bolted up the stairs as fast as her injured legs would carry her until she stood in front of the door. She knocked on the door, lightly at first, but louder after she didn't get an answer.

Sam came up behind her, reaching past her to turn the knob. To her surprise, the door swung silently inward. They stepped inside the dark apartment, and as Lucia flipped on the entryway light switch, the bedroom door at the end of the short hallway opened. For the briefest moment, Lucia's tension melted from her limbs, her shoulders slumping in relief.

At least until Matt stepped into the circle of light cast from the entryway. She straightened and froze as Sam stepped swiftly around her.

"What are you doing here?" Lucia demanded, her tension flooding back and doubling now.

"Lucia? And..."

"Sam."

"I could ask you the same."

"Where's Shelby?"

Matt scratched at his short blonde hair and looked around the corner into the living room, then poked his head into the bathroom. He peeked in the kitchen to confirm she wasn't there either, and by that time, his sleepy disposition had hardened to worry.

"Last time I saw her was in the..." he let the words trail off, simply throwing a thumb over his shoulder toward the bedroom.

"How the hell did that happen?" Lucia asked. Sam gently squeezed her arm, but she ignored him.

"We didn't have sex if that's what you're worried about. But it was a hell of a night for Shelby, and now that you two are here, I'm officially worried. You seriously didn't see her on your way up here?"

Sam turned his body away from Matt and grumbled in Lucia's ear. "We need to go."

"What happened?" Matt asked, his voice firmer this time. "I care about Shelby."

"Maybe." Lucia crossed her arms and studied him. "Are you telling us you were the last person to see her last night?"

Matt's eyes turned cold. "Don't think for a second you can play that game with me, sweetheart."

Sam turned slow, his eyes fierce, and he took a step toward Matt. The air was thick with friction as they faced each other down.

"I'm pretty sure I've been in this business longer than you, Sam." He nodded. "That's right. Shelby told me Lucia's man was a statey. I know more than you think."

Lucia grabbed Sam by the shoulder and stood on her tiptoes, drawing herself close to him. "I don't think he knows. Let's just go—"

"Go where? Is she in trouble?" Matt asked, spreading his hands. "I'm not the enemy."

"You have no idea what you've gotten yourself into," Lucia said.

Sam turned and walked toward the door, pulling Lucia's phone from his pocket.

"Like I said, I know more than you think. I know..." Matt hesitated. "I know what happened to her last summer. I read the reports."

"How?"

"Beyond databases?" He shrugged. "It's a small-town kind of area. I'm sure you're aware of that. Word travels fast, especially in our circles." He nodded toward Sam.

"I just can't believe she trusted you—"

"I've been here, Lucia," Matt snapped. "You've been planning your wedding, taking care of your fiancé, starting a new job, and whatever the hell else you're doing. I'm here on her smoke breaks, I was the one to help her quit. I listened while she opened up about her friendship with you and Sam. It was slow, but I come here whenever I'm not working. For the past month and a half, I haven't gone more than two days without seeing her."

"Why?" Sam asked abruptly.

"Why do you think?" Matt arched an eyebrow. "I know all about that asshole McNamara, the one that did all that horrible shit to her and you, and how he got his case thrown out. And I was there again last night when her biological father showed up out of nowhere, and she completely lost it."

"What?" Sam and Lucia asked in unison.

"Yeah. He showed up last night while she was on break. I was with her. Just pulled up to the pub and said he needed to talk to her. She sent me to get a cigarette from Ginger, and by the time I came back out, she was screaming bloody murder at the guy."

Lucia's jaw went slack, and she simply stared at Matt, dumbfounded.

"Do you think he would come back and bother her?" Sam asked.

Matt shook his head. "No. He's a cop too. Looked like he wanted to throw himself off a bridge after she chewed his ass out."

"A cop?" Lucia asked.

"Yeah." He fished in his pocket and pulled out a card. "A detective... Mitch Ward."

Lucia turned and locked eyes with Sam. "What the hell is happening right now?"

"Uh, fate? Coincidences? I don't fucking know," Sam grumbled while tapping at the screen of Lucia's phone. "Oh, shit. That's not good."

"What makes you think something is wrong? Maybe she just needed some time alone, especially after what happened last night," Matt said. "It was all I could do to keep her from drinking herself to death."

"Really?" Sam asked, his tone genuinely interested.

"I had to pour that shit down the drain."

"Why?" The edge in Lucia's voice softened considerably.

Matt hesitated and ran his hand over his short blonde hair, seeming to rethink sharing so much too freely. He was tired, groggy even, if she had to guess by his bloodshot eyes and the crumpled clothes he'd obviously fallen asleep in. "I didn't want to watch her kill herself trying to numb all that pain. With all the hell she's been through, I didn't trust her to moderate herself."

"No kidding." Lucia quietly thought over the situation as she pieced it all together.

"I'll show you why we're worried," Sam said, and he held out Lucia's phone for Matt to see.

Chapter 46
CHAPTER FORTY-SIX

S am flipped through the series of pictures he'd taken outside, and Matt's face paled as he interpreted the scene.

"No," he whispered, swiping at the screen to move back and forth through the photos. "Too many different footprints."

"A set of prints indicate someone was dragged through the fallen snow," Sam said. "And all those tracks will be covered with new snow very shortly."

"Holy shit," Matt waved on his feet and stepped backward, steadying himself. "I never heard a peep."

"Shelby," Lucia wet her lips before continuing, "she's not a screamer."

Matt's cheeks turned red, and he clenched his fists at his sides. Lucia knew how hard it was to know that some stranger had put their hands on the person they loved. And Shelby had already been through so much. But someone—at least two someones—had grabbed her off the street and taken her.

"What?" Lucia asked, stepping toward Sam.

"She's on the move." Sam flipped the phone screen toward her.

Lucia froze, and Matt moved closer again so he could see it too. The pulsing blue dot on the device location map indicated Shelby's phone, and it was traveling rapidly west on some backroads.

Fear sank heavily in Lucia's gut as she stared at the map. She shook her head and tried to push past Sam and head for the door. "We have to go after her. We're wasting time."

"Hold on," Sam said, stopping her with a firm but gentle hand on her shoulder. Before he could say anything else, the phone buzzed in his hands.

"What the hell? It's... It's Shelby."

Lucia and Matt watched intently as Sam accepted the call and activated the phone's speaker function.

"Shelby?" Lucia asked.

"No," a man replied slow and smooth, his voice gravelly but firm. "Miss Lucia Sorenson?"

She hesitated.

"I've heard so much about you," he continued.

"Who is this? Where's Shelby?"

"Oh, I'm a friend... of a friend. Some call me the Fear Doirich. As for Shelby? Well, I think we'll become quite close as well."

"Put Shelby on the phone," Sam interjected when Lucia didn't respond.

"I assume this must be the young state trooper, Samuel Frost."

"And you are?"

"I think it's best if we become acquainted in person. Then we can have an honest and fruitful discussion about our way forward."

"Let me talk to Shelby," Lucia demanded, struggling to keep her cool.

"No," the man said simply. "I'm going to give you directions, and if you don't follow them exactly, I will put a bullet through her brain."

The air left Lucia's lungs like she'd been punched in the gut.

"If you call the police, she's dead. If you take a wrong turn, she's dead. If you move too slowly, she's dead. If you go over the speed limit, she's dead. Are you seeing a pattern here? One wrong move and, well... if you don't understand by this point, I'll just put the girl out of her misery right now."

"No!" Lucia cried out, ripping the phone from Sam's hand. "We understand, damn it. Don't hurt her!"

"You will watch your foul tongue with me, young woman. Now, apologize, and we'll move on."

Lucia grit her teeth, seething and afraid, her eyes stinging with frustrated tears. Sam shook his head and squeezed her arm.

"I apologize," she ground out the words, fighting the urge to vomit. Sam locked his eyes on Matt and held a finger to his lips. Matt nodded.

"Do you have a pen and paper ready?" the man asked.

Matt rushed silently to the kitchen, then reappeared with a small notebook and a black pen. Lucia sat at the dining table, and Matt followed. Sam stood behind Lucia and placed a reassuring hand on her shoulder.

"We're ready," she said, and the man delivered his instructions and rules coolly and quickly.

"Whatever you wrote on, whether notebook, journal, or tablet, bring it too."

"Why?" Lucia asked before she could stop herself.

"Because if you don't—"

"Fine," she interrupted. "We'll bring the notebook."

"I'm glad we have an understanding. You have 96 minutes to reach your destination, Miss Sorenson. Don't arrive earlier than 90 minutes from now or after 100 minutes."

"It sounds impossible to be so exact. What if there's traffic or we get pulled over?"

"I trust you remember the theme of our conversation. Do not get pulled over, and don't let anyone follow you. I have friends that will find out if you call for help. If you do, there will be no chance for reconciliation for all the harm you've caused my family. And there will be no chance of you ever finding Miss Ford's remains."

"I-I understand." She barely choked out the words, her mind dragged from the task at hand by the mental image the man had implanted of Shelby's lifeless body.

"I'll see you soon," the man said before hanging up.

Lucia's fingers shook, and she let the phone fall onto the table before dropping her head in her hands. Sam reached over her shoulder and picked it up. He took a paper napkin from the center of the table and hastily scribbled down Shelby's phone number, the time and details of the call, and a copy of the instructions the man had given them.

"What the hell is going on?"

Lucia, Sam, and Matt all jumped, turning to find Lee standing in the darkened living room and glowering at them in his baggy t-shirt and flannel pajama pants.

"Shelby got kidnapped, and none of you asshats thought to wake me up and tell me?"

Chapter 47

CHAPTER FORTY-SEVEN

Matt said nothing for a long minute, but neither did anyone else as Lee walked past the trio to start the kettle on the stove.

"Amateurs," he muttered as he pulled a mug from the cabinet. "I heard everything. You better get your asses in gear. Don't you dare fail that woman."

"I'm sorry, Lee," Matt said, rising from his chair and stepping forward as he apologized. "It all happened so fast that I didn't even think—"

"Now you only have about sixty seconds to think. I know Shelby doesn't want me involved in any of this, but it's too late for that. And I can't sit by. I'll help however I can."

"We can't bring anyone," Sam stated firmly. "If we make one wrong move, step outside of the lines even once, Shelby pays the price."

"I have to go," Matt said.

"No, you don't. And you can't. He never heard your voice, so he has no idea you're involved in any of this. And it's better that way. We can't call the cops yet, but someone needs to know where Lucia and I are going, just in case..."

Sam's eyes seemed to lose focus, then his gaze locked on Lucia, her head still in her hands, fingers tangled through her messy dark hair. Matt could imagine how Sam felt then, knowing that they were going into the lion's den without any backup, any security, or any assurance of seeing the woman he loved come out alive.

Lee interrupted. "I might just be a cook, but I think I see something you don't. That man said Sam's and Lucia's phones have to stay here. He doesn't want either of you tracked to where he's sending you, no cell tower pinging, no GPS location history."

"We don't have time to restate the facts." Sam nudged Lucia and tipped his head toward the door. "We have to go now, or we're going to miss our window."

"Stop, Sam. You should take Matt's phone and let him take yours after you enable location sharing for each other. Unless you both enabled that function with Shelby's, he can't track your phone, he can only track Lucia's. And I'll track all of you while using Lucia's phone to keep track of Shelby."

It was just about complex enough to confuse Matt, but he agreed with Lee's suggestion. "Let's do it." He wrote down his passcode on a napkin and handed it to Sam, then pulled out his phone. The three shared their numbers and hastily enabled the location-sharing function.

"We have to go. Now." Sam hurried to the door, and Lucia followed.

"Wait." Matt jogged after him. "That's not a plan. I can't just sit here on my hands."

Sam and Lucia hesitated, glanced at each other, then Sam shrugged at Matt.

"I don't know what to tell you. You can't come with us and risk Shelby. If you care about her safety, you won't insist." Sam glanced at his watch. "And we're already going to have to make up minutes on the road."

Sam took one last hard look at Matt, then shook his head, turned, and headed down the stairs after Lucia, disappearing as Matt closed the door behind them.

He stood there for a moment, staring at the closed door in helpless silence, then headed back to the dinette and slumped into one of the chairs. Lee placed a steaming mug in front of him, then sat in the chair opposite with his own mug.

"It's ginger green tea," Lee said. "It'll help your brain."

"You don't really seem surprised to see me in your apartment at three-something in the morning."

Lee grinned over his mug. "I've been shipping you and Shelby all along. Sam and Lucia may not trust you yet, but I think I've got a pretty good feel for people. I trust you. You're one of the only cops that ever treated me like a person when I was homeless, rather than some vermin or nuisance."

"Like recognizes like," Matt said softly, barely above a whisper, then sipped his tea. He'd prefer coffee, but it was a petty desire at a time like this. "I haven't always been where I am now, or who I am."

Lee stared at him, his dark gaze curious and piercing. "That is a story I'll draw out of you some other time. For now, you need to figure out how we're going to help Shelby. What's your take on that conversation with the mystery man?"

Matt cleared his throat and thought about it. "I think it's pretty obvious this man knows more than he shared. I thought it was odd how he gave the exact expected travel time for Sam and Lucia to the minute. Was he only basing it off her location showing on Shelby's phone? Or something more?"

"What else?" Lee prompted.

"Lucia didn't hide that she knew Shelby was missing. She let him know, and he wasn't surprised at all."

Lee took a fresh notepad out of a drawer and started taking notes.

"He's sophisticated, thoughtful. He knows what he's doing, and he's prepared. I'm not sure if he knows about me, but I think he knows everything else about Lucia, Sam, and Shelby. Which means he knows about this apartment. And you."

The pen stopped scribbling, and Lee looked up, his brow furrowing.

"I don't think you're safe here."

"But if I leave, they'll see Lucia's phone on the move and..." Lee let his words trail off.

"Leave it here."

"But I can't track Shelby's phone without Lucia's—"

"Leave it. It might not be any good to us anyway."

"Why not? That's our only link—"

Matt held up a hand to stop him. "Where is she showing up right now?"

Lee unlocked Lucia's phone and refreshed the location data. "She's at a party store in..." he paused to zoom out over the map area. "Hardy-Croton Dam."

"Let's figure out these directions that Sam copied for us." They pulled up a map and followed the directions, tracing their eyes along the backroads meandering through farmland, forest, and river valleys. The destination Sam and Lucia had been directed to was a campground a few miles away."

"The best we can do is note where the phone is showing up now and keep that information for later. Can you drive?"

"I don't have a license."

"I guess I'll take you to my place then."

"No way." Lee crossed his arms over his chest and leaned back against the sink. "You're not leaving me out of this. I have to help her. She saved my life, and I owe her everything."

"You realize she'll kill me and kick your ass if I agree and bring you along, right?"

Lee sighed, then headed for the entryway and put his shoes on.

"My first time up here was last night, so if I had to bet, I'd say they don't know how involved I am with Shelby. At least not yet."

"And she wouldn't reveal that bit of information," Lee observed. "She's too smart for it."

Matt smiled thinking of her, though it was a bittersweet feeling. "Let's go. You can help me figure out what I'm going to do while we're on the way to drop you off."

While Lee gathered all the napkins and the notebook from the table, Matt grabbed his coat from the hook near the door and shrugged it on before tying on his boots. They left quickly, Lee engaging the lock and deadbolt, though they both knew if someone really wanted to get in, that wouldn't stop them.

As they reached ground level and crossed the parking area, Matt spotted a small lump lying under a frozen blanket of snow near Lucia's snow-covered truck. Mitch came to mind, and Matt remembered watching him leave something on the hood. He paused to pick it up and when he brushed off the snow, realized what Mitch had left last night was a teddy bear, undoubtedly for Shelby.

Logically, it wasn't important right now, but Matt couldn't leave it behind. He wasn't sure of the story behind this particular toy, but he knew it wasn't a happy one. One day, this bear might be the only thing Shelby had left from her father, and when that day came, Matt knew how much things like this would matter.

He took the bear with him as he climbed into the driver's seat of his own truck, fully aware of Lee's questioning gaze as he placed the bear on the middle seat and buckled himself in.

Sticking his hands into his pockets to find his truck keys, the sharp corners of card stock jabbed into the palm of his right hand.

Withdrawing the card and studying it, he recalled once more the heart-broken detective who'd given it to him. "Maybe we have one more card to play."

Chapter 48

CHAPTER FORTY-EIGHT

S am had insisted Lucia drive so he could sit in the passenger seat and snoop through Matt's phone, skimming his texts, calls, browser history, and social media accounts. He spent around twenty minutes opening apps and searching Matt's accounts before deciding he couldn't find anything damning. At least not yet, and this wasn't the appropriate time for a deep dive.

"What are we going to do?" Lucia asked, her voice weak but calm. "I can think of a hundred things, but this guy has us by the balls, Sam."

Sam smirked despite the gravity of the situation. "He sure does. But we're going to get through this. The last time I spearheaded our mission, we got our asses kicked, and it was because I refused to listen. So it's time for me to eat a little more crow and ask what you and Shelby would do."

"It wasn't your fault, Sam."

"It was." He nodded, easily swallowing his pride as he remembered the sight of the bruises on Lucia's face and neck. "But we're not going to play that game right now, Luce. Just focus. How would secretive Lucia and Shelby handle this?"

"I'm the planner," she said, then sighed. "Shelby's light on her toes and quick in her thoughts. She always adapts fast when the plan goes off the rails."

"A plan never survives first contact," Sam muttered. It was a phrase he learned early in his military career. Plans were necessary, but the unpredictability of an ever-evolving situation on the ground required contingency planning as well. In this case, they didn't have the time to do it properly and had very limited information with which to plan.

"I think Shelby and I would find some way to scope the place out, hunker down, and start taking out targets."

"Targets? That's a little gung-ho. Shit! Turn right here!"

Lucia laid heavy on the brakes without slamming them and turned north onto Crystal.

"Anyway, we don't have time to do all the planning I normally prefer to do. Like that mission down in Southfield."

Sam bit his tongue, wanting to snap at her, but knowing it wouldn't help. His anger over that one still burned bright.

"We were just supposed to scout it out and see if we could get enough evidence to call the cops. But things went sideways. If we hadn't followed our instincts, and if Shelby hadn't pressed me to follow that car, we never would have found Natalie and Kaylie. They might not have even lived through the night, the way Natalie explained it."

Sam nodded and kept his mouth shut, unable to think of anything constructive to say.

"But given how little margin we have for time," her eyes darted toward the clock on the radio, "we don't have time for any kind of recon. At least, not with our own eyes."

"Don't leave me hanging," he prodded.

"It might be tough, but in between directions, use Matt's phone to scout ahead on the map and see where we're going."

Damn. That is a good idea.

"Of course." After reviewing the directions and getting her turned down the next road, Sam started following the directions along the map. "We have five miles before our next turn, west onto Blanchard. Then it gets a little intense."

"Turn it off!" Lucia shouted, taking one hand off the steering wheel to curl her finger around the sides of the phone and click the side button to turn off the screen.

"What the hell?" he snapped, raising his gaze to glare at her. But her free hand, hovering just below the dash, pointed forward and to the right.

They were quickly closing the distance on a car parked on the shoulder of the road, its hazards flashing and dome light on. Lucia drove over the centerline to give the car plenty of space, but she didn't slow. Even driving at fifty miles per hour, Sam could clearly see a man's backlit head, his darkened face staring back. A chill ran through his body, and he watched in the side mirror until the car disappeared from view.

"Why—"

"How else would he know if we followed his instructions?" Lucia interrupted.

Sam considered the question. "You think that was someone working for this guy?"

Lucia nodded, though it was almost imperceptible in the low light of the cab. The area was too rural for streetlights, and the thick, snow-heavy cloud cover kept the ambient light low.

"Then why isn't he following us?"

"I don't know."

"So maybe that person back there just broke down on the side of the road and isn't marking our progress?"

"Better safe than sorry. If that guy back there does work for the man who has Shelby and he calls back to tell his boss that we have a cell phone, she's..."

Lucia let the words trail off. "We're not supposed to have any phones with us. And if he finds out we do, that endangers Shelby and reveals that we might have help."

"I guess your paranoia is paying off," he admitted, albeit begrudgingly. "We still have another four miles until we turn onto Blanchard. Keep an eye out for any more suspected checkpoints while I check out the map."

He covered the phone screen with his parka and lowered the brightness. It was uncomfortable to be so tightly hunched over, but he was determined to keep any light from escaping because Lucia was right. If her paranoia was more deeply based in instinct than he'd first expected, then they needed to be careful.

With the directions fresh in his mind, Sam quickly dragged the map and followed the twists and turns to their destination.

"Looks like... an orchard?" Sam zoomed in on the area with the satellite layer enabled. It appeared to be an active apple orchard, complete with a large warehouse, various smaller outbuildings around it, and a plowed driveway and parking area.

"Who do you think this guy is?"

"I'm not really sure," Lucia said softly. "But I think it's best not to underestimate him."

"Why's that?" Sam asked before Matt could say anything.

"Natalie warned me about him, this Fear Doirich."

"What the hell kind of name is this?"

"Shelby looked it up while you and I were being treated in the hospital. It translates, essentially, to "the dark man," and it's from an Irish fairytale. Apparently, some bossman down in the straits sees himself as powerful as an old god of lore, so he takes the name. He's the one responsible for kidnapping Natalie. She swore he'd come after us, and said we should prepare for when he retaliates, not if."

"Luce, that was only a couple of days ago." Sam scoffed. "It's not impossible, but with the way Mitch... handled things, nobody would even know we were involved. Not yet."

"I don't know, Sam. What about this orchard?"

Sam ducked his head back in his coat and studied the area of their destination. "Looks to be about twenty acres of orchard, and it's surrounded by forest. West and north a few miles away is Hardy Dam. South is the Tamarack."

"What if this is it?" she whispered, stealing a glance at Sam.

He locked the phone screen and set it down, reaching over the console to taking Lucia's right hand in his. "Don't think like that."

"If he's sophisticated, he's not alone. And if he's not alone, he's controlling the key terrain."

Sam couldn't help but grin. "It sounds like you've been reading through my collection of Army field manuals."

To his relief, she grinned.

"Voraciously."

"We have to trust in our instincts, especially yours," he squeezed her fingers, "and in our friends, Shelby included. If anyone can get out of a shitty situation like this, it's her."

"Agreed. But how many times can you escape before they finally figure out how to keep you? Tell me again why we're not just calling the cops."

"Remember. I'll text Matt when we're close, then he'll make calls to the right people."

"And we're on our own until the cavalry arrives."

"Yes. If they get wind the cops are coming, I'm afraid of what will happen, and not only to her."

"This can't end well for us. You know that, right?"

"It will, damn it." He grit his teeth and tried not to think about the worst case scenario. "At some point, we all have to face our problems. We can't run away from this forever, and if we do, we teach them they can bully us and win. We're either backed into a corner and fighting for our lives now or weeks, months, years down the road. None of this will stop unless we make it stop."

"And what if they make us stop. Are you ready for that?"

"If we die, at least we'll die together, fighting against evil men." He kissed the back of her trembling hand. "You're tougher than you think you are, Luce. And I'll be with you through whatever comes."

Chapter 49
CHAPTER FORTY-NINE

M itch had the unpleasant experience of coming to consciousness yet again as a damnable sound roused him from a deep, dreamless slumber. Did he fuck it up and pull the trigger too hard, yanking it away from its intended target—his brain? He must have done something wrong, as he wouldn't be waking up at all if he'd put a bullet through his gray matter.

A glassy clanging vibrated through the room, shrill and painful in his foggy head, and he recognized it as the sound that had brought him back from oblivion, where he wished he was now. He opened his eyes and lifted his head.

Pulling himself to the pillows, he rolled onto his side, thankful he hadn't thrown up and choked to death on his own vomit after all he'd drank. It was starting to come together in his mind: the pain, the alcohol, the trigger he'd pulled.

The gun.

He pushed up into a sitting position, fingers fumbling for the lamp switch on the nightstand, and finally turned it on. There was his Smith and Wesson, its black body sinking like a shadow into the duvet. Loathing and longing both filled him equally, vying for dominance as he hesitated to grab his trusted firearm, his protection, his long-held tool for keeping himself and others safe.

The same one he'd attempted to end all of his pain with before passing out like a fool.

Drunk or not, it was time to get the job done. The wheels were already set in motion, his texts to Collins already sent. He picked up his duty pistol, and it felt heavier than ever as he examined it.

Mitch quickly found the problem. The sliver of a safety switch had been flipped on, preventing the gun from firing.

"Moron," he spat. He flipped the safety switch off, and it clicked lightly into place. It was ready.

The silence of the room grew heavy, suffocating even, as he stared at the black pistol and imagined what kind of mess it would make for the people who found him. He had to remind himself that it didn't matter. There were plenty of people who undertook crime scene cleanup as their line of work, and he wasn't about to deprive them of another job to pay their bills and feed their families.

He hefted the heavy pistol and held it firmly against his temple, only the sound of his own sharp inhale disturbing the thick quiet of the room.

Cl-l-l-l-l-ang!

Mitch jumped so badly his hand twisted, and he almost accidentally pulled the trigger.

"Damn it!" he wheezed, flipping on the safety and doubling over on the bed. "Can't a man off himself in peace?!"

He waited, listening to see if it was a call or a text message, but nothing happened. It must have been a text, easy enough to ignore.

Mitch dropped backward into the pillows, lifted the muzzle of his gun to his temple once more, and clutched one of the pillows against the other side of his head. He wasn't sure it would make a difference in reducing the mess, but it was worth a shot.

With a good, clean grip on the Smith and Wesson, he flipped the safety down with his thumb and seated his finger on the trigger, ready to pull.

Cl-l-l-l-l-l-lang!

"Fuck me." Mitch sighed, exasperated. He dropped the pillow from his left hand and flipped the safety off yet again before rolling off the bed.

He dropped the gun near the pillows and grabbed his phone from the desk against the opposite wall. Although he'd turned off the ringer, he hadn't turned off the vibration feature, and the damn thing was too close to the bottle, rattling against the thick glass in the most annoying and noisy way possible.

"I'm sorry, Collins," he muttered as he opened the phone screen to turn off the ringer. But the notifications that greeted him weren't all from Collins. There were a dozen messages from a number he didn't recognize with a 989 area code.

He would have ignored them, but when he expanded the collection of messages, he noticed they all read the same message.

Shelby is in trouble, kidnapped.

Short, succinct. Perhaps too few words, with too little context. Mitch instantly craved answers to the questions raging in his mind.

A sick feeling rolled through his body, and he couldn't help but shiver. His mind was more awake now, and he glanced at the bed and his gun lying among the pillows. He shouldn't reasonably care if the daughter who'd disowned him was in trouble.

But he did care.

The sick-sweet fear seeped into his bones, and he was far more afraid at the idea of Shelby being hurt again than he was of blowing out his own brains all over the linens at a cheap motel.

Could he finish the job he'd started, off himself and leave her to whatever fate some vicious bastards had in store for her? Or would he do whatever he could to try to save her, having to face her wrath and fury when she saw his face again?

His body moved before his mind acknowledged the only course of action he would accept, his fingers tapping deftly over the screen as he called the number.

"Detective Ward?" It was a man's voice, the man who had been with Shelby last night.

"What happened?"

He pulled on his boots as he listened to Matt Douglas rapidly explain the series of events that occurred after Mitch's visit to Merrill the night before.

Lucky for all of them, Mitch hadn't driven all the way back to Southfield. Somehow, he wasn't keen on explaining that he'd found the nearest place suitable to end his sad, empty life.

Instead, he kept asking Matt questions as he cleaned and emptied his room, then left his key in the drop box near the office door.

"No. Don't call anyone else," Mitch instructed. "Not yet. Where can I meet you?" He holstered his pistol, flipping the safety on, and dropped into the driver's seat of his car.

Chapter 50

CHAPTER FIFTY

Shelby opened her eyes to total darkness, but she wasn't afraid. At least not at first. Not until she tried to move and found her hands and legs had been bound to the chair she was seated on. She tried to speak, but her mouth wouldn't open. Duct tape, she guessed, or something like it.

The air was cold and dry, and she shivered lightly.

As she became more conscious, the aches and pains in her body grew stronger. She could barely remember being grabbed from the parking lot in front of her apartment. The soft, stuffed toy bear she'd held in her hands. The low, dull whir of an engine. Her body being encircled by the arms of two strong men and pulled into a white van.

The pinprick and pinch of a needle into her neck.

Then nothing. No dreams, no thoughts, no pain.

She took her time now, breathing deeply to fight her grogginess, and wiggled a little, testing her bonds. Nothing gave, not even a little.

Footsteps thudded against the floor, growing louder as they came closer, and she froze, trying not to tense up as they stopped just in front of her. The other person's energy was palpable, and she felt the warmth radiating off their body as they leaned in close, coming near her ear.

The cover over her eyes was pulled from her head, and suddenly, she could see, squinting against the sudden bright light.

"You're awake now," a man said. She didn't bother trying to reply. "I've heard all about you. I'm delighted to finally meet you."

Her eyes finally adjusted, and an older man's face snapped to clarity in her vision. Short black and silver hair topped his pale head, and he donned a navy parka, black jeans, and dark brown work boots. He stood over her, arms at his sides, angry blue eyes sparkling as he studied her.

"Don't scream," he instructed, his words low and firm. Then he reached out and ripped the tape off her mouth.

Shelby flinched and groaned, but she didn't cry out.

"I assume our boys didn't rough you up too badly."

Her stomach knotted as the gravity of the situation settled in, but she maintained her silence, only staring back up at him and forcing a lop-sided grin.

But the older man didn't react at all. He turned and walked a few steps to a metal chair set in the middle of the concrete floor. She took her gaze off him to survey her surroundings as much as her bindings would let her. Four corrugated steel walls boxed in the large rectangular space, complete with a steel roof. A few space heaters were scattered around the corner they'd set her in. Larger boxes and crates crowded the opposite long wall, and parked near the wide bay door at the front was the white van and a new-looking black Escalade with tinted windows. Salt spray covered the bottom of the otherwise clean and undamaged vehicle.

She counted at least half a dozen men standing in the large space. A couple were smoking, others chatting quietly near the vehicles.

"Nice ride," she said, keeping her gaze on the SUV.

"Are you thirsty?" The man twisted open a bottle of water and held it out.

"Are you serious?" she asked flatly, not hiding the lack of amusement from her voice.

"I can help you—"

"No," she cut him off, shaking her head even though it made her vision swim. Whatever drug they'd given her hadn't completely worn off yet. "What the hell do you want?"

He frowned deeply, his cold gaze piercing through her as he screwed the cap back on the water bottle.

"You have a foul mouth, don't you?" He nodded his head, dropped the bottle on the floor, and walked toward her languidly.

She sneered at him. "When I'm dealing with monsters who kidnap women and tie them up, I make it a point to deal with them in a language they'll understand."

"You, an uncivilized little peon, want to call me a monster?" He shook his head and tapped his toe against the cement floor. "You'd have to be at my level and have my respect for your words to mean anything."

His gaze left her as he faced the vehicles. "Bring my son out." When he turned back to her, he was grinning. "It's time for him to learn how to deal with little people like you."

A tingle crawled down Shelby's spine as men stirred at the back of the Escalade. They lifted something out of the back, and she realized in horror that it was a person in a wheelchair.

He rounded the SUV and began rolling himself toward Shelby. She gasped when she recognized him, her stomach twisting and rolling at the sight of him.

Phil glared at her, a sneer transforming his once youthful-looking face into one weathered and jaded. He stopped at his father's side but never said a word, never took his eyes off her.

As Shelby took in the sight of him, the state of him now, fear crept into her gut and threatened to spread. She needed to keep it from taking over, but a man with a vendetta was a dangerous one, especially when he had friends and money.

"Your friends are on their way," the older man informed her.

Her breath halted, and if she could have moved, she would have searched her pockets for her phone.

"They'll be here soon, so we don't have long to get acquainted. I'll start. My name is Richard McNamara. I'm Philip's father." He waited for a moment, then lifted his open palm to her. "And you are?"

"Eat shit." She growled the words, narrowing her eyes and steeling herself. The quiet ones were the scariest, but if there was anything worth spending her last breath on, it was defying rich assholes.

Richard did not sigh, frown, clench his fists, or show any sign of anger. He stepped toward her, slow and calm. Once he was close, he stared down into her eyes and drew back his hand, then brought it full force with his open palm against her left cheek.

He'd hit her so hard that the chair Shelby was tied to rocked, and she was left seeing stars. Her breath came fast as she shook her head, trying desperately to clear her vision.

"Language," he scolded her. "I won't be so gentle next time. Now. Introduce yourself."

Her chest heaved, and she looked away as that sickening fear crawled through her veins. He hauled his harm back and slapped her a second time, the chair rocking again.

She fought the urge to groan and was left dazed, but she kept her mouth shut.

"You're not a very smart young lady, are you?"

Shelby kept her gaze on the floor, breathing in through her nose. She didn't fight her fuzzy vision this time, knowing for certain this sadistic asshole might be just getting started.

"Introduce yourself, and politely," Richard instructed, the frigid edge in his voice cutting through the eerie quiet of the space as his son and his men watched in silence.

Shelby let her gaze drift up just as her vision cleared, and her eyes met Phil's. In her periphery, she could see Richard's hand raised to strike her again, but she didn't turn to him. Something about Phil had changed; something softened in his face, sadness threatening the edges of his soulless gray eyes.

Maybe the bastard is a little less sadistic after his own brush with death—

Richard struck her so hard he knocked her on the floor, and her head hit the cement as she fell. She groaned audibly now, her vision dark and her body limp in its bonds.

"Pick her up," Richard instructed. Multiple pairs of boots clunked over the floor toward her, and hard hands picked her up with the chair.

Her head swimming and mind fuzzy, she struggled to stay upright in the chair as they cut whatever material had bound her.

"Last chance," Richard said. "If you don't learn like this, then we'll have to find other ways to discipline you. Now, a ladylike introduction would be greatly appreciated by all of us." He waved to his men. All of them were now standing in a circle surrounding her.

"Fuck off," she said with a hiss, spitting in his direction. It didn't reach him, but she quickly learned that spitting pushed his buttons.

His left hand held her shoulder to keep her up, and his right formed a fist before barreling into her stomach. She cried out finally, and he let her go, standing calmly as she tumbled to the floor, clutching at her midsection as the pain arced through her like electricity. It hurt to breathe, it hurt to move, it hurt as her pulse thundered through her veins. Her face, head, neck, and now her core ached and throbbed.

She watched through one half-open eye as Richard pulled a knife from his pocket and passed it to Phil.

"It's your turn. You train them, or they train you. She needs to be punished for what happened to you."

Chapter 51
CHAPTER FIFTY-ONE

The heavy silence unnerved Matt, and he had to battle his talkative nature to keep his mouth shut as much as he could. But he couldn't stay entirely tight-lipped, as there were relevant questions to ask and answer, ones that might give them the edge if all of this was leading up to some conflict.

And it damn sure felt like they were on a freight train straight to hell.

After dropping off Lee and giving him quick instructions about how to arm the security system, Matt headed back to Merrill to meet up with the detective from Southfield. It was odd, meeting the father of the woman he was falling for like this, but he also recognized how ridiculous it was to think of something like that.

But what could he do except grit his teeth and stay just five miles per hour over the speed limit to make sure he didn't get pulled over on M46. He sure as hell wouldn't have let Mitch drive. Not only was he in the wrong state of mind to not drive recklessly, but he also reeked of liquor.

"So, why'd you stay in the area?" Matt asked, repeating the question he'd asked on the phone.

Mitch stayed quiet, staring at the map on his phone's screen as they sped toward Hardy Pond. The body of water was created by the hydroelectric dam installed on the Muskegon River and was a recreational hotspot. But not in December, and so close to Christmas. It wasn't quite the haven for skiing or winter sports. Only the most dedicated fishermen would be out on the ice, and only if the ice was thick enough. The area's summer homes, lodges, cabins, and shoreline cottages would be emptied or rented to low-income rural folk.

In Matt's mind, it made the situation all the more dangerous. The more isolated and removed from dense population centers they were, the longer it would take to call in the cavalry. Even if the state troopers or county cops came from the nearest posts in Newaygo, they'd need to travel a maze of snow-covered routes, unpaved roads, and two-tracks to navigate to get to the obscure location where Shelby's phone had last pinged.

"I can hear the gears working in that brain of yours," Mitch said, breaking the silence. "It's probably best we share what's on our mind."

Matt nodded, choosing to ignore the hypocrisy, at least for now. "I'm worried about how out of the way this place is. Even from Newaygo, it's a trek if all these roads haven't been plowed yet."

"It looks like we have to take at least two seasonal roads to get to this point," Mitch agreed.

"And what if she's not even there?"

Mitch lifted his head and gazed out into the darkness beyond the truck's headlights. He soon returned his gaze to the map on the phone screen. "Why are you worried about that?"

Matt shrugged. "These guys seem sophisticated. If not for the snow and the phone call, we might not even know she was missing. And if they know what they're doing, then they know they need to get rid of her phone because it can be tracked."

"Let's just take it one step at a time. You might have the energy for speculation right now, but I don't." Mitch sighed. "What I wouldn't give for a hot cup of coffee."

"Sorry, pops, you're going to have to wait on that. Where are Sam and Lucia?"

"I'd guess they're about ten minutes away. We're still another thirty-five minutes out."

"Damn." Matt squeezed the steering wheel between his fingers as if he were wringing out his tension and anxiety. "They might barely make it."

"I'm taking us along a more direct route, so we might catch up sooner than expected. The directions this man gave them are very specific. It's odd that it doesn't take them along the most direct route if time is so important to him."

"It sounds like this is more about control. He knows he's got all the leverage, and he wants to make sure they know it, too."

"Lucky for us, he doesn't seem to be expecting us."

"I still have a bad feeling about this."

"Don't get swept away by your feelings. You have to bury all of that and walk into this with your head clear and focused on the task at hand. If you get sidetracked, people die."

"I know." Matt sighed and ran one hand over his hair.

"We're going to need both our heads and all our firepower to get through this alive and come out the other side with Shelby, too."

"I can't stop kicking myself. If I'd heard her get up and walk out, I would have gone after her. And then none of this would have happened."

"Seems like she's the kind who does what she wants and doesn't ask permission from anybody to do it."

"That's hitting the nail on the head pretty damn good for not knowing her all that well."

"I'm sure you've heard the saying about apples not falling far from trees." Mitch fell silent.

Matt let the silence stretch, still running through the scenarios in his head where he could have stopped all of this from happening. Finally, he broke the silence. "I wasn't even that far away."

"Listen, kid. You can't do this to yourself. There's nothing you could have done to stop it, and the sooner you realize that, the sooner you'll be ready to do what needs to be done."

"And what needs to be done, Detective?"

"Just Mitch. I think we're in for hell and high water if we want to keep everyone alive. If we even have a shot at doing that."

"Sam and Lucia might be toothless, but at least we're bringing the armory." He threw his thumb over his shoulder toward the backseat of the truck. When he dropped off Lee, they'd both grabbed an armful of guns and ammo from his basement and packed it in the truck just before Mitch had shown up.

"That's great, but if any bodies come out of this, we're going to have a shit-ton of questions to answer and paperwork to do. I'm on the verge of retirement, but even I won't be off the hook entirely."

"With me being much earlier in my career, I'm guessing my chances of coming out unscathed are—"

"Slim," Mitch said, nodding his head. "You better focus on the road and lay that pedal down, son."

"Got it." Matt sped up as much as he dared, praying they wouldn't get noticed by state police patrols. With the omnidirectional radars, he had to worry as much about a moving duty vehicle as he did about a speed trap.

"They've stopped moving. Now, hopefully, they do a good job of hiding your phone, and they can keep themselves out of trouble until we get there."

Chapter 52
CHAPTER FIFTY-TWO

T he blade of the KA-BAR reflected the fluorescent lights overhead, and Phil squinted against the sudden flash of light. His hand shook as he accepted it from his father, so he wrapped his fingers tightly around the grip to steady himself.

When he looked at Shelby, face to face now, he didn't see the same young woman he'd roughed up all those months ago. He saw the fallout, his own pain, the loss of his mobility, and how close he'd come to death.

Suffering was far more real to him now, and the thought of slicing open her flesh forced him to imagine how that pain would feel if the same was inflicted on him.

He lived in almost constant pain and misery, what his physicians called "chronic" lately. Healing would take a long time, he knew, but no one could tell him if the pain would ever fully disappear.

Aching, angry, and cold, he shook his head. As pissed as Phil was, he didn't have the stomach for violence anymore. All this was for him, and he knew his father's wrath would be awful, but he couldn't do it. He would indulge in his violent sexual fantasies about his physical therapist, that bitch Lucia, or even Shelby the way she'd been when he first laid eyes on her, but he couldn't carry them out anymore.

Hell, he couldn't hardly sleep at night anymore. All the torment, pain, and death he'd caused before the shooting came back to haunt him, one memory and one night at a time. It was getting harder to pretend he was worthy of the moniker he'd given himself.

"What on earth are you waiting for?" His father's voice broke through his rambling thoughts, and he shuddered.

The terrifying, heavy knife slipped from his fingers and clattered on the cement floor. Phil could only shake his head.

"Philip!" His father growled his name as he stepped in front of Phil's wheelchair and gripped the armrests.

Phil hated this part the most, knowing that his father was on the verge of humiliating him, and this time in front of the men who were supposed to work for and respect him.

"Don't we pay people to do this sort of dirty work?" Phil finally looked up, locking eyes with Richard.

His father released the armrests and straightened, shaking his head at his son. "I've always insisted that we shouldn't order others to undertake work we're not willing to do ourselves. Here's where you prove what you're willing to do, how far you're willing to go for yourself." He knelt and stared into Phil's eyes, making him feel more like a petulant child than ever. "And for your family."

Philip tried to swallow, but his throat was too dry. "I'll do whatever I can, everything I can, sir. But for fuck's sake, look at me." He gestured to his legs, the limbs he could no longer feel or control. "If I lean too far out of my chair to play with her," he gestured at Shelby, "I'll fall face-first out of it and onto the floor."

Richard raised an eyebrow, but Phil continued before his ruthless patriarch could say anything.

"I need to have some dignity left if I'm to command any respect from the people who work for me, who work for our family. I don't want them to feel sorry for me, but I don't want to be the butt of their jokes either."

His father seemed to consider this, his cold eyes searching Phil's face before glancing up at his men.

Shelby's breathing had calmed now, and Phil found her staring at him. That burning hatred was still alight in her dark eyes, and she seemed almost relieved.

But only for now.

Even if he couldn't do it himself, he wasn't about to defy his father and stop anyone else from having a go at her. She'd brought nothing but ruin to his life, and she kept finding ways to take down piece after piece of the operation he'd worked so hard to build. If she wasn't stopped now, everything would unravel sooner or later.

He was afraid of pain, but he was more afraid of prison, especially in his current state. It could only be that much more difficult to be incarcerated as a paraplegic than an able-bodied man.

But now he had her, and two of the other troublemakers were on their way, handing themselves over like the idiots they were. Depending on what his father decided to do with them, the trio could last hours or weeks. Either way, they would pay the piper for all the loss they'd caused, all the legal trouble and financial drain.

"I'll wait in the van." Phil didn't wait for permission, turning his chair and wheeling himself away from Shelby and his father. Hard things had to be done, and even if he wasn't able to hold the knife, he was fully capable of giving the orders and trusting that it would be done. To his great relief, his father didn't object this time.

With this understanding set straight in his mind, he closed his senses to the impending horror that would soon envelop Shelby in a new, agonizing reality.

Chapter 53

CHAPTER FIFTY-THREE

S am exhaled noisily as he turned off the Bluetooth and WiFi features on Matt's phone, then stuffed it into the narrow space behind the plastic mold of the glove compartment before closing the door. The device was slim enough to fit in the space without falling out either way when the compartment was opened, and it was the only place he could hide it without tearing open the side panels. There wasn't enough time for it since they were less than a mile from their destination. Plus, they were being followed closely by a truck or SUV now, likely occupied by the Fear Doirich's men.

"Almost there," Lucia said, gripping the steering wheel so tightly that her fingers hurt.

"Are you ready?" he asked, zipping up his jacket.

"I'm ready."

"You sound more confident than usual."

"I am more confident. We've been through hell and back, and we keep coming out of it. Singed and beat to shit, but out of it nonetheless."

"So far. But I gotta be honest with you, Luce." He reached over and took her right hand from the steering wheel, caressing the back of it with his thumb. "It doesn't look good. Maybe our luck has run out."

She said nothing at first, unhappy with his assessment, but she didn't take her hand away. "I know," she admitted. "But there's no other way. We don't have time, we don't have options, and he doesn't want to negotiate. I think this is... It's..."

"Say it."

"Revenge."

Sam nodded and let her hand fall from his. "Just remember. Your will to live must be stronger than someone else's will to kill, or you don't stand a chance."

"Those are some pretty wise words, Sam. Are you turning into some kind of philosopher?"

"Honestly?" He cocked a grin as she glanced over at him. "I saw it on an anime show that I watched as I kid."

Lucia burst out laughing, laughing so hard her still-sore ribs ached from the effort, and Sam laughed with her. Their mirth faded into silence as they approached the driveway to the orchard. The vehicle behind them flashed its lights, so Lucia flipped on her blinker and turned onto the freshly plowed road. Clearly, the drive hadn't been plowed or used at all until tonight, and a pickup truck with a plow attachment on the front sat midway as if to confirm her assessment.

The vehicle behind her rode hot on her tail, and she hated every second of it. When her headlights illuminated the warehouse, her heart began to race, and she surveyed her surroundings as much as she could through the darkness. There were all the things Sam had described to her, but it was all too new for her to feel at ease.

"Are you buckled?"

"Of course. Why?"

Lucia didn't answer. She increased her speed slightly even as they got closer to the warehouse. But the men behind her wouldn't see that, as intent as they were on kissing her bumper.

She laid her foot down on the gas just enough to rev the engine but not enough to let the tires slip on the snow.

"Get ready to run."

"Luce—"

She jammed her right foot on the brake pedal before he could try to talk her out of it, and the tailgating vehicle slammed into them. Her head jerked backward from the force of the impact, but her fingers gripped the steering wheel as her truck was propelled forward despite her foot anchored on the brakes.

The pair of vehicles, metal bumpers tangled together, now skid across the freshly plowed drive over a thin layer of slick, hard-packed snow. With her left foot, Lucia slammed on the emergency brake, then unlocked the doors and unbuckled her seat belt.

"Get out!" she cried as she threw open her door and flung herself out of it before the truck came to a complete stop. She landed on her feet, but the momentum threw her off balance, and she rolled several times before getting up and sprinting for the warehouse.

Pulling her gun from its holster, she turned off the safety and gripped it ready in her hands. Avoiding the giant bay door, she bolted for the side door, ripping it open as soon as the handle turned.

She slid inside, fast and quiet, chest heaving as her eyes adjusted and she sought a target.

The lights were on but, as they say, no one was home.

Empty wooden apple crates filled the cement floor of the warehouse, and a single fluorescent light buzzed overhead. Only one of eight was either turned on or operational, and it cast a dim light over the dusty, clearly deserted space.

Lucia's heart sank as realization hit her. This wasn't where Shelby was being held, and her advantage of surprise had been wasted.

Voices outside caught her ears, bringing her mind back to the most immediate danger. She flicked on her pistol's safety and tossed it into the nearest crate. It landed with a thunk, and she put her hands up before turning back toward the door she'd entered.

The door flew inward, and a man burst in, pistol drawn and gripped strongly in both hands. He pointed it at her and grimaced. Blood dripped from his swollen nose, and red rash marks covered parts of his face around his nose.

She guessed part of her plan had worked, and she'd successfully made his airbags deploy.

"Don't fucking move," he shouted at her as he approached. His right hand dropped from the pistol grip and drew handcuffs from his coat pocket. "Kneel."

It was near impossible to swallow her fear, but she did as he instructed, knowing that she'd already disobeyed instructions. This terrible miscalculation might get her, Sam, and Shelby all killed. All she could do to try to salvage the situation was comply.

At least for now.

She flexed her wrists as the man with the bloody nose secured her arms behind her back with the cuffs.

Chapter 54
CHAPTER FIFTY-FOUR

Matt sped as much as he dared, carefully maneuvering his truck around sharp corners and through twisting curves, over paved streets and dirt roads, while Mitch alternated between scanning the road ahead and behind and checking on the pulsing blue dot that indicated the location of Matt's phone.

The entire drive had been filled with tension, and Matt knew all this time imagining what horrible things might be happening would only fray their nerves. All they could do was try to maintain awareness as they sped toward an unknown fate.

"Your phone is still active," Mitch said, worry edging his voice. "And it's been almost ten minutes since they stopped moving."

"How far out are we?"

Mitch's fingers tapped the screen. "Looks like five minutes. Maybe."

"Turn on the map and let the GPS guide me," Matt instructed. "I'd appreciate if you prepped our backup." He nodded toward the weapons in the back seat.

Mitch sighed but didn't say aloud whatever he was thinking. He set the GPS and laid the phone down on the center console. Then he unbuckled, twisted in his seat, and pulled himself into the back to load weapons.

The clicking of safety switches, sliding of bolts, and snapping of magazines being loaded followed as Mitch made quick work of preparing the firearms and additional ammo.

"Are you in love with Shelby?" the older man asked, breaking the silence.

Matt froze for a fraction of a second, even lifting his foot off the gas pedal, before recovering his composure. "Well, shit. We're not dating or anything. Nothing is official right now."

"That's not what I asked."

Behind him, another magazine was fed into its well, snapping into place with a heavy click. What could Matt say to a man about his daughter while he was armed?

"Now's not really the right time..." Matt hesitated, then grit his teeth. "Hell with it. Yes, sir. I'm in love with her. Started falling hard the first time I talked to her."

"How long ago was that?"

Matt shrugged. "A few months ago. I've been coming by and keeping her company more and more ever since."

"Does she like you back?"

"That's an excellent question. I think she does, but she's... well, do you know what kind of hell she's been through? She doesn't exactly trust men, and I can't blame her."

"I..." All sound from the back seat ceased for several seconds. "I just found out."

"I've been standing by in case she wanted or needed me. But I'd never force the issue. If it's meant to be, it'll be. If not, well, I'll still be there for her. As a friend."

"That's an unusual commitment for a young man. You sure know how to say all the right things."

Matt rolled his eyes, disgusted at the insinuation, but the mechanical voice giving the map directions cut him off.

"Your destination is on the left in five hundred feet."

"Are we ready to roll?" Matt asked, braking and pulling to the side of the road. He cut the lights and put the truck in park, waiting for his eyes to adjust in the sudden darkness.

"What are you packing?"

"The Glock and..." He thought back to what he'd grabbed in a hurry. "Is there Browning SA-35 back there?"

"There is," Mitch replied after a few quiet moments, passing both pistols forward. "Safety's are on."

Matt strapped the Browning into his shoulder holster and the Glock into the leather at his hip.

"Try to avoid firing," Mitch said as he took the front seat again and picked up the phone. "We all have a lot better chance of getting out of this without any blood being spilled if we can avoid a shootout."

"True." Matt grit his teeth as he surveyed the trees around them. The snow fell silently, accumulating in the branches of the pine trees. "I don't see any cameras. Do you?"

While Mitch searched the trees, Matt pulled a sheathed hunting knife from under his seat and snapped it to his belt.

"Nothing," Mitch said.

Matt turned on the headlights again and turned down the narrow dirt drive surrounded on either side by thick forest. The truck rolled over the uneven surface, dipping and rocking, the headlights bouncing into the mix of tall evergreen and deciduous trees and their dense undergrowth.

"Cut off your lights," Mitch said. "It goes straight."

Matt was about to argue, but Mitch dropped the glovebox and pulled out a flashlight, then rolled down his window.

He slowed the truck to a stop. As soon as the lights darkened and only the orange running lights cast their glow into the shadows, Mitch flicked on the flashlight and shined it forward, lighting Matt's way, however dimly. It was risky, but it was a good idea. If they could get any advantage of surprise, they needed to try, however slim their chances.

It wasn't long before the trees fell away and the drive opened into a clearing. Lucia's truck was parked in front of a large warehouse. Matt cut the engine and the running lights, and let his truck roll to a stop while Mitch turned off the flashlight.

They sat very still, surveying their surroundings and looking for any sign of light or movement, but all was quiet, all was dark.

Matt opened his door and slipped out of his seat, closing it as gently as possible behind him to kill the dome light. He unsnapped his holster and drew his Browning but kept the muzzle pointed to the earth as he started toward Lucia's truck.

Every step crunched and squeaked through the combination of old and fresh snow, and he cringed as he attempted to walk more softly.

It didn't help enough.

He paused to listen, only hearing Mitch's footsteps. They locked eyes, Mitch shook his head.

Taking a deep breath, Matt strode toward the truck despite the noise and placed his hand on the hood. It wasn't warm anymore, but it wasn't freezing yet, either.

Matt turned toward the warehouse, his eyes searching in the darkness before his vision finally focused on a small door. He crept toward it, cursing that if he approached it from the side instead of straight on, he would risk making even more noise.

At this point, he didn't expect anyone to be there, but he wanted to play it as safe as possible.

He continued forward, and Mitch followed at an angle, shuffling his feet quietly through the deeper snow to the sides of the natural path to the door.

Reaching forward, Matt held his breath as he squeezed the knob in one hand, then counted to three and flung it inward before stepping to the side and flinging his back against the side of the building. The corrugated steel sides of the barn were more concealment than cover, but it was better than nothing.

Nothing happened for several seconds, only the creaking of trees from the nearby forest as a gust pushed through their empty branches. Mitch clicked on his flashlight and pointed it into the building. After several more seconds, he approached the doorframe and stepped inside, sweeping his flashlight left and right as Matt glanced in at an angle.

Mitch fumbled in the dark for a moment before lights flared to life inside the warehouse and in front of it.

Stepping inside behind him, Matt scanned the large space, his heart racing as the truth sank in.

"They're not here," Mitch said, his voice sullen as he broke the truth like glass in the dusty warehouse.

"No," Matt whispered as his vision blurred. "This can't be right. We must have missed something." He spun on his heel and raced out of the door they'd just entered before Mitch could say anything else.

He holstered his pistol as his feet hit the snow and sprinted for his truck. Grabbing his phone, his fingers fumbled as he opened the screen and pulled up the tracking app that showed his phone's blue dot. It was still there, pulsing brightly and unmoving. With a few taps, he initiated a call to the device and listened carefully. Despite the single bar of signal, the call went through and his phone started ringing on the other end of the line.

He held Sam's phone away from his ear so he could listen for his to ring, but he couldn't hear anything. Pulling up the map screen, he let the phone ring while he oriented himself and walked toward the blue dot. It only took a few steps before he found himself nearly on top of it.

Matt opened the passenger door of Lucia's unlocked truck and rang his phone again with Sam's. The device didn't ring, but it did vibrate, shaking the dash. He searched on top of it, under the carpets, and in the glovebox before finding the slender opening at the back of the compartment and withdrawing his phone.

"Is that yours?" Mitch asked.

Matt only nodded, grinding his teeth as a whirlwind of thoughts stirred in his mind.

"Have you called Shelby's phone?"

"That's an idea," Matt said, hope rekindling in his chest as he opened his phone screen and initiated a call to her device. A ringing noise erupted from within the warehouse, and his hope suffocated as fast as it had reappeared.

Both men rushed into the building, whipping aside empty apple crates to dig for the phone. Mitch found it, taking it from the bottom of a giant empty apple bin.

"No," Matt repeated, defeat sinking into his bones now. It was real this time, and he strode back out into the snow, pacing until he stood beneath the gooseneck light illuminating the snow.

He dropped to his knees, the snow reaching mid-thigh, as he thought of all Shelby had already been through. Visions filled his mind of the footprints in the snow outside her apartment, and he imagined the fight she must have given them. His colorful imagination couldn't be kept from the darkness of what she'd been through when she'd been kidnapped before, according to the reports, and what she might be going through now.

"Dead end, son." Mitch sat in the snow next to him. "Time to call in backup."

"Backup," Matt repeated, trying to focus on a fragile thread teasing the edge of his mind. "No. It'll take too long."

"We don't have a choice, and we've lost too much time as it is."

"They were here, damn it!" He swiped his hand angrily through the deepening snow, spraying it in an arc toward the edge of the semi-circle of light that ended at his truck.

"Without another device on them or something, we don't have a snowball's chance in hell of figuring out where they went from here." Mitch took out his phone and started tapping on his screen.

"Wait!" Matt leapt to his feet and stared out over the snow. "Stop. Where's the flashlight?"

Mitch extracted it from his pocket, and Matt snatched it from him before clicking it on and sweeping the beam over the open area. He walked away from the warehouse and examined the area behind his truck and then Lucia's.

"The snow is falling," he said as Mitch approached. "But it's not falling that fast. Look at their tracks."

"No shit."

Together, they surveyed the snow and found the tracks of a third vehicle which had come in the same way as Lucia, then Matt, but hadn't appeared to exit the same way. All around them, the forest seemed a dark, impenetrable mass, save for the way they'd entered from the east.

"Because we know it's there," Matt mumbled, searching until he isolated the third vehicle's tracks with Mitch on his heels. "There." He pointed the flashlight north, tracing his glowing column along the tracks that led away to the north of the clearing and into the forest.

"Let's roll," Mitch said as he turned and sprinted for the truck.

Chapter 55
CHAPTER FIFTY-FIVE

S helby watched, too dazed to try to run, as Phil left for the van. His
father watched him for a moment before his gaze crawled back to her,
his blue eyes raging with icy fury.

"He's presented a fair point," he said, louder than needed, and she
guessed it was for the benefit of the men around them.

She shook her head, wishing it was as easy to shake off the dizziness from
her hit to the head, but she felt nauseous and more weak than ever.

Richard walked toward her, the gleaming knife held casually at his side.

"No," she muttered breathlessly as she struggled to focus her vision.
Throwing herself sideways, she tumbled off the chair, crying out at the
sharp pain as she hit the floor hard on her right hip. Despite the pain, she
scrambled forward. She didn't know where she was heading, only that she
needed to get away from the blade that was coming at her.

"Damn it," Shelby cursed as she stumbled. She couldn't move straight,
couldn't even think straight.

"Bring her back," Richard ordered, his voice strong and unconcerned.

Footsteps clunked toward her, and she thrust herself forward again.
Strong arms caught her around the waist and lifted her from the floor. Her
reflexes finally kicked in, and she made herself small and dropped her full

body weight toward the floor. Her captor clearly hadn't anticipated the move, so she slipped from his grasp, and he toppled forward over her as he lost his balance.

Shelby kicked out at his legs as he went over, catching his right knee and causing him to scream as it bent outward. He crumpled to the floor, but another one grabbed her by the jacket and lifted her from the floor again. Her vision was beginning to clear, which she attributed to the adrenaline, and she found the man's face twisted in fury, his dark eyes sparkling with anger.

She wasted no time once her eyes were on him, fingers scrambling forward to grasp the T-shirt shirt beneath his jacket. He gave her a wicked grin as if her feeble attempts to free herself amused him. It only lasted until she crossed her arms and used her natural leverage to twist the sides of the shirt's neckline around his neck.

"It only takes three seconds for the darkness to start," she whispered, sneering at him as he realized what was happening. He let her go, and she landed on her feet but kept pulling the shirt tightly against the jugular veins on either side of his neck, effectively cutting off the blood flow to his brain. He dropped to his knees, his arms faltering as his fingers grasped weekly at her neck.

"Fuck you," she hissed the words, spittle flying as she pulled harder.

Footsteps jogged toward her, so she dropped the man and spun, turning away from the men running at her. Maybe she had a chance, a shot to get out of this.

All she could do was run, run for her life, but as the tunnel vision of her violence faded, she realized she was running toward a corner of the building with no door. She surveyed the walls, desperate for any exit, but there were no windows either.

"No," she muttered, her voice feeble as she sucked in oxygen. Unable to go any farther, she pushed off the balls of her feet and sprinted right along the wall, spotting a door in the next corner. She couldn't guess if it was unlocked, and she didn't even believe she could open it before the many pairs of feet behind her caught up, but she wasn't about to give up.

Shelby would never surrender.

She would fight to her dying breath if she had to, and she'd take as many of these bastards with her as she could. A chest-high stack of crates wasn't exactly in the way, but she vaulted over it instead of skirting it and kicked a few crates at her pursuers. It wasn't that she thought the crates would stop the men, but she hoped they might be slowed and help her gain a little more distance.

On the other side of the stack, her foot rolled over a crowbar lying on the floor, and she fell to her knees as it clattered and rang against the cement floor. In a split-second decision, she grasped the crowbar in both hands and pushed herself back to her feet before sprinting the final distance to the door.

Her boots felt like cement shoes as she slid to a stop near the door, grasping the handle to turn it.

But it didn't budge. The door was locked.

Shelby spun and hurled the crowbar at the men, only seeing the taser after she'd released her weapon. The damn thing must have been a lucky crowbar because it hit the nearest man in the face, sending teeth flying from his mouth before bouncing into the nose of the man holding the taser. He spun wildly, gripping the taser and accidentally tasing the third man who'd tried and failed to avoid crashing into the others.

Richard startled and began walking toward her, muttering something she couldn't hear over the sound of her own blood rushing in her ears.

Sprinting again through her breathlessness and the ache in her bruised hip, Shelby made a beeline for the bay door and the vehicles in front of it. The sounds of groaning men reached her ears, then the pounding of sturdy boots across the cement floor. Instinct and fear drove her harder, her thigh muscles burning as she gave every ounce of everything she had left.

She had almost reached the bay door when Phil wheeled his chair from around the corner of the white van and leveled the barrel of a gun at her.

As shocked as she was, there was no way to stop in time, her tired legs hurtling the mass of her forward.

Freedom, she told herself, just as she had when Phil had first held her captive the summer before. Or death.

Shelby pushed off and leapt the remaining distance, flying at him knees-first. Time seemed to slow for that fraction of a second, and she watched helplessly, surrendering to fate, as he yanked the trigger.

The shot went wide, but not wide enough. Fire lit through her left side near her ribs just before she crashed into him. She grasped for him, snatching the back of his coat as she took them down. They tumbled together briefly, but she pushed herself into a crouch and, despite her disorientation from the fall, searched for the gun. It had landed near Phil, who was gasping for air, likely having had the wind knocked out of him.

Dropping to her knees, she fumbled the gun in her quaking hands, lifting it just as Richard approached. He still gripped the knife in his white-knuckled fingers, face twisted in a sneer as he halted.

"This is your last chance. Put the gun down or—"

"Or what?" she railed at him. "You'll kill me? You'll slice the flesh from my bones? Toss me to your men for their fun? Fuck you. FUCK. YOU!"

She got to her feet, hands trembling as her short burst of adrenaline began to crash. Steady or not, she'd take at least one of these bastards out before they got to her. Stepping backward slowly, she stopped when her back hit the bay door, then pointed the muzzle of the pistol at Phil.

"How much do you love your kid?" she asked, her voice a half-growl.

Richard froze, and his face paled.

"I'm happy to see something scares a monster like you."

"I'm not a monster, Shelby. I'm a man with a family. I only want to protect my family."

"By destroying other families?!" she retorted, spit flying. Shelby could hardly contain her rage. She wondered if she could shoot them both without risking one of them getting to her. "Fuck your family!"

"Calm down," Richard urged, albeit gently. "You're absolutely right. Now, I'm going to drop this." He waggled the knife in his hand. Slowly, he bent at the knees and lowered himself until he could place the blade on the floor.

Shelby felt her eyes couldn't get any wider, her entire body trembling in anticipation of some deception, some trick or attempt to hurt her. She expected him to throw the knife at her, but he didn't. He rose again to his full, commanding height, his blue eyes finally showing some hint of fear, glistening at the corners.

"Tell me what you want," Richard prompted, his piercing gaze unblinking.

"What do I want?" she hissed. "I want to be left alone. I don't want to be kidnapped in the middle of the night and have some old asshole beat the shit out of me."

His eye twitched at the curse word. He was truly bothered by the language, and she was tempted to aggravate him even more but knew her position was precarious enough.

"I suppose that's fair."

"I want this door open, and I want to drive that pretty black Escalade out of here," she continued.

He raised one eyebrow. "Are you sure you wouldn't prefer the luxury of the cargo van?"

Now Shelby twitched. "Maybe I should tie you up and beat you, see how much you appreciate it."

"It sounds like fun," he said, enunciating every word and forcing a grin.

But the men she'd stopped with her lucky crowbar were getting up now, and the least injured one began limping toward her.

"Keys, now!" She pointed the gun at Richard now.

Phil moved then, and she pointed the muzzle at him again. "Don't move!"

He fished in his pocket, and she heard the plastic jangle of a key fob. "I can't drive it yet, but I like to hold onto it anyway."

She used her nondominant hand to swipe the keys from his fingers but still kept the gun pointed at Phil. "Someone open this damn door. One wrong move, and I fuck up your family." The curse was indulgent at this point, now that she finally had a little leverage.

"All right, you win. No need to rub it in," Richard admonished her. He glanced over his shoulder and waved at the man who'd started limping toward them. "Do as she asks. Quickly!"

The man attempted a jog, but it was merely a faster limp. He made a beeline for Richard and stopped by his side. "It's..." he stopped to catch his breath, holding his side. "Right behind her."

"That's a good one." Shelby was not amused and didn't enjoy the creeping vine of doubt invading her mind.

"To your right, next to the rail," Richard directed her and glanced to her right before locking his eyes on her again. "I can assure you. I want you out of my life just as much as you want me out of yours."

She had to risk it. With a few furtive glances, she found the switch on her right. Careful to keep her aim locked on Phil, she sidestepped until she could hit the button with her elbow. An electric motor came to life, and the bay door began to lift.

"Now, how do I drive out of here without being shot at."

"We can either enjoy this standoff until one of us falls asleep, or you can take your chances." Richard shifted his weight and crossed his arms over his chest. She was quickly losing her position of power.

"Shoot your shot," Phil encouraged, forcing a grin up at her from the floor. He was still lying on his back, but now his hands were laced behind his head as if he was enjoying a relaxing evening out.

Shelby had to admit, his words about summed it up. She waited until the door had raised up high enough for the Escalade to drive under, then shifted her feet, ready to dart behind the vehicles and make her mad dash for the driver's seat.

"Why don't you stay?" Richard smiled at her, his shoulders falling, the furrow between his brows relaxing now. "I'd like a chance for us to start over."

Something rigid jabbed into her scalp from behind, and Shelby froze, her pistol still aimed at Phil. A hand took her left arm in a vice grip, and the warmth of a large body stepped close, pressing against her and sending a cold chill down her spine. The last flicker of her hope died out as someone's hot breath warmed her ear.

"Put that down," a man whispered, his deep, razor-edged voice shattering her vision of any future beyond this night.

Chapter 56
CHAPTER FIFTY-SIX

The men who'd taken Lucia and Sam had cuffed them, placed black cloth bags over their heads, and fitted them with noise-canceling ear muffs. Someone hefted Lucia over his shoulder, walked for a bit, then dropped her hard on a flat surface. She couldn't hear if Sam had joined her, but she wiggled around enough to know there weren't any bodies near her.

The forced silence from the ear muffs was almost painful, that sudden and unwelcome void of sound growing like a black hole in her mind. She needed noise, any kind at all, to ease her anxiety and desperation. This wasn't a situation in which she could afford to lose her head, figuratively or literally.

But this was exactly the sort of dire circumstance she and Shelby had trained for months to be prepared for.

Vibrations through the surface told her she was lying on the floor of a vehicle, and she felt every bump as it navigated the ragged two-tracks and unpaved roadways of the Michigan backwoods.

She squirmed around, rubbing the side of her head against the floor until she got one side of the ear muffs off. The sudden massive influx of sound caused her entire body to jerk, but she welcomed the pain of roaring with the noise of the vehicle's engine. Eventually, her mind cleared, and she recognized the rap metal music blasting through the speakers.

Maneuvering her body in the small space, Lucia rolled onto her side and pulled her knees toward her chest until she could just barely squeeze her feet through the space between her cuffed hands. It was a painful contortion of her body, but she finally got her legs through.

Although she was still cuffed, she was more capable with her hands in front than behind. She slowly peeled the hood off her head, careful to move slow and quiet, even if she doubted anything could be heard over the raging mosh-pit music.

Low light greeted her eyes, soothing in an odd way, and she breathed deeply of the fresh air. At least it was fresher than what she had breathed through the bag. It smelled like she was one step closer to freedom, even if it was a tiny one.

Every bump in the road jostled her as she sought a comfortable position from which she could survey her surroundings. A large, dimly lit space greeted her, and criss-cross shadows covered everything. Searching while she oriented herself, she found the source of the soft light as she came to recognize the vehicle.

She was in the back of a large work van, surrounded by scattered tools and debris, and the light casting its weak glow was coming from the radio and dashboard. A wall of wire stood between her and the front, backlit by that light and creating the crosshatch shadows. Beyond the wire, two shadowy heads sat in front, one driver and one passenger.

They were already moving at a snail's pace, but the driver braked suddenly, forcing Lucia to lay flat on the floor and brace her arms against the mounted toolboxes on either side to keep herself from rolling. The red glow from the brake lights added illumination to the interior, and she spotted the long, unmoving shape of another body lying against the wire barrier and facing her.

Lucia's heart pounded in her chest, and her throat tightened as she low-crawled across a few small, scattered tools on the thinly carpeted floor toward the body.

She wanted to throw herself toward him and scream his name.

It took every ounce of control she could muster, but she kept her mouth shut and moved slowly in case either of the men in the front might be paying the slightest attention to their human cargo. Once she was close enough to reach him, she interlaced her fingers with his, and he immediately squeezed back, seeking, desperate, comforted despite the terror.

Staying low, she grabbed the same tools that she'd already used to free herself. Quietly, she used them to free Sam while being jostled by the van's bouncing over the rough roads. When she removed his ear muffs and the bag over his head, she held her finger to her lips, hoping he could see her signal despite the darkness.

But she should have trusted Sam to know better, as he never said a word. Despite the darkness, she was able to make out his eyes locked on hers and the outline of his face. Thankfully, the dark hood had made it easier for her eyes to adjust to such limited ambient light, and she could use that to her advantage now.

Crawling backward as slowly as possible, Lucia felt around for the scattered tools on the floor of the van, eventually wrapping her fingers around the handle of a flathead screwdriver. She slid her fingers over the tool but already knew it was too big to pick the lock or slide into the teeth of the handcuffs. It couldn't break the chains either without breaking her arms, so she pushed it toward Sam as he reached behind his legs and slipped them between his arms.

Lucia returned to searching with her hands and squinting into the shadows, searching the scattered trash for anything useful. The van took a hard turn, then started to slow, and her pulse quickened with the fear of what was to come. She was almost ready to give up when her fingers grasped a pair of sunglasses.

Feeling along the arms of the wire-frame sunglasses, she pinched the temple ends and grinned into the shadows at her last-minute luck. She tore with her fingernails at the plastic covering the ends, shredding them and clearing one of the arms fully before twisting her fingers to maneuver it between her hands.

After bending the tip of the end into the keyhole, she inserted it into the mechanism and fished around until the cuff on her left wrist snapped open. She was less dextrous with her left hand, so it took a little longer to pick the right cuff, but only by a few seconds.

Lucia had just unlocked one of Sam's cuffs when the van hit a final bump and slowed to a stop. She pushed herself backward and hastily covered her face with the bag as the van was shifted into park.

The music was turned completely off suddenly before one of the men in the front spoke. "What the hell? Is that Victor?"

"Oh, shit!"

Both front doors were flung open, letting in a frigid blast of winter air. Two pairs of footsteps sprinted away through the snow, so Lucia slid the bag from her face and dared a glance at the front. They hadn't even bothered to turn off the engine.

The van's dome light was on, and Sam glanced up at her as he fished the metal arm of the sunglasses into the lock on the other cuff.

"Go!" he hissed at her in a whisper.

She scrambled into a crouch and lunged toward the back door, fingers grasping the simple handle and pulling it toward her. There was a split moment of dread, the fear that it wouldn't open, but the latch released, and the door popped open.

It was louder than she would have liked, but the noise from the van's engine drowned it out. Sam was right behind her, scrambling over the scattered tools and trash as they dropped onto the snowy ground.

She shivered as the cold air hit her. Combined with the adrenaline, it tightened her muscles and made her vision tunnel.

Dark, thick forest surrounded the open clearing they stood in now, and she was struck by how similar it was to the place they'd been taken from. Crouching, she pinned her back to the rear bumper of the van after Sam closed the door quietly behind them.

He crouched next to her and leaned close. "You thinking what I'm thinking?"

His voice comforted her, his hot breath warmed her neck, and her trembling body quieted.

Lucia nodded. "Shelby might be here."

"Either way, it's win or die, love."

She turned her head and cocked an eyebrow at him. That wasn't a term he often used.

Sam held up the screwdriver she'd found earlier, then lowered it and locked his gaze with hers. "I do love you. You know that, right?"

All she could do was nod as the knot tightened in her stomach again, and she barely resisted the urge to bolt away into the forest with him. But neither of them could live with doing such a thing, and that was the simple truth.

Sam caressed her cheek with his free hand, pulling her face to his and kissing her deeply before pulling away. He spun and rounded the other side of the van, gone from her vision in a split second, and that was all she needed to remember that he was counting on her.

They didn't have the luxury of surrendering to fear.

Lucia followed suit, listening only for a moment before rounding the corner of the van and surveying the situation. Being unarmed, she felt almost naked but knew that if she could maintain the element of surprise, she'd still have an advantage.

Some fifty feet away, the two men from the van were standing in front of the half-opened bay door of a steel-sided warehouse like the empty one she'd burst into before they grabbed her. There were more vehicles to the left and right, and two just inside the door.

One of the men from the van had a gun in his right hand, hanging at his side, and the other, a balding man, held a pistol straight out in front of him.

Squinting but still unable to see what he was pointing at, she moved forward at an angle while staying crouched to get a better look. She swayed suddenly, falling to her knees in the snow as her new field of vision revealed a woman with short black hair and tawny-brown skin.

Chapter 57
CHAPTER FIFTY-SEVEN

L ucia brought her fist to her mouth and bit into her knuckles, stifling her urge to scream out a war cry and tackle the man holding the muzzle of his pistol against Shelby's head.

There were more people inside the well-lit warehouse, moving fast toward Shelby. Lucia didn't know what to do.

If she rushed them now, she risked getting both herself and Shelby killed.

She glanced at Sam, armed with the screwdriver, and he shook his head slowly, his eyes locked with hers. He didn't want her to go bursting into this situation, but she didn't have time to do all the planning she preferred. It was time to fight like Shelby: swift and savage.

Steeling herself, Lucia crouched on the ground, tensing her muscles and digging the toes of her boots into the snow, ready to leap forward into a sprint. Before she could push off, the revving of an engine echoed through the barren trees.

Turning, Lucia sprinted toward Sam instead, joining him behind another vehicle closer to the building and hoping the men hadn't spotted her when they'd looked toward the forest.

It could have been a vehicle passing on a nearby road, but everyone froze, and all sound fell to silence in expectation of whoever might be coming.

Lucia flattened herself into the freezing snow and gazed beneath the SUV's undercarriage, squinting until she found two pairs of legs standing together, clearly Shelby's and the man who held her hostage.

The sound of the unknown vehicle rose, then faded away until it disappeared altogether. Voices picked up from inside the warehouse, but Lucia couldn't hear well enough to make out what was being said. She only knew that a man had a gun pointed at Shelby's head.

Sam nudged her, and when she turned, she found him nodding toward the side of the building. As with the previous warehouse she'd busted into before being taken by the men, there was a door on the side. She considered it but remembered the squealing hinges of the other door and shook her head.

He didn't seem to care. He reached over and squeezed her hand, then quietly padded through the snow toward the door, keeping a low profile to keep his cover behind the vehicles.

But Sam hadn't been quiet enough.

"What was that?" one of the men asked, voice becoming a startled hiss.

All movement stilled, and an eerie silence settled over the clearing.

"Check it out. Walk the perimeter and make sure we're alone." The order came from the deep, gravelly voice of an older man. Shelby cried out suddenly. "I'm going to need more time with this little bird."

Lucia's stomach twisted, and a sick feeling snaked hot through her core. Two pairs of feet limped in the opposite direction, but one pair of legs was coming straight for her. Carefully, she dug her fingers into the snow and pulled herself under the SUV, thankful the owner hadn't paid to have the frame lifted. As it was, her slender body could just barely fit beneath it, and she simultaneously fought the urge to groan as she scraped her back against a piece of metal and the nerve-wracking fear of being crushed should it suddenly fall off its tires for some ridiculous reason.

She held her breath as she watched the beam of a flashlight sweep left and right over the snow where she had been until it turned toward the side of the building. The man now walked toward where Sam had headed. All she could do now was pray he had found somewhere to hide.

But she couldn't simply wait and see. It wasn't in her nature.

Lucia clenched her teeth and glanced between the open bay door of the warehouse and the direction of the side door Sam had gone for. No one was standing near the bay door entrance anymore, and the two men who had gone the other way hadn't reappeared yet. She couldn't even hear their footsteps crunching loudly through the snow anymore.

"Damn it," she whispered, keeping her eyes toward the side door as she slid out from under the SUV. Pulling herself to her feet, she kept her profile low in case anyone looked out from the bay door or if the other two men reappeared suddenly.

Even if they were making a complete circle around the building, she was running out of time to do something. The man searching nearby had his back to her, and he was shining his flashlight at tall stacks of snow-covered apple crates.

"Is someone there?" he asked as he raised a pistol toward the crates. "Move slow, and keep your hands where I can see them."

Staying in the man's deep boot tracks through the snow, she crept up behind him just as Sam slowly rose from his hiding spot. The man searching for them was too distracted by Sam to hear or sense her approach, but Sam noticed. He squinted his eyes as the cone of light found him and immediately shook his head.

She knew that was meant for her, but she wouldn't let Sam be taken, not after all that had happened to him already, and considering whatever they probably had in store for the two of them.

Jumping on the man's back, she wrapped one arm around his neck, quickly applying a carotid restraint. He threw himself backward and fell on top of her in the snow.

Lucia grunted as she was crushed between his body and the hard ground, but she held on for dear life despite it, knowing that if she let him go, then she and Sam might both die in the seconds that followed.

The man dropped his gun so he could try to peel her arms away, but she held the position, the fingers of her nondominant hand wrapped in his thick, medium-length hair to keep his head pressed forward against her other arm.

His fight left him as the blood flow to his brain was successfully cut off, and within a dozen seconds, he was barely moving. She held him a dozen seconds more until he stopped fighting entirely, not knowing if she'd only rendered him unconscious or killed him.

Sam ripped the man's body away from her and grabbed her by the arm before pulling her to her feet. He nodded his head toward his hand, which now held the man's gun, then moved toward the open bay door.

"Hide!" he ordered.

Lucia was about to argue when the bloodcurdling scream of a woman tore through the winter air. They both froze, and her heart sank. It had to be Shelby.

Before she could bolt for the opening to try to save her friend, the two men who had circled the building came around the corner, their flashlights honing in on Sam and Lucia almost instantly.

They dove and scattered just in time to evade a volley of bullets fired at them.

There was no hiding under the vehicles anymore, but as she was presently unarmed, she had to keep moving until she thought of some way to level the playing field.

She didn't have many choices, and she didn't have much time, for Shelby and Sam's sake as much as her own.

Even as she made her decision, she knew her chances of making it out of this alive had dropped so low they were now dancing in the depths of hell.

Pushing off the balls of her feet, she shot forward and sprinted toward the bay door, ducking under it and holding her hands up in surrender as she passed between the two vehicles parked closely inside. She squinted against the bright interior lights, willing her vision to clear so she could assess her situation.

Two men stood opposite of Shelby's motionless, bloody body sprawled on the floor. They looked up as Lucia skidded to a halt on the smooth concrete floor, nearly kicking Shelby as stopped herself.

"What did you do?" she choked out the words. Her eyes stung, but she was too full of adrenaline to cry.

"There's the woman I've been waiting for," one of the men said with the deep, gravelly voice she'd heard earlier. He was tall, slender but athletic, had silver-flecked black hair, and icy blue eyes that struck her as eerily familiar. "Miss Lucia Sorenson."

Lucia said nothing as she locked eyes with him, studying his posture and their surroundings through her peripheral vision. The second man, obviously a lackey, stepped close, holding a pistol up and pointing it at her head.

"On your knees," the older man ordered.

She ignored him. "And who are you? Your name can't actually be 'Fear Doirich'."

"Why not? It is whatever I say it is. And if you want your parents and your big brother to live much longer, you'll do exactly as you're told."

The mention of her family hit her like an unexpected punch to the gut. She thought he'd offer to let Shelby or Sam live if she cooperated, and the lack of such an offer struck fear in her heart.

"They don't know anything—"

"And they won't have to know death just yet if you finally behave yourself, young woman." She shook her head, knowing in the core of her being that this was it.

Her end had finally arrived, and the monsters would win after all.

"My son was right," the Fear Doirich said, clucking his tongue as he looked her up and down. "You *are* a fine woman. Even I would like to enjoy your company for a few weeks. It's a shame you're so much trouble."

The realization struck her then, and she connected the man's icy blue eyes with all the men she'd been alternately running from and chasing for the past six months.

"Are you..." she hesitated, studying him carefully before continuing. "Are you Phil McNamara's father?"

The older man grinned at her. "Yes, I'm Richard, father to the young man whose life you ruined."

Richard stepped forward suddenly, startling her. His hand shot forward, and he grabbed her by the neck before she could back out of his reach.

Fear took hold of Lucia as his hands squeezed her throat.

"So delicate," he rumbled near her ear, his hot breath fluttering loose strands of her hair even as her throat ached and her lungs begged for oxygen.

He released his grip, and she stumbled backward slightly before he caught her by the wrist. "Now that we're done with your friend, I think it's time for you to tell Mr. Frost to surrender."

"Sam?" she whispered. "No. He got hurt and ran."

Richard released her, then stepped backward over Shelby's body and shook his head. "That's sweet, honey. You have three seconds to call out to him."

"Or what?" she challenged, relaxing her shoulders. "You'll kill me?"

"Me? No. My man here," he gestured to his lackey standing beside him, "will put a bullet in your pretty little friend."

"Sh-she's alive?"

He nodded, then pressed the toe of his boot against Shelby's shoulder and rolled her onto her back before stepping back again.

All three of them fell silent, and Lucia choked back a sob when she saw Shelby's chest rise and fall.

Richard began to count. "Three. Two..." he raised his eyebrows at Lucia. "One. Time's up."

"Now?" The man with the gun grumbled the simple word.

She turned her gaze on the lackey as he stepped closer to her from the opposite side of Shelby's unconscious body, his eyes narrowed. Dried blood was smeared around his swollen red nose and busted lips.

They stood eye to eye, Shelby between them, glaring daggers across the divide. He didn't break eye contact when he pointed the muzzle at Shelby's chest.

Lucia surrendered to the impossibility of the situation, relaxing into the dark embrace of an unknown fate as she let out her breath and expelled all her worries about what could go wrong. The world seemed to slow, and her vision darkened, focusing on her target, and she let muscle memory take over.

Shooting her left hand forward, she grasped the gun by the end of the barrel and pulled it to her right, pointing it beyond and away from her body. She stepped into the man's space as she pulled him forward, almost tripping him over Shelby. With her right fist balled up, she came off her right heel, rolled her hip, and threw everything she had into a right cross straight to the lackey's already-broken nose.

A geyser of blood spewed from his face, and he choked on a muted scream as his fingers released the gun, and she spun it in her hand to point it at Richard. His lackey dropped to his knees, holding his face as he groaned unintelligibly.

Dropping her finger to the trigger, Lucia steadied her arms, braced her hands, aimed at Richard, and exhaled.

Chapter 58

CHAPTER FIFTY-EIGHT

After Lucia had saved Sam by choking out the man who'd spotted him, they were separated under a hail of bullets. He bolted for the van they'd escaped from and lost track of Lucia in the process, holding fast to what little faith he had left that she would be okay.

The two men who'd shot at them stopped firing their weapons, and Sam could hear them approaching as they plodded through the snow toward his position.

Sam yanked the back door of the van open and clawed through the tools scattered haphazardly over the floor until his fingers wrapped around a blue, cast iron pipe wrench. He let himself grin as his eyes quickly surveyed the rest of the tools in the warm glow of the van's dome light. He wouldn't normally bring a wrench to a gunfight, but he couldn't see that he had any other options.

At least if he was going to die, he'd do it standing on his own two feet and go down swinging with all the fury he could muster.

Gripping the wrench in his hands, Sam psyched himself up as the hurried footsteps of the men came closer. He imagined the way it felt to kiss Lucia, to hold her and love her, tangle his fingers in her silky dark hair.

He remembered a younger version of himself, a hopeful, idealistic teenager who had joined the Army to be part of something bigger, to stand for his country's call to arms so others wouldn't have to. And he couldn't forget the reason he'd left the service to become a law enforcement officer in his own community, so fuckers like these would have one more good man to stand against them as they sought to bend and break good people for their own gain.

It was no comfort to know that he would die tonight at the hands of evil men, but he was bitterly grateful that he could stand and fight in spite of the hell his body had already been through.

He could never kneel. He would never surrender.

Relaxing his shoulders, he exhaled long and slow, then hefted the pipe wrench to one side like a batter at home plate, ready to swing.

Footsteps jogged past the opened back door of the van, and Sam swung as hard as he could. The man never saw it coming, his pistol raised as if to shoot Sam, but he was too close. The head of the wrench smashed into the man's cheekbone, caving in his face. Blood and gore splattered the van and Sam's exposed skin as his enemy crumpled to the ground, body twitching as it settled into the snow.

Before Sam could wind up for another hard swing, the second man rounded the door.

There was no time to wait and think. Sam dropped the wrench and threw himself forward, striking the gun barrel down and away. In the small space, the shot's report deafened Sam, and he went tumbling to the ground with the second man. They tussled for the gun, and every muscle in his body ached as he fought for each and every moment of life.

Two shots were fired from somewhere, but they sounded far away, and Sam didn't dare look up while locked in a life-or-death struggle with the second man. With a sudden burst of power, his opponent pushed hard and rolled on top of Sam, straddling him as they each grabbed the gun.

Sam's energy began to wane, and a wave of lightheadedness threatened to steal what strength he had left to fight, so he gripped the pistol from the bottom of its barrel in his left hand and slid the fingers of his right down until he found the safety switch, hoping to God he made the right choice.

In a matter of seconds, Sam bent his knees, dug his heels into the snow, let go of the gun, and bucked his hips upward, sending the other man flying overhead. Sam rolled onto his stomach and tried to push himself upright, but another wave of dizziness stole his will, and he fell face-first into the snow, heaving breaths.

"Drop it!" a man roared, and Sam looked up to find two figures emerging from the trees and running toward him.

It was over, he knew now.

One leg burned more than the rest of his body, and the adrenaline he'd been running on was crashing now. There was nothing left in his tank to keep him going.

He lay there in the snow, sucking in air and thinking only of Lucia and the fire in her touch while the men's words turned to fuzz in his brain.

Chapter 59
CHAPTER FIFTY-NINE

Lucia squeezed the trigger. Someone tackled her from behind, and she went sprawling over Shelby, sending the shot wide before hitting the floor, her elbows slamming against the concrete floor.

He held her around the chest with both arms, but she easily shrimped out from under him and twisted onto her back. She lifted her pistol and took aim at the man who tackled her as she propelled herself backward across the smooth floor. Richard started toward her, heedless of the gun, fury twisting the refined features of his face, but halted when two shots sounded from outside the warehouse.

"Damn it, Father," Phil screamed. "Get out of here now!"

Lucia didn't dare glance at the man yelling, not with the threat of Richard's rage within a dozen feet of her, but he sounded somehow familiar.

Richard surveyed the room and then ducked to view the scene beyond the bay door before he bolted toward a back door in the corner of the warehouse, snaking a key ring out of his pocket as he reached it. Within seconds, he had unlocked the door and run through it, letting it swing open behind him. A frigid draft of winter air blew in after him.

Lucia scrambled to her feet and glanced back and forth between Phil and the door Richard had left through. Phil lay on the floor, glaring up at her. She needed to make a decision fast. If she didn't go after Richard now, she might not be able to catch up to him, and he had threatened her family.

Phil was unarmed as far as she could see, but she didn't trust him enough to turn her back on him, and she couldn't leave him alone with an injured and unconscious Shelby. If she was awake, Lucia wouldn't have worried–Shelby would have flayed Phil alive–but there was no such luck.

"Where is he going?" she demanded, walking toward Phil, her pistol hanging from her trembling right hand.

"He's going to fuck your world up," Phil grunted as he rolled onto his side and pushed himself up into a sitting position.

"No. Get back on the floor, face down."

He narrowed his eyes and stared back at her. "No."

"Do it, or I'll put a bullet in you."

"What are you going to do? Paralyze me? Oh, wait. You already did that. Did I say thank you yet, bitch?"

"You came after me," she screamed, channeling her pent-up rage at him, raising the pistol and pointing it at his face. "You just kept coming for me. What the hell was I supposed to do? And I didn't even shoot you, asshole. Liam did!"

Phil shrugged. "It's still your fault."

"Are you kidding me?!" Her body ached, and her brain buzzed, but her rage began to cool as the winter air crept across her cheeks and chilled her fingers. She lowered the pistol. "I can search you for weapons and secure you, or I can shoot you. What's it going to be? Because, frankly, I'm sure every prosecutor in the State of Michigan would decline to charge me after the living hell you've put me and everyone else through." She returned his shrug with a grim smile.

The smug expression faded from his face, and his icy eyes lost their shimmer. "Would you make it quick? A headshot?"

His willingness to die surprised her, but she had to admit he looked exhausted, tired, older than she remembered. For a split second, she almost fell into the trap of pitying the man who had bought, sold, trapped, exploited, and murdered so many.

Lucia smiled. "No, I won't make it easy on you. In fact, I hear gut shots are painful as hell, and if I manage to avoid hitting anything vital, it could take a long time for you to die. So how about I shoot you in the stomach so we can test that theory."

The color drained from his face. He nodded and lowered himself back onto the floor, face down.

She kept her weapon ready as she approached in case he tried anything, but his body remained entirely relaxed as she searched him. She dug in her heels and dragged him by the feet toward the vehicles near the bay door.

She left him there and sprinted back to Shelby, crouching on the opposite side of her so she could keep Phill and the unmoving lackey whose broken nose she'd punched in view.

"Shelby?" she said softly at first as she tried to rouse her friend to consciousness. Lucia flicked on the safety switch on the pistol she'd taken from the man lying not a dozen feet away from her. "Wake up. We have to go now."

Shelby didn't even flinch as Lucia's hands swept from her head to her feet, searching for wounds. She'd been beaten to hell and had bruises all over her body, including a few nasty lumps on her head and face, but there weren't any open wounds, for which Lucia was immediately thankful. Now, she only had to worry about whatever head trauma Shelby had suffered.

Lucia sighed and started to rise, but movement in her periphery caught her attention, and she hesitated. Turning, she found the lackey's steel-toe boot coming straight for her face. She pulled back, hurling her body away from the incoming kick, though it still caught her.

The force of the blow on her left shoulder sent her spinning, and a popping sound barely preceded the explosion of pain that flooded her body and mind. A scream erupted from her throat, a sound she barely recognized as her own.

She fell and groaned, blinking back tears only to find the lackey had retrieved his gun. His face, splotched with bruises and sticky with blood, had swelled, leaving his right eye closed and his left eye only open a slit.

He stepped toward her and pulled the trigger.

The gun only clicked.

While he studied the gun, Lucia tried to crawl backward but faltered when she attempted to put weight on her left arm.

She fell to her side on the floor and pushed herself up clumsily with only her right hand, but even the dead weight of her left arm, hanging useless and awkward, sent bolts of pain through her shoulder, back, and chest.

"Drop it!" a man yelled from near the bay door, and she turned just in time to see the lackey flick off the safety and swing the muzzle toward the sound.

Two shots echoed, ringing in Lucia's tender ears. The lackey dropped to his knees, blood blooming on his jacket. The gun clattered to the floor as he slumped onto his face.

"Lucia!" This time, she recognized Sam's voice, and her stomach twisted as she registered the fear in his tone and the slurred way in which he spoke her name. She turned, and they limped toward one another. He wore a makeshift bandage around his left thigh.

In spite of their wounds, they embraced quickly, squeezing each other so tightly it hurt.

Sirens resounded through the woods beyond the warehouse as dawn began to lighten the sky, and after a few desperate moments of holding Sam, Lucia pushed back and looked up into his eyes.

"Shelby's not waking up," she barely managed to choke out the words. Turning, she held onto Sam with her good arm and tried to limp toward her unconscious friend.

Lucia froze as two men rushed to Shelby's side.

"Matt," Sam explained. "And Detective Ward."

She was stunned but grateful. "They shot him?" she asked, nodding instead to indicate the lackey now lying in a growing pool of blood on the cement floor.

"Ward did."

"Did they already call for an ambulance?"

It was Sam's turn to hesitate as they both looked toward the open bay door and the driveway beyond. The sound of the sirens was getting closer. He furrowed his brow, then fixed his gaze on the other two men as they assessed Shelby's condition. "Who called for backup?"

"It wasn't us," Mitch said without looking up, his full attention on caring for Shelby.

The sirens were almost deafening now, and Lucia spotted a vehicle moving outside just before two uniformed officers came shuffling under the half-open bay door.

"Everyone on the floor!" one of the officers roared the order.

With their injuries, it wasn't smooth or easy, but they did as they were instructed, fear filling Lucia's heart.

This couldn't be right.

Chapter 60
CHAPTER SIXTY

It took over an hour to get out of handcuffs, with a flurry of calls made between the local dispatch and the various departments Sam, Matt, and Mitch belonged to. Clearing their names wasn't easy because Richard had escaped through the forest and had been the first to call 9-1-1, claiming that Lucia had held him and his son hostage for ransom and threatened to murder them if her demands weren't met.

It was preposterous, but it was the story Richard stuck to.

To Lucia's surprise, Phil hadn't tried to escape. In fact, he was found right where she'd left him. Unfortunately, he wouldn't speak to the police except to insist on his right to a lawyer.

An ambulance made it through the woods on the rough two-track from the road, and the paramedics evaluated everyone, clearing only the uninjured Mitch and Matt to meet Shelby at the hospital after she was evaluated. They suspected a severe concussion and couldn't make any promises about when her father or friends might be able to see her.

As Lucia and Sam waited in the ambulance for the paramedics to load Shelby's stretcher into the back, she was touched to see Mitch by her side the entire time, never straying more than an arm's length away.

Matt found Mitch standing beside the stretcher in the morning light, his eyes closed and head bowed as he muttered a quiet prayer for his daughter. When Mitch opened his eyes, Matt drew something from inside his jacket and passed it to Mitch. Lucia spotted the same teddy bear she had seen earlier that morning. It felt as if it had been days rather than hours since they'd first found Shelby had been taken.

Mitch hesitated, then accepted the bear, squeezing it in his fingers before placing it on top of Shelby's blanketed body. He looked up into the ambulance and locked eyes with Lucia. "Will you make sure it stays with her?"

Lucia nodded, her eyes stinging with the threat of tears. "I will."

⁕

Shelby's doctors had put her into a medically induced coma for five days to protect her brain from swelling after diagnosing her with a traumatic brain injury and performing surgery to drain the hematomas they discovered upon her initial evaluation.

Matt and Mitch had become fast friends while taking turns, splitting the visitor hours between them to make sure someone was always with her in the first week. Then, they started spending more of the overlapping shift times together until one or the other had to return to work.

Matt made sure the teddy bear was seated upright in front of the flower vases on the window sill. After Mitch's shifts, he would find it hidden or set aside, and he always replaced it. Whatever the older man's demons, Matt knew it was too important to let him try to hide it.

The day she was roused from the coma, the pair were sitting near the window. Matt was entrenched in a conversation with Mitch about his experience investigating homicides.

"Do you want to advance–" Mitch was saying, but Matt held up a hand to stop him.

He had the better view of Shelby, and he froze, holding his breath as he waited to confirm what he thought he saw.

Slowly, almost imperceptibly at first, her eyelids began to twitch and flutter. Matt rose smoothly from his seat and rounded the hospital bed, quiet but quick, as Mitch scrambled to his feet.

Matt knelt next to the bed while Mitch stood near Shelby's shoulder, grimacing as tears glistened in his eyes. Clearing his throat, Matt caught Mitch's eye and tipped his chin up, hoping to remind the older man to keep calm and hope for the best. But the older man shook his head and strode out the door.

Shelby blinked slowly, then pinned her unsteady gaze on Matt as he gently took her hand in his.

"Matt," she said, her voice hoarse.

"You're okay." He rubbed his thumb over the green, faded bruises on her knuckles.

"Who walked out?"

"It was Mitch." Matt glanced over his shoulder at the door before returning his focus to her. "Your father. He's been here every day. We've been watching over you, waiting for you to come back to us."

Shelby's eyes flitted toward the doorway, then to her hand where Matt was rubbing it. "Water, please." Her words were barely a whisper.

"Of course." He jumped to his feet and spun toward the door just as a nurse walked in, Mitch trailing behind her with a white styrofoam cup in one hand.

"Ice water," Mitch muttered as he passed it to Matt.

Matt held the straw up to Shelby's mouth so she could sip.

The nurse reviewed the myriad screens and equipment, checking Shelby's vital information and examining her eyes. "How are you feeling?"

Shelby stared at her, groaned, then released the drinking straw from between her teeth. "Pain," she said simply.

"I know. You're going to feel some aches and pain in your body after all you've been through. What's your name?"

"Shelby," she hissed in a whisper, then swallowed hard. "Ford."

The nurse proceeded through a standard battery, asking for the year, the current president, and other easy questions until she seemed satisfied. "I'll be back with the doctor as soon as she's available."

When she left the room, Mitch stood nearer to the bed. Matt waited for him to say something, but silence filled the small room.

Eager to break the tension, Matt rose and headed for the window, grabbing the teddy bear from the shelf before dragging a chair closer to Shelby.

He laid the bear in her open hand and brushed his fingers against hers.

"We almost lost it." Matt rubbed the back of his neck with one hand, his gaze falling to the white blankets covering her battered body. *We almost lost you.* That was what he wanted to say, but he couldn't speak the words, knowing how fast he would fracture beneath the weight of those words.

Shelby's fingers caressed the bear's face as she examined it in silence. "Thank you," she said softly.

Mitch shifted uncomfortably on his feet. "Matt has my number saved if you want it. If there's something... anything at all, just call me."

Matt held his breath, waiting for Shelby to explode. The medical staff had warned both of them that waking up from a coma was difficult for patients, and most were irritable and quick to anger. That was already Shelby's default setting most days, not to mention the last time she'd spoken to Mitch.

"How... how are you here?"

"We found you, Lucia, and Sam," Matt interjected. "Without Mitch's help, I don't think I could have made it in time, and I wouldn't have made it out alive."

She squeezed her eyes shut, then opened them, turned her face to Mitch, and held her free hand up toward him. It trembled until he closed the distance and wrapped it in both of his hands.

"Thank you," she said, staring up at the father she'd never known.

Mitch gave her fingers a gentle squeeze, his eyes brimming with tears, then he laid her hand gently on the bed before turning away. He hesitated in the doorway. "Anything you need, Shelby, just call me."

Before being discharged from the hospital, Lucia and Sam had spent time by Shelby's bedside, too. Lucia had never imagined she might see a future son- and father-in-law getting so far ahead of themselves, but she was glad Matt and Mitch had each other to lean on while they waited for Shelby to recover.

Lucia was released after only two days with only a few more painkillers than what she'd already been given after the incident at the cabin in Knowland. Sam, on the other hand, had to stay longer. He'd been shot in the thigh during his tussle with a gunman outside the van, and though it had barely missed an artery, it had done irreparable damage to his leg.

He'd undergone surgery within hours of his arrival at the hospital, and they kept him a few days longer to monitor whether he would need another surgery before he could be released.

Both he and Lucia would require physical therapy for months–maybe even years–to come.

To her disappointment, Lucia learned from Guzman that Phil was already working with prosecutors on a plea deal. He gave up all the information on every woman and child he'd ever taken, and most of them were found within days of him spilling his secrets. Lucia had broken down in tears when they told her they'd found Jordan, and all the women that Shelby been taken with the summer before. All the known victims had been found alive and brought home to their families after being provided the necessary physical and mental health services and support.

Unfortunately, Phil and his expensive lawyers had latched onto some of his father's lies, absolving the elder McNamara of all criminal liability. According to their official story, Richard had come to talk Phil out of his evil ways, getting caught off guard by Lucia and Sam as they fought back to save Shelby. An investigation into Richard was opened, but any man on Phil's side who lived through the night vouched for Richard's innocence in their own plea bargains.

Maybe it was the money that kept their mouths shut, knowing whatever families they left behind would be cared for while they waited behind bars for parole. Or maybe it was some sense of true loyalty to the man who had paid them exorbitant fees for their services.

Lucia didn't know why they wouldn't turn on him, and after Phil's previous skate, she wasn't confident that Richard would be successfully charged and convicted of any crimes.

He was a tiger released back into the wild, one who might still want to make her his meal if he was stupid enough to follow through on his threat of coming after her or her family.

She no longer held any allusions of safety and comfort, knowing that any day—any moment, really—could be her last.

Chapter 61
CHAPTER SIXTY-ONE

L ucia sucked in a steadying breath and peeked through the crack in the door to survey the room beyond.

"It's almost time," her mother said.

Turning, she locked eyes with her mother, who was barely holding back tears.

A light knock sounded on the door, and Lucia stood bolt upright. "We're ready out here." It was her brother, Robert.

"Okay, thanks," she replied before turning to her mother. "I have a stupid question."

Mayra rolled her eyes before proffering a gold tube of lipstick. "Touch up your lips."

She accepted it, hesitating. "How do I look?"

"Like an angel, Mija."

Taking the lipstick, Lucia moved in front of the vanity mirror and did as she was instructed and gave her face another spritz of setting spray while Mayra smoothed pieces of her carefully styled hair. The stylist had helped Lucia choose a thick, loose braid and decorated it with small white pearls and crystals.

After adjusting the A-line lace and tulle skirt, she traced her fingers down the beaded lace V neckline and the princess bodice. It wasn't what she had imagined when she'd been planning her wedding only weeks ago; it was better. Boho, simple and elegant, and it perfectly accentuated every curve of her body. It was beautiful but not extravagant. Even the tiny pearls and crystals were subdued, achieving a look more dewy than flashy.

She tested a few smiles in the mirror and snuck a few happy glances at her overjoyed mother. Deciding on a smile, she turned and gently kicked the train of her dress behind her as she turned toward the door.

"Flowers," Mayra said, passing her a modest bouquet of white and pink roses surrounded by dried lavender and pampas grass tied in pink silk. They were so light in her hands she worried her nerves would ruin the beautiful composition.

After her mother smoothed out the train, she opened the door, and Lucia stepped out into the warm light of the rustic venue. The 150-year-old renovated hip-roof barn had been strung with long ropes of Edison lights alternated with long white banners overhead while thick bunches of fairy lights wrapped every column in the intimate space.

Everything was bright, warm, and twinkling in the early evening air.

Lucia's chest tightened as faces turned toward her, a hush falling over the crowd. The faces all blended together, and she felt a tingle of fear inching up her spine.

Too many people.

Then her eyes found him, standing tall and proud before the arch at the front of the room. His dark blue Michigan State Police dress uniform stood in stark contrast to the pink and white flowers, soft string lights, and white cloth draped over the arch. His figure was imposing in that uniform with his hands clasped before him, but his face was soft, his eyes as gentle and warm as ever.

Her breath came back, the fearful tingle dissipated in an instant, and her natural smile filled her face before she could try to force any of the ones she'd practiced. She remembered all they had been through–all they still would endure–and knew in her heart they needed one another beyond comprehension. Together, they could handle anything.

A violinist played the melody to the song Sam had chosen, "Crazy" by Shallow Side. She had objected until she read the lyrics and listened to it. As she remembered the heart-felt words and how much they meant to Sam, she fought the tears stinging her eyes.

An arm was presented then, and she looked up to find her father waiting for her, a gentle grin softening the hard lines of his face. She beamed up at him, took his arm, and they walked together down the aisle toward Sam.

When they reached him, they halted, and the officiant spoke. "Who gives this woman to this man to be wed?"

"She gives herself," William answered. "And she has her family's blessing."

He turned to Sam, who snapped to attention and offered a salute. William raised his hand slowly in salute, then lowered it again before stepping away. Sam dropped his salute, standing statue-like until William took his place in the front row next to Mayra.

Then he offered his hand to Lucia and cracked a smile, his green eyes twinkling. She stepped onto the platform, glanced into the crowd, and spotted Shelby.

Although she'd refused to wear a dress, Shelby looked sharp in her mauve satin blouse and black slacks. She was flanked by two familiar faces: Mitch on her left and Matt on her right. Shelby clung to Matt, whose arm was wrapped around her. Although Shelby might say it was mostly for support because her body was still weak, they both looked suspiciously happy. She smirked up at Lucia, and a sense of relief filled Lucia's mind. Her friend's validation was something she hadn't realized she'd needed until now.

"Please be seated," the officiant instructed.

Lucia turned her focus back to Sam. The intensity of his gaze as he drank her in and the way his lips curled into a soft smile made her knees weak. His shoulders relaxed as he held her hands lovingly in his own.

She barely registered the words of the officiant as he spoke, trusting that he would read the poetry and philosophies they had provided. Instead, she lost herself in visions of the future that lay ahead of them.

"Lucia," the officiant repeated.

"Yes?" she asked, then laughed nervously. A soft wave of chuckles swept through the gathering.

"It's time to share your vows."

She squeezed Sam's fingers, tried to wish away the warmth in her cheeks, and then focused on him solely again.

"Sam, my love, my life, I swear to you my whole heart. I take you as my husband, loving you as you are, your strengths and your faults, as you do mine. I will always be yours, in times of plenty and in times of want, joy and sorrow, sickness and health, and in both failure and triumph."

He cocked a teasing eyebrow, and she smirked, knowing how much more those words meant to them after all they'd been through.

She continued. "I promise to always be faithful, to support you, and to prioritize our love and life together."

"Sam?" the officiant prompted.

"Lucia, my love, my life, I swear to you my whole heart. I take you as my wife, loving you as you are, your strengths and your faults, as you do mine. I will always be yours, through want and plenty, sorrow and joy, sickness and health. Together, we can only triumph."

He winked and grinned at her, melting her heart all over again. It took every ounce of discipline she contained to keep herself from jumping into his arms.

"I promise to always be faithful to you, to support you, to prioritize our shared love and life." He paused, looked down at their hands, then lifted his eyes again to meet her gaze. "Come hell or high water, I promise to always choose you."

Chapter 62
EPILOGUE

B rennan switched on the lights as he walked in the door, his arms full of shopping bags. He poked his head around the corner of the room and looked into the open areas beyond, but all was dark.

Good, he thought, jogging sneakily up the stairs to take his purchases to the bedroom. Thankfully, he and Cynthia had their own walk-in closets, and he could expect a certain level of privacy while he laid out the stash he'd long hidden over the long island countertop that filled the center of the space.

He didn't turn on any music as he prepared to undertake this important work; he needed the quiet to warn him of any prying eyes that might sneak up and catch him in the act.

Scissors? Check.

Tape? Check.

Wrapping paper? Check.

With skilled hands, he wrapped the horde of presents he'd gotten for his wife and their little girl, Lizzie, and marked most of the tags as 'From: Santa.'

Cynthia would give him that playful side eye, and Lizzie would be as delighted as ever at the mystery of the hefty man in the red suit with a reindeer-drawn flying sleigh.

What he was doing was practically selfish because Brennan couldn't get enough of their squeals of delight at all the thoughtful or exciting presents he'd found for each of them. This was the family he'd always dreamed of having, the one he wished he'd had as a kid. However, his imagined family had been filled with siblings eager to play and tussle with him.

He and Cynthia only had one child now, but they'd been talking lately about giving Lizzie a little brother or sister, and he was more than ready to expand their family.

Brennan finished wrapping everything in just under an hour, tucking all the presents in various drawers and cupboards throughout his closet since there were still two days until Christmas Eve when he would sneak out after Lizzie's bedtime and fill the blanket under the tree with "Santa's" gifts.

Satisfied with his gift-pick, gift-wrapping, and gift-hiding skills, he walked out of his closet and closed the door behind him as he loosened his tie and detached his cufflinks. He dropped both on his dresser as he listened to the heat kick on. All else was quiet.

Too quiet, considering Lizzie's car was out front, and she always found him as soon as he came home.

Brennan glanced in the mirror over the dresser and frowned at himself through the dark of the room. The bathroom light was on, so he checked but found it empty. His heart rate picked up, but he tried to dismiss the niggle that tickled in his chest.

Failing to keep his cool, he nearly tripped as he descended the stairs before striding through the entire first floor, looking for his wife.

There was no sign of her.

The kitchen was clean, the TV was off, and the study was tidy.

Not a single thing was out of place.

Taking the stairs two at a time, he headed back up to the second story and scoured it, looking through his bedroom and the guest bedroom before heading toward his daughter's door.

His heart thudded in his chest as he approached the door, dread spiking his veins with fear. He pushed the door open silently, felt for the light switch, and flicked it on.

Lizzie's bed was perfectly made and empty.

Brennan's mouth went dry, and his hands trembled as he turned from the room and pulled his phone from his pocket. He dialed his wife's phone as he flew up the stairs to the third level and searched for any sign of his wife and child.

On a table in Lizzie's playroom, a single piece of folded paper sat under a china tea cup.

He hesitated, wishing he could ignore whatever pain waited for him inside the paper, but he picked it up anyway, tipping the cup over. It clinked on the table and rolled off the table, hitting the thick rug with a thud.

One wrong move, and you will have to start a new family. No cops. Wait for contact.

Brennan's knees gave out, and he collapsed to the floor, crumpling the paper in his hands as the air left his lungs.

Cynthia's voicemail recording picked up over his phone's speaker, and he listened as her beautiful voice asked him to leave a message.

There was a beep, then silence. It took him several seconds to force his hands to work, but he finally ended the call.

He sat like that for... minutes? Hours? All night?

Brennan didn't know how long he'd been sitting there, but when he finally rose, his legs were numb. Pins and needles spread like a hot wave through him, and he staggered to the chair Cynthia had used while nursing Lizzie when she was a baby.

His phone rang, startling him, and his shaking fingers barely held it as he accepted the call and brought the receiver to his ear.

"Son?"

Brennan had expected to hear a mechanically altered voice with ransom demands, but it was his father's voice that greeted him.

"Dad?"

"Where is Cynthia? And Lizzie?"

"Th-they're..." Brennan squeezed his eyes shut and bit into his knuckles as hot tears slid down his cheeks. "They're gone."

"Damn it! I know who did this. We can—"

"What do you mean? How do you know?"

"Because they just tried to kill me, and they threatened to kill my entire family."

"I thought this was a money thing."

"It's partly a money thing," Richard conceded. "Partly revenge."

"Revenge for what, Dad?"

"For what Phil started. They said they would start with my grandchild and work their way up."

Brennan's thoughts were coming too fast, and it was too much to process.

"They said no cops."

"That's what they told me, too. And it's better that way because they've got a network of corrupt officers all over the state."

"This is your fault," Brennan whispered through his tears.

Silence ensued.

"You and all your schemes. You ruined Phil. He could have been a good kid. You ruin everything you touch, you bast—"

"Watch your tongue with me, boy," Richard warned, his voice a low growl. "I'm the only one who can help you get your family back now."

"And how can you possibly do that?"

"By staying calm and taking a very clean, tactical approach. But I can't do this alone, son. Phil will be in jail for the rest of his life, and Ash hasn't come home in years." He paused, holding Brennan's gaze.

Brennan said nothing. He willed himself to wake up from this nightmare, this circle of hell in which his beloved wife and daughter had been kidnapped due to his father's criminal engagements. And the one where he was forced to break his promise and join forces with his old man to save them.

"Are you with me?"

"Yes," Brennan finally said as he clasped his trembling hands together.

"What are you willing to do to get them back?"

"Anything, Dad. I will tear this world apart to get them back safe."

READ MORE

In chronological order:

- Desecrate the Darkness - Book 1

- Walking in Darkness - Standalone short story available on Amazon.

- Stand Against Darkness - Standalone short story.

  - Would you like to read it for FREE? Head to www.akhughey.com/freestand

- Hunting Darkness - Short story originally featured in the Make Them Pay thriller anthology.

  - Would you like to read it for FREE? Head to www.akhughey.com/freehunt

- Together Against Darkness - Short story featured in the March For Justice anthology.

- Falling Into Darkness - Book 2

- Rising From Darkness - Book 3

Would you like updates about upcoming releases, live events, giveaways, and reader parties?

- Join my Dark Angels Reader Bulletin at akhughey.com.

- Get access to Bonus Content like flash fiction, more short stories, books, audio, and more when you join me on Ream: https://re amstories.com/shadowsandscreams

Acknowledgements

I would like to thank the members of the Author Transformation Alliance for actively providing feedback and support; Julie Wild for beta reading; Nan Sampson for editing; Mary B. Knapp for being my publishing inspiration and support throughout my writing journey; K. McCoy for sensitivity reading and for being my accountability partner; Emily Burch Harris for proofreading; Shawn Smith for pressuring me to write faster; my husband for his support; and my parents, for encouraging me and instilling within me the belief that I could do anything.

I must also express my endless gratitude for my incredible cover designer, Kristen of Kristen Lee Design. Visit her at Kristen Lee Designs on Facebook and Instagram.

About the Author

A.K. Hughey writes psychological thrillers and gritty vigilante stories from her home in the northern Shenandoah Valley, where the mountain-ringed landscape remembers more than it reveals. With a B.A. in English and an M.A. in Ancient and Classical History, her work reflects a sharp eye for patterns and a deep reverence for consequences. Her perspective is shaped by more than sixteen years in the military and defense, and by the years that followed, building stories, raising a family, and learning all the ways in which the silence can hold more than just secrets.

In her stories, the right to survive is earned, justice is a quest, and no one escapes unscathed. Her characters bleed, bend, and break as they battle the darkness. Sometimes, they are even forced to fight the ones they trusted the most.

A.K. HUGHEY

CONNECT

Website: www.akhughey.com

Ream: https://reamstories.com/shadowsandscreams

Facebook: www.facebook.com/audreyiswriting

Instagram: www.instagram.com/audreyiswriting

Twitter: www.twitter.com/audreyiswriting

TikTok: www.tiktok.com/@audreyiswriting

www.ingramcontent.com/pod-product-compliance
Lightning Source LLC
Chambersburg PA
CBHW021958260626
47156CB00018B/2267